Praise for Darrell Kastin's
The Conjurer & Other Azorean Tales

The mysticism that lies within the land draws us to it. *The Conjurer & Other Azorean Tales* is a collection of short fiction surrounding the Azorean Islands and the island's certain beauty and majesty, and the wisdom that seems to float about it. Drawing on the naturally supernatural, this enticing collection of short fiction, is very much recommended reading.
~ The Midwest Book Review

A story of mystery and magic—magical appearances and mysterious disappearances, mysterious women and magical islands—beautifully and lyrically told.
~ Karen Joy Fowler, author of *The Jane Austen Book Club*

What a wild, big, gorgeous book! Amazing, amazing. Metaphor and myth turn into history and history explodes into human connection... the pages are saturated with such fine sea mist...
~ Katherine Vaz, author of *Our Lady of the Artichokes*

Shadowboxing with Bukowski

Darrell Kastin

Fomite
Burlington, VT

ISBN-13: 978-1-967022-21-2
Library of Congress Control Number: 2015956979

Fomite
58 Peru Street
Burlington, VT 05401
www.fomitepress.com

09/23/2025

Dedicated to the baby in the bookstore window.

"I'm not even what you might call a real human being anymore," Nicholas Kastinovich said.

I wasn't about to give him an argument. I merely shrugged. We all have our problems, why should *he* be so special? He must have read in my expression that I had no idea what the hell he was talking about, because he added, "I've been reduced to a mere character. A caricature of my former self, the product of a twisted, perverted mind."

Mentally, I kicked myself, and wondered how I might give him the slip.

"Yeah?" I said.

He nodded several times. "It's payback, you see, for what I did to Bukowski."

That stopped me. "You mean *Charles* Bukowski?"

"Buk. Alias Hank Chinaski. The very one. He got back at me."

"But Bukowski passed away. Years ago."

"Ho, ho, yeah, you just go right on telling yourself that," he said. "That's a rich one." He turned around as if Bukowski might be sneaking up on him that very moment.

"What did you do?" I asked.

"Listen, and I'll tell you."

This was what I got for letting Ron Voss—an acquaintance of mine, a busybody, know-it-all with his own bar and grill and a troubling aspiration to be a matchmaker for lost friends and missing family members—for letting him talk me into meeting this oddity, this so called Nicholas Kastinovich—who, by the way, has the look of someone who has crawled out of a ghetto or a gutter, a troubled soul, like the Wandering

Jew himself maybe, or the accursed narrator of the "Rime of the Ancient Mariner"—simply because my name happens to be Kastin.

"Say, Kastin and Kastinovich," Ron said. "Sounds like a law firm. You two are probably related. This is great! Come meet him."

Beware the bartender who knows everyone's secrets.

"What makes you so sure we're related?"

"Your names are practically the same," Ron said. "Besides, you look like you could be brothers—maybe your old man fooled around a little, eh? You both have that Jewish look."

"What does a Jew look like?"

"Well, you know...like a Jew. Like Dustin Hoffman, like Woody Allen."

"Ron, there are Jews from Ethiopia, and Jews with blond hair and blue eyes, Hispanic Jews and Jews you couldn't tell from Arabs. You should stick to darts from now on. You just might hurt yourself."

"Thanks, I'll remember that." He was wiping some glasses, but absentmindedly.

May no one ever think of doing me another favor again so long as I live, I thought. "You're a writer," Nicholas Kastinovich continued, giving the word as much inflection as if he were referring to someone who emptied septic tanks or dug graves. "So, go ahead and write this in a book. You might think it considerate to choose a less offensive name for the narrator, a name that might endear me to the reader. Forget it. Keep my name what it is."

I may have muttered something—I'm not sure. But he paused for a moment, as if getting up his wind for another verbal assault; he gazed at me with an unpleasant expression, a combination of suspicion and disdain. A restless sneer lurked around the corners of his mouth.

"*What?*" I said.

"Your face. I've seen that look before. You have that, what-have-I-got-myself-into,-stuck-here-talking-to-this-raving-lunatic look."

"You're imagining things," I said, brushing aside his comment with a wave of my hand. "I'm not making any face. If I made a face, it was only because this coffee is bitter as arsenic."

"Humph."

I wondered if he was psychic. I watched his thin upper lip curl even more, while his lower lip twitched.

"Look," he said, "the only reason I'm telling you this is because you might be a Kastinovich, too. And if you are, then you should listen to what I have to say. Everyone should listen and beware!"

He poured three packets of sugar into his cup of tea, and stirred and stirred until I was ready to grab the spoon out of his hand and hurl it across the room.

"Just look at me," he said. "This is what I've become." His outstretched hand swept over his agitated body, seated at the edge of his chair, twitching and looking like a coiled spring about to be set loose.

It was difficult not to pity him, but I had no idea what to say. He was a nonentity, someone no one would notice if they passed him on the street, totally devoid of charm or personality. Still, I wasn't exactly sure what he meant, so I raised my eyebrows.

"Trust me," he said. "Write it up and let them wonder. They'll ask questions, sure. They'll think you deliberately named me after yourself to cast doubt and confusion on the whole venture. Is this a story or a confession? Is the author real and this tale merely fiction as it purports, or is he hiding behind a screen? Who is more real, you or me? Leave that to others to sort out. I also hear you only use an initial, the letter "D" alone. That'll keep them wondering. I'll be able to say in my defense that at least I have a proper first name, Nick, while you go about with merely an initial, "D" for a name! As if *you* are a character out of a Kafka story, a nobody, and *I* am a person of flesh and blood."

Jesus, he was strange. "You let me decide what to name whom," I said. "If I even decide to go along with this. Besides, my name *is* Kastin."

"*Kastin*," he spat. "I suppose that was your grandfather's pathetic attempt to escape his own name. He wasn't the first, nor the last to try that. Where did you say your grandparents come from?"

"Somewhere in the Soviet Union," I said.

"Of course!" he said. "Where? Moscow, Petersburg, Kiev, Odessa?"

"Belarus."

"Ahah! I tell you I knew it. And what was the original name?"

"Not sure," I said. "It was changed but no one knows from what. Could have been Kastinovich, or maybe Kastinovski, or perhaps Kastinokov."

"Bah! You're a Kastinovich just as sure as I'm sitting here talking to you."

I didn't want to tell him that I had already put two and two together, and that—much as it pained me—I had already drawn my own conclusions that we were probably related. I mean, what were the odds? Grandparents who came from the same region, the similarity in our names, the physical appearance, such as it was. Peering into those watery, washed-out eyes of his, which if they did have a specific color could only be called dingy, I felt a painful twinge of recognition; it was like peering into my own ancestral past, a reflecting pool wherein I saw all my own sins, my father's sins, as well as the sins of countless generations preceding, all the way back to the very first schmuck to ever tell a lie, to filch a neighbor's cow, or cheat on his wife.

Still, I thought, let's get this over with. "So, what about it then?" I asked. "Am I going to hear your story or not?"

"Okay, listen," he said. "There are a few things I should tell you about the Kastinoviches. First, we are prolific, and so virile, we could impregnate a sack of flour or a mound of mud. There are more of us out there than you might think. Years ago the Kastinoviches multiplied in such numbers they were practically considered the thirteenth tribe of Israel. It was fitting that such an unlucky number should be ascribed to us! Our ancestors went off, scattered to the four winds, some to Odessa, some to Poland, some to the United States, and some to Germany. Most changed or shortened the name to try to fit in unnoticed. One took the name of his wife, another took his mother's name. Not that this helped—you are who you are, and there's no getting around it.

"After centuries of persecution, how many of us are left, God only knows. If we weren't killed by Gentiles, we were betrayed by our own. I'm telling you, even the Jews hated us!"

"Why?" I asked.

"Why what?"

"Why would other Jews hate your family?"

"Listen, many of them married non-Jews, trying to hide from their disastrous fate. Other Jews looked down on us, and would've rather married a goy or the town drunk than a Kastinovich. We were regarded as something of a cursed lot. As a result of all this mixing and matching, I'm not even a Jew, but a half-Jew—or a half-assed Jew—as my father would say. I was sixteen before I even knew I was Jewish, after my friends at school taunted me, and I rushed home to find out what a dirty Jew was, and why the kids at school called me such a thing. It must be like one of those babies the Germans took from Jews and raised as a good Nazi, suddenly finding out those people he was taught to despise, that he was one of them.

"What chance did any of us have when from the get go we were saddled with Kastinovich for a name, and everything that name entails? The stigma of its sordid history, a name that has wrought catastrophe and caused us to flee from one country to another, leaving ruination behind us. There are good reasons why each new generation of Kastinoviches brings new dire consequences and a general worsening of an already pretty bad world situation, each sowing the seeds of destruction, like so many malevolent Johnny Appleseeds. There are reasons why to this day in certain places in Belarus and Poland the word Kastinovich is a curse, a term of the utmost derision. Go to Minsk or Pinsk, call someone a Kastinovich and see what happens!

"So, go on, write it all down, but for heaven's sake do not say the word aloud. Not unless you want to bring misfortune raining down upon your own head. Meanwhile, I'll do what all characters do, take up the reins of the story and go along with the ruse, as if I don't know full well how it all will end.

"'Write,' people told me, when they learned of my acquaintance with Chinaski and the fact that he hadn't come to murder me even after the terrible things I did—at least not so far. 'Write it all down,' they said. 'Use a pseudonym, hide your identity.'

"But then I knew it wouldn't do me any good. Once a Kastinovich, always a Kastinovich. There is just no getting around it."

And so I let Nicholas Kastinovich talk. He did so for over an hour, hardly taking a breath. Lucky me, I'd brought a tape recorder and merely listened. I've written here exactly what he said. I can't vouch for its veracity. You'll have to judge that for yourself.

1

The Big Shebang

Try as I may I can't recall the first time I saw Hank Chinaski. His face appears out of nowhere, a loiterer who lurks on the edges of memory. He flits and stretches through a thousand different alleyways—a pervasive, irrepressible shadow: the very breath or spirit of Los Angeles.

Trying to remember the first time I saw Hank was like trying to remember the first time I had thought seriously about death, a subject I wasn't keen to ponder, if I could avoid it. Death left me with a vague but no less disquieting, gloomy premonition that gnawed at my heels. A feeling I couldn't easily shake. It was similar to the emanations of heat that rose like waves from the asphalt and concrete of Los Angeles, suspended in the hazy, particulate air: a dark prophecy that loomed and threatened to descend. It left me with suspicions that the whole sprawling mess that was L.A. was little more than an ornate mirage concocted by the desert sands, the lack of water, the scrub that grew—if that near cactus-like existence could be referred to as flora—like scabs on the soil, the accumulation of all the years of Hollywood scripts and film productions, the nameless actors and actresses who had disappeared in the cracks of its sidewalks, and to top it off, those unholy Santa Ana winds. You could almost hear its choked whispers on the quietest nights: *Nothing here is real.*

I watched for Hank from my perch at The Little Big Bookstore on 6th Street, in Downtown San Pedro, a neglected half-forgotten little corner of Los Angeles. There, I studied the sea with alarming regularity, convinced it posed a fair amount of danger. I noted with some satisfaction, however, that San Pedro would be the first to go. The way I figured it, if you had to be annihilated there wasn't much sense in waiting around until the bitter end watching friends, family and loved ones, to say nothing of the rest of humanity, swallowed up before your number was called. What was the advantage in being the last to go? Would the first to take the plunge have it any rougher than someone who saw everyone else go before him? Nah, best to beat the crowds, be the first to check out the lay of the land, so to speak, see what kind of refreshments are available in the nether world. Grab a good seat, if at all possible, and hang on for the ride.

I suspected a far more pressing danger was the desert, those treacherous sands and the heat that could easily snuff out any and all signs of life, so tenuously held. Hadn't the Mojave and the Sahara once been garden paradises? Los Angeles itself was little more than a glorified desert, a painted wasteland, little different from the backdrop scenes I had often stumbled upon when my friends and I sneaked into the MGM lots in the backwoods of Culver City years before. All the swimming pools and steel and glass buildings couldn't camouflage the fact that Los Angeles essentially had no water, was dry as a mummy's corpse. The Los Angeles River was nothing more than a trickle, but for one or two weeks a year, and the only river I'd seen with a bed of concrete. Shut off the water that flowed down the California Aqueduct from the north, and the water piped in from the Colorado River to the east, and all of Los Angeles would blow away like a dead dandelion caught in a sandstorm.

Whether to die by drowning in a flood or to die suffocating on desert sands? Which was nobler in the mind to suffer? These were some of the burning questions that kept me awake at night, amid frets and worries over the bookstore. Los Angeles stood poised on the brink of imminent disaster, facing nature's own supermarket of catastrophes: one good tidal wave would suffice, but then there were also potential floods and mudslides, earthquakes and fires, even volcanoes were possible. Hell, the whole thing could be sucked into the La Brea Tar Pits for all anyone knew. And there I was calling L.A. home, or rather San Pedro, for we tried to avoid acknowledging the ravenous monstrosity that was Los Angeles. I counted the minutes, the days until that final moment of reckoning came.

Chinaski had a face you couldn't soon forget. At the same time it was a face that was naggingly familiar; a face mauled by life. I'd seen him around Venice Beach, passed by him in Hollywood and Downtown L.A., around Santa Monica and Long Beach, Fairfax, Inglewood—especially in and around Hollywood Park—simply because Hank Chinaski wore the streets of Los Angeles upon his face. Peering at Hank's mug was no different than crawling into the dingiest dive L.A. had to offer. I called him Hank like everyone else. Though he signed his books "Charles Bukowski," Chinaski or Hank, his alter ego featured in his novels *Ham on Rye* and *Women*, was how most everyone referred to him. The only ones who ever approached him with, "Hello, Mr. Bukowski," or called him "Charles," were those who had never stepped through the suburbs, let alone the squalid, seedy downtown of Hank's world; who hadn't drunk from the same fetid trough as he, those who tiptoed through his poetry and stories now and then the way some people on occasion give themselves a thrill by driving—with windows rolled up and doors locked, of course—through some god-awful section of Downtown Baltimore or East L.A.

I wasn't one of those who went up to pester him. I didn't gawk after celebrities, follow limousines, or chase ambulances. If I saw Hank betting on the horses in Hollywood Park, believe me I had sense enough to leave the man alone, even if it was only an acute sense of self-preservation that kept me at a distance. But it was more than that. I sure as hell wouldn't want people coming up to me simply because they recognized me, liked a record I'd recorded, a book I'd written, or a movie I'd starred in. People didn't see a building they admired and go off half-cocked and track down the architect, follow and hover round him or her, haunt their environment, phone them, ask for their autograph, try to find out where they lived, want to have their baby, did they?

Who knows? Perhaps there are anonymous groups out there that meet on a weekly basis to discuss their secret obsession with architects: gathered in a tight circle beneath a dim light in some borrowed attic or cellar, they sit, eager to share their problems of living in a society that is too quick to cast aspersions, and in which they are misunderstood: "Hello, my name is Marcia, and I am a recovering obsessive/compulsive with a fixation on architects." A hum of acknowledgement, rich with empathy, emanates from the entire group, before they continue, going round and round each confessing their dirty little secret shame.

Besides, having had some experience of my own, I knew that people went to the racetrack to get away from it all, to dream big impossible dreams, and to feel some otherworldly affinity with those impressive thoroughbreds, those haughty fillies. Disturbing Hank at the racetrack would be like shouting out something obscene at someone on the other side of a cathedral: "Hey, Louie, you get laid last night?"

No, I'm telling you, it just wasn't something you wanted to do.

Nevertheless, people approached him as if they were the very best of buddies, as if they'd both been weaned off the same bottle of muscatel or Ripple wine. Fans swarmed the man. They wanted to let him know they liked his stuff, that his was the only writing they read, that they had a thing or two in common. "Hey, Bukowski, I love your poetry." "Will you sign this racing program?" "Can I buy you a beer?"

Was a writer different from any other schmuck? Was it something similar to the Native American who avoided having his image caught in a photograph; these people felt that in owning what the artist produced, they owned a piece of his soul as well?

Meanwhile, I beat a hasty and embarrassed retreat, perhaps due to my being a Kastinovich—anonymity being the preferred status of our family, for in that name lay a thousands insults and injuries, a thousand years of crimes and assaults and persecutions.

I cherished my inconspicuousness. I regularly practiced the art of being invisible, though, in reality, it was an innate ability I was born with. I didn't have to try. I was regularly overlooked in stores and restaurants. If I spoke up in my pipsqueak voice, I'd get no response. I could be there for hours waiting for someone to assist me in my own bookstore. If there was anyone else around, the customers would walk right past me and up to them thinking they were the person who worked there. Even the baby in the window commanded more authority than yours truly.

While I waited for Hank to make an appearance, I gazed through the door of my bookshop, awaiting the eager throngs of book reading, book loving, more importantly, book buying customers—far too numerous to count—that San Pedro had to offer. The signs were favorable. Soon the Reagans would retire from office. New blood would turn things around. Young blood. People would wake up, wondering how it had happened, how the country had been allowed to slip into that deep dark sleep. Video games would become passé; America would regain its lost soul. The intelligentsia would rise again.

I merely waited for the trickle-down theory to reach me. In the meantime, I patiently dismembered time, compared and contrasted reality with expectations. I surveyed the shop, found it overflowing with enough fiction, nonfiction, art books, etc., to educate and enlighten a small country, books which all those potential I'll-believe-'em-when-I-see-'em, customers could feed their muchdeprived heads. And I bit my fingernails down to the quick, hoping to make enough sales to pay the rent.

I planned the future as though it were a paint-by-numbers kit. I designed ornate connect-the-dot games in my search for an avenue toward achieving a modicum of success, a means of staying afloat. Never mind that one or another of my Jewish aunts or uncles constantly remarked: "You want to make God laugh? Make a plan." Every other month had so far brought an imminent catastrophe of unpaid bills, surprise expenses, and forgotten or overlooked problems wreaking havoc in all corners of the store. I dreamt glorious dreams of buying out the shop next door, perhaps upstairs as well; we'd expand, fill the entire building with books, used right now, sure, but how about a rare book room, and a new book section? How about shelves rising to the ceilings? A basement filled with subversive material? So what if there wasn't a basement. Hell, I'd get down there with a shovel and dig one myself.

I dreamed of having a literary Winchester Mystery House. I'd expand the bookstore downward and outward, room after room, filled to the brim with books.

I kept one uncertain finger on the pulse of the leading economic indicators, monitored the unemployment rate, business failures and inflation. During the Great Depression people had flocked to the movies. But how had book sales fared? People had sought escape, diversion, and, after all, used books were an inexpensive commodity. On top of that, the best of them were works of art; they enriched the soul, were objects of beauty.

I wasn't sure, however, whether it was best for the economic situation to improve so that people would have more money to spend, or for things to worsen so they would rush to buy books in order to alleviate their problems. It was another quandary in which I found myself befuddled. Something I couldn't seem to unravel.

Hank regularly sat and chatted with the old Romanian at the Kabob place directly across the street, two relics in a modern world, the Sphinx and the Cyclops, a lovely sight to behold. Most of the time the Sphinx sat with a newspaper, while the Cyclops stood guard, or wiped the counter with a soiled rag. I watched, noting that they had no need for speech.

Hank smoked his slender, brown, foreign cigarettes, the Romanian his hand-rolled smokes. There they chewed the fat, snarled at passersby, shared a laugh or two. The two of them older and meaner than sin itself.

I watched them with an undying fascination, a sense of awe. I had a strong affinity for anything and anyone old. I relished decrepit buildings, ruins, shards of ancient pottery, and relics of any kind.

I brought out my binoculars, to have a better look. Hank sipped a cup of something, coffee, probably the thick, bitter, European style the

Romanian brewed up for himself. It was a dark gooey brew I couldn't even get down. He smoked. There was a paper on the table in front of him. A racing form, perhaps. I strained to see what horse he might be betting on, but, due to the angle of the paper and the distance, couldn't make out anything. The thought of walking up with Hank to cash our winning daily double helped buoy my spirits.

The combined viciousness on their side of the street was, of course, in marked contrast to the sheer youth, inexperience, and innocence on our side. I watched the Cyclops and the Sphinx spit, smoke and swear, communicating mostly with grunts and snarls, a few monosyllables thrown in now and then. I listened, and must admit I did attempt to mimic, to join in on the exclusive language they shared. I even practiced it when alone in the shop: how to sit like Bukowski, the gestures, the look, the voice. But I failed miserably, except to entertain my one-year-old daughter, who occupied the crib in the bookstore window. The kid was my cohort, my partner, and sometimes bouncer. My wife's presence was sporadic, as she often had to find a job so we'd have money to pay the rent, put food on the table, and of course buy books with which to stock our shelves.

I struggled with how to overcome my purity, my innocence. I didn't smoke, drink, or do drugs. I didn't cavort with prostitutes, or even gamble with any enthusiasm. God, I was green.

Hank's voice went with his face. It was the voice of a mountain, if a mountain could or would talk. I, on the other hand, had the voice of a sparrow. And aside from maybe sticking a lit cigar down my throat I had no idea how to attain the ability to speak like a mountain. Besides, it was tricky to escape the banal, the pleasantries, hello, how are you, what's new? I could handle the monosyllables okay. But I couldn't get around the problem that one word led to another, a question begged a response, which led invariably to another question.

Unbearable long stretches of time passed wherein the Sphinx and the Cyclops didn't utter a single word.

Whenever I saw Hank on the street, or in my bookstore, or across at the Kabob stand, I'd wave. He'd wave.

"Just got back from the track," Hank would say, flashing a grin that led me to believe he'd had a good day. Then I faced the obvious, glaring question of what, if anything, to say next? "Gee, how'd you do?" "What horses did you bet on?" "You going back tomorrow?" Or just nod and grin? Silent pauses made me squirm. It was a vicious cycle. The grunts and other noises also gave me trouble. I could neither decipher nor utilize them correctly—that specialty of saying so much by not saying anything. Perhaps I could convince the Cyclops to write a dictionary of grunts and other sounds for me on the three-and-a half by five-inch notepad on which he jotted down his daily totals.

The Romanian's saving grace was that he never ever asked Hank about his writing, never once mentioned books; words were intended to adorn a menu or a sign, nothing more. Books were the equivalent of someone who not only talked too much, but who couldn't stop; who could possibly have that much to say? About anything? He would no more read a book than he would listen to someone spill their guts about their lifetime of sorrows. He looked at books the way I looked at Pet Rocks, or Cabbage-Patch dolls; they were ludicrous, utterly without merit, useless.

"Anything I need to say," he informed me, "I can say in one or two sentences. Who needs a whole book?" He was among the many who were eager to inform me, a bookseller, why they didn't buy or read books.

The times I sat down to eat in his establishment, instead of taking the food to go to enjoy in the refuge of my bookstore, the Cyclops joined me more or less by sitting down at one of the other tables, or at least rested one foot on a nearby chair as he leaned on his knee and smoked a cigarette. He sighed such weary, heavy sighs. While I ate he gazed up at the ceiling, blew smoke rings and watched them dissipate, picked up a newspaper, looked at his hands, his fingernails, stared at the door. He sighed again, then spat on the tiled floor. He closed his eyes. If I was thoughtless enough to ask a question or make a remark like, "Seen Hank lately?" he snarled at the intrusion, the disturbance to his train of thought. And for all I knew he was thinking about grand unforgettable events: recalling his youth, past joys, the name of the gorgeous girl he had kissed one night at her window—what had ever happened to her?—the friends he had grown up with, those rare moments in his life when contentedness and happiness had paid him a short visit; moments far too fleeting, too remote, and too few.

The Romanian greeted his customers with a shout, "*Vhat do you vant?*" in a thick accent. He'd tell them what they could or couldn't have with their sandwiches, what was acceptable to put between two slices of bread and what was not, and ran people out of the place if and when they annoyed him, which wasn't infrequently. Other than that he was quite lovable.

I liked the old man. Every day I waved, "Hey, Svevo, how's it going?" He'd wave back and snarl. A gesture indicating things were rotten as usual.

"Vhy you always call me that?" he sometimes asked.

"Call you what?"

"Svevo?"

"Isn't that your name?"

"No," he said, sizing me up with a look that made it clear that he was considering the removal of my head. "I never told you my name."

I didn't bother to ask what his name was either, and he never did tell me. I liked the one I had picked out for him just fine. He seemed like a Svevo, acted like a Svevo, and so for me he would always be Svevo. There were plenty of other things I didn't ask him about, though I was definitely interested in knowing: what the faded tattoos that adorned his arms were; what he had seen and done during his long life; what was the secret of his friendship with Bukowski? But all that would have entailed conversation.

I stepped outside the bookstore and watched for potential customers, some unwary strays I might lure into the shop. A sporty couple in their early thirties, very trim and squeaky clean, looking every bit as though they'd just stepped off their catamaran, entered the ka-bob shop, looked over the menu and ordered something. Perhaps they would stroll over to my shop after they enjoyed their meal.

"Say, how about putting some of that sauce on the sandwich?" this foolish tourist fresh off the boat asked.

"No!" the Romanian answered.

"Look, I'll gladly pay extra, I don't mind, I just want some of that sauce."

"You know vhat?" the Romanian said. "I no put that sauce on that sandwich. That sauce don't go on the sandwich. The sauce is for salad. You vant sauce, you order salad."

Get the man riled up and he says more in one minute than he has said in a whole month. There was no arguing with him. There was no shaking him from his convictions. These people simply did not know how to eat. He'd send them off in search of another establishment, or they'd become so indignant with his behavior, his mannerisms, his smoking as he cooked their food, that they would leave.

"Come on, dear, let's go somewhere else!"

"*Fine*, you go." He dismissed them with a wave of his hand.

I watched them jump back into their sports car and drive off without so much as a glance toward the bookstore. I called out to my friend, who stood in his doorway glaring after his errant customers. "You sure got rid of them, all right."

"Idiots. They vant to tell me how to make my food."

My daughter spied him from her crib in the window. "Look, daddy, it's the funny old man," she said. He scowled and waved his fat fist at her, but she laughed and pointed at him. "Funny old man."

She wasn't the least bit afraid of this man who made a regular habit of yelling at potential customers, leaving them cowering with a sudden loss of appetite, eager to flee from his shop, about to soil their pants. I, too, always prepared to defend myself, ready to duck or run, whenever I asked for one of his Greek salads or one of his beloved gyros sandwiches, never knowing if he was going to chew me out, slap me upside the head, or throw the food at me.

My daughter, on the other hand, thought he was amusing.

He came over still shaking his fist at her. "Who's a funny old man?"

"You are," she said, standing her ground, her tiny hands grasping hold of the wooden rails of her crib.

"I'm not a funny old man. Your father, *he's* a funny old man."

"No," she said with a giggle. "You're the funny old man."

He held up a packet of crackers, dangled it like a carrot in front of her face.

"You vant crackers, huh?" he said, gruffly. She nodded her head, yes, yes. "I punch your face!" He touched her face with his clenched fist and handed her the crackers. "Vhat you say?"

"Thank you, funny old man," she said, laughing, as she watched him cross back to his side of the street.

I'm telling you, the girl never once laughed at Hank Chinaski.

The old Romanian was a regular cigar-store Indian who stood guard outside of his Ka-bob place. He looked one way, then the other, huffed, then puffed, and finally turned to me with a shrug.

"Vhat's wrong with this place?" he asked. "Vhere are all the customers?"

I stood in the doorway of the bookshop, faced him across the street. I noted that we two spent an inordinate amount of time gazing with dubious hope up one side of the street and down the other, waiting, looking for someone, anyone headed our way.

"Don't worry, things will change," I said without much conviction. "They'll come once they get the revitalization going."

He shot me a dubious look. "Maybe," he muttered, mashing out his cigarette butt on the sidewalk. The proposed revitalization project had suffered delay after delay. But it was on which we hung our hopes, our future. "For this, I should have stayed in the old country."

I thought about that. Would the old man go back? Maybe if things didn't work out here I could join him. Imagine, the two of us living the good life back in the old country; days of hard toil, nights of hard liquor. Were there books and bookstores there? Perhaps, instead, I could tend sheep on a hillside, live in a shack, return to the simple way of life. Something far removed from the unnatural complexities of profit margins, taxes, business licenses, advertising and customer relations.

Hank and I were the old Romanian's best customers, and while pleasant company we may have been, we two certainly didn't eat enough to keep a business afloat, although compared to me Chinaski had a powerful stomach. Me, I was scrawny, a wisp of nothing.

In the deathly eerie quiet and stillness of the bookstore—as if a deep dark winter had descended overnight, especially when the kid was napping peacefully, or teething on some vile hardcover by William F. Buckley Jr.—I pondered the very thing the Romanian had asked. Where were the people, the customers? There was a clothing shop, a toy store, and a stationery nearby which seemed to do a good amount of business. I watched people pull up and enter those shops and come out again with their hands full of bundles and packages. Why would they patronize those shops but not ours? Why did they jump into their cars and drive off as if muggers or rapists were in hot pursuit? Did they know something we didn't?

I knew the answer had to be simple: Buy more books! I was sure that the more we had the more people would come. So I scoured the city, borrowed money, spent savings. It was just a matter of numbers, a simple equation of getting enough books in, and letting people know about it. We put banners up, proclaiming a Grand Reopening. And I filled the shelves with all the books I could find. I didn't care what they were or how much I paid for them.

A Crown Bookstore had just opened up the road on Western Avenue, but I was unconcerned, even though everybody dropped by to inform me that a Crown Bookstore spelled death for our establishment. Let them have their puny shelf of bestsellers, their books for forty percent off. We would deal with it by the sheer overwhelming numbers of books, the scope and breadth of our selection.

2

In the Belly of the Beast

The day my pregnant wife and I married, my father took me aside. His face wore the expression of immense sadness and disappointment with which he often greeted me. Once more, I had let him down, not that I did anything. It was what I didn't do. He didn't approve of my life. As if I did. He didn't approve of my wife, either. He didn't approve of our having a child. And he didn't approve of the direction I was headed, which was no direction at all.

"You haven't amounted to much of anything," he said, shaking his head. I was going to ask him to tell me something I didn't already know. "You're not going anywhere. You're drifting. And schtooping. It doesn't take brains to do that." I couldn't argue with him there. He sized me up with his usual look of reproach. "Just look at you. You've got a family now. You need to do something with your life."

"I'm doing what I can." I realized it was pitiful, a man of twenty-eight years working minimum wage jobs. When I could keep them.

He made a sound to show what he thought of my efforts.

I had tried my hand at various jobs, all without success. My stint as a driver was short-lived because for the life of me I couldn't avoid running over curbs, or backing into buildings or walls. "I have problems with visual perception," I told the boss, who quietly told me to find work somewhere else, as he surveyed his smashed-up van. I was employed for a while in a sail loft, the monotony of which I enjoyed because I spent the time dreaming of sailing away to far remote corners of the globe, like my mother's Portuguese ancestors once did, those sailors of the far Azores, but the savage abuse my body suffered, the pain in my arms, knees, and feet, finally won the upper hand and I had to quit and search for something less strenuous. There was my three days of employment at a Fotomat, and a short stint, too, in a burger joint, but it was only a stopgap measure until something better showed up.

"I've decided that in lieu of giving you two a honeymoon," my father continued, "I'm going to do you a favor." He paused to let this sink in. I gulped, unsure of what to expect.

"Yeah?" His words made me uneasy, knowing as I did that everything my father did came with strings attached. While he gaveth with one hand he withheld with the other. More strings than a harp.

He nodded his sage head. "Yes, I'm going to help set you up in business. I saw an ad in the newspaper, a bookstore running a going-out-of-business sale. I'll make them an offer, and I want you to run the shop. You like books, so it makes sense. You'll learn something about running a business."

Much as I hated to be handed anything from the old man, my predicament was so lousy. There was nothing good that loomed on the horizon. I was without natural talent, or training. I knew nothing about anything. So I agreed. It would be mine in name only, while he could boast that he had saved me from a life of perdition. "Okay," I said, shrinking, cringing. I watched the magnanimous man puff out his chest. "Thanks. It beats flipping burgers." He snorted and proceeded to tell me the all-too familiar tale of how as a young man he'd worked at a grill all hours, until he got himself a better job at a carpet warehouse. "It was backbreaking work, but I showed everyone I was made of the same stuff as they were." He too was tough, and he'd worked until the sweat ran down the crack of his ass, as he repeatedly informed his progeny of no-necked varlets.

"Okay, okay, I get it," I said, disturbed by his overly graphic description.

"That's what I want to see from you, see? With a wife and kid and this store you'll have to work hard," he intoned.

"I know."

"Sure, you know. You know nothing." The faith he had in his first born son was nothing short of inspiring.

We took over the bookstore, ran several ads announcing, "Still in Business," and hung signs and banners proclaiming the same. They had run their going-out-of-business sale for many months, so the stock, while large, had been picked over. It was called the Little Big Bookshop, after the title of *Little Big Man* by Thomas Berger, and was appropriately named considering its size, which was large, and the fact that all of us who worked there stood well under five-foot-six.

On occasion Hank moseyed over my way, and in his I've-got-Time-by-the-throat-deliberateness signed a few of his books, and left. Now and then he bought something: a magazine, a book on Hemingway.

"How're things going?" he'd ask.

"Okay Hank. We're keeping our nose to the grindstone."

He'd nod, smile, and leave saying, "May the gods be kind."

There was never any sense of urgency to Hank. Every move, every gesture indicated that he was content to sit back and wait it out with the best of them. He took his own sweet time, spoke ever so slowly, walked with a leisure gait, a casualness, if not grace—like the Pope himself—as he smiled at you, waved his hand, mouthed his holy offerings. And like the Pope, people hung on his every word, waited for him to utter a benediction or condemnation. "This is shit, this is good," all in that voice, that intonation that bespoke, "I've had the last laugh. There is no need to rush. Not when you have outlived so much good, so much bad. Not when you've got time by the balls."

By the throat, by the balls, Hank gripped them both.

I gazed at this man who had survived so many close calls with death, who had ingested so many poisons he was now inured to them, and used those very toxins to his own advantage. They fueled his writings, particularly the more vile and disturbing tales and poems. Perhaps he was immune to death. Nothing could kill him. Invulnerable after a lifetime of depravity, the man who had written, *Crucifix in a Deathhand* and *Confessions of a Man Insane Enough to Live with Beasts* and *Flower, Fist and Bestial Wail*, like some flesh and blood inverse version of *The Picture of Dorian Grey*, the painting, not the man. One look at his face and you could see he had escaped nothing. Every moment of debauchery, every sin Bukowski ever committed, was etched upon that unique mug for all to see.

There was little that compared to catching sight of Hank as he drove past the bookstore, the black steed he rode, his BMW, Bukowski's own Rocinante glistening, in the bright San Pedro sunlight; he waved and grinned, his arm stretched out the window, a cigarette stuck in his mouth. *Hello, my people.* The slow wave, *bless you my son.*

It was reassuring, comforting in a way, for anyone who had done even half the things he had purportedly done, anyone that old, who had debauched in extremis, and survived, inevitably made one feel that they not only had so much life yet to live, but that they had an awful lot of catching up to do, as well.

Hank always looked at me as if he was about to reach right out and pat me on the head. He invariably called me "baby," because like most people, compared to him that's about all my nearly thirty years amounted to. He always said it as if he was truly surprised to see anyone so damned innocent, so green, so fresh; as if he could in no way imagine himself having ever been as young. I amused him. Had he ever seen anyone more deserving of being called baby?

Thus, I worked frequently at coming up with a manner, an expression, something to show I had lived, I had traveled, had seen the world, that I had done things. Not withstanding my feeble attempts, the deeper tone of voice I used whenever he was around, Hank remained unconvinced.

He departed saying, "Hang in there, baby," giving a slight wave of his hand, a gesture at one and the same time of both acknowledgment and instant dismissal.

I liked him, though I admit I squirmed uncomfortably beneath his gaze. I never felt so wet behind the ears as when Hank was around. Sitting in my bookstore where I was the purported owner, if not master, where for all intents and purposes I didn't have to answer to anyone, I felt proud. I had the desire to accomplish something good, something worthy and beneficial. Here, I was contributing something to society, if nothing more than the dissemination of ideas, dreams, information and beauty. But if I stepped outside to see Hank standing nearby, I suddenly had to suppress the urge to stick my thumb in my mouth and say something pithy and wise, like "ga ga."

I thought for a while of knifing someone; say an evil pawnbroker or landlord, or better yet one of our fellow shop owners, who looked down their noses at us as if they couldn't wait to be rid of these outlanders who didn't belong in San Pedro. Then, perhaps, I might not appear quite so god-awful young to the old man. If nothing else it was discouraging to be looked at as some harmless, sweet bird of youth. It rankled me to no end, and I began going out in the evenings, and driving round and round a five or six block radius. I informed people that I was spending my nights on the docks, hanging out in bars with pimps and pushers, taking notes as a witness to San Pedro's most violent scenes.

I dreamt up vivid tales of depravity that I might very well have witnessed during the long cool San Pedro nights on the waterfront, around the fishing boats, tugboats and cargo ships. If I saw a fight break out on Pacific Avenue, if I sidestepped a spike-heeled hooker on 6th Street, or encountered a rough looking specimen with more scars than charm careening down the sidewalk after happy hour, I spiced up these incidents to resemble more closely the life I imagined for myself. A life wherein I witnessed beatings, muggings, murders, consorted with hookers, freaks and thugs, and brawled with stevedores.

Perhaps I took it farther than I should have, for I yearned for those days of yesteryear when sideshows roamed the countryside, revival meetings, medicine shows, traveling preachers. I longed to accompany third-rate freak shows, which promised unnatural sights for the curious: viewings at midnight, after the ladies and the kiddies have gone, *Pay your buck at the door, and see things you won't believe are true! Come feast your eyes on Wondrous Wanda the Contortionist as she performs her sensational act! Guaranteed to thrill every man out there! And some of you ladies too!*

I discovered I was an adequate liar, and then some. No doubt due to the fact that I was a Kastinovich. My family had honed and developed this particular talent to a fine art over the centuries, in order to insure our survival in an otherwise hostile world. No one doubted me, no matter how wild and outrageous the story; no one even so much as questioned whether I had done or seen what I claimed. It appeared I could say anything and be believed.

I donned a new hat.

"Where'd you get that?" I was asked.

"Fight last night," I improvised. "Some drunk started trouble. I relieved him of this. He's now wearing a trashcan lid."

They shook their heads. My nocturnal activities only confirmed the worst of their long-held suspicions. "You'd better be careful," they warned. "You'll end up in jail, if not dead."

"Don't worry about me. I can take care of myself."

"I don't want to get a phone call at two in the morning asking me to come bail you out of jail."

I grinned, and tisk-tisking their concerns. Their tacit acceptance of anything I said spurred me on to ever more unbelievable lies. I concocted a tragic tale about Joe, the fisherman, who fell in love with a transvestite stevedore named Willy, who ran off with San Pedro's only one-legged Hermaphrodite, Doreen, and that was only the beginning.

Family and friends observed me in a new way: that of someone who might go off half-cocked at any moment, and say anything, do anything.

"He's headed for trouble," they murmured behind my back. "I wouldn't put anything past him."

I drove through the toughest areas, so at least I able to honestly say I had been there, and therefore might in truth have seen the things I described, and where I could at least try to absorb some of the unsavory atmosphere of the place. I considered how I might be regarded if only I had a decent scar running the length of my cheek. Maybe if I walked with a limp, something that would raise me up a notch in estimation and respect whenever Hank deigned to gaze upon me with that appraising eye of his, in which I looked about as harmful as moss.

I took small comfort in the fact that Hank liked me, or at least tolerated me in the way that nature had arranged things so that the old were forced to make room for the new. It was probably similar to how the dinosaurs in the twilight of their reign as top of the food chain looked upon the surging hordes of mammals, which were quickly evolving to usher in the eventual age of the bipeds. It was easy to imagine tiny furry mammals swarming through the forests, proliferating like rabbits, while the dinosaurs nonchalantly surveyed the scene, much in the way we might note a sudden upsurge in the cockroach population; mildly interesting, perhaps even annoying, but hardly threatening.

Hank's ravaged face dredged up so much of San Pedro. This was where he now resided, his adopted home tucked away in this neglected corner of Los Angeles, bypassed by the major freeways, those flowing rivers of traffic and populace that filled to maddening congestion all other parts of the city. Most people didn't take the 110 Freeway beyond the 405. The 110 dead-ended in San Pedro, where people drove in order to catch the boat to Catalina Island or a cruise ship, but little else.

Because of its location at the L.A. harbor, on the underside of the hump of Palos Verdes, San Pedro had grown at a slower rate than L.A. proper; it lagged a couple of decades behind. Life moved at a much more leisurely pace.

Here Hank had settled, nestled in the bosom of San Pedro's ethnic minorities: the Italians, Mexicans, the Filipinos, the Croatians, Japanese, the few Portuguese—my other tribe by way of my mother—who manned the everfewer fishing boats. Someone told me that long ago some Azoreans had called San Pedro "Little Faial," coincidentally the very island on which my mother was born. Where were their descendants, I wondered. The Azorean men and women who'd left behind those tiny volcanic islands?

Bukowski's face conjured up the docks and Terminal Island, the L.A. Red cars sunk in obscurity beneath the murky waters of the harbor; the numerous dives and restaurants; Old Front Street, with its speakeasies, bars and flophouses, which clung so precariously to life for so long, and was demolished before my disbelieving eyes, to make room for fancy office buildings and grand hotels.

San Pedro, so the newspapers proclaimed, was slated for renovation. In the meantime it was still a haven for secondhand stores, Thrifty's and Woolworth's, bars, pawnshops, and empty storefronts. The nouveau riche hadn't yet gotten to it, which would possibly partly explain why things were so rotten in the bookstore, far removed from the economic upswing which, we repeatedly heard rumors, was just around the corner.

Down along Pacific Avenue and Gaffey Street, hordes of Latino, Asian and other minorities, men, women and children, mingled with the down-and-outers and drunks, the pickpockets, prostitutes, and occasional poet, and the wandering tribes from the halfway houses, all of which gave San Pedro a sort of carnivalesque, fiesta-like feel. You always expected the unexpected, nothing could surprise you, not the gangbangers, a sailor on crutches, or the thirty-something-year-old tourist with money growing out of his pockets. I anticipated the arrival of hawkers of strange wares, soup kitchens and bread lines to feed the hungry, and feats of daring and bravado performed by self-taught street urchins.

San Pedro was some kind of off-kilter "Brigadoon." Okay, so it wasn't exactly filled with beautiful women who could carry a tune, magic ambiance, or riches and good times. Still, it was a pleasant and charming haven, for the most part, though here and there were places that had I the means I would have leveled. It retained some echo of its former charm: a sleepy café at Land's End, where everything they served was flavored with the tang of the sea; quiet streets, lined with quaint 1930s homes and palm trees, the older buildings of downtown, the wharf.

The touristy Ports O' Call Village and the port, the Santa Catalina boat and the cruise ships, aside, San Pedro was an otherwise sleepy little beach town. It was a place where someone like Bukowski could more or less live in peace--at least his neighbors didn't give a flying fig about who or what he was. Poetry? What did they know or care about poetry? Most had no clue of the celebrity in their midst. But San Pedro was also a strange, dark, twisted little realm, in its own subdued sort of way. Muffled, strangulated whispers assaulted me whenever I chanced to catch a catnap at the bookstore, before or after hours, informing me that beneath the entire town were interconnected tunnels, as if legions of gigantic moles had riddled the hills with their burrows, and that these tunnels led to the underground bunkers near Land's End, built during or before World War II. I spent many an hour searching for these lost secret tunnels; they drew me in a manner of a recurring dream you never forget and which you will yourself to try and recapture, to experience yet again; the call of a siren you'd follow without thought or hesitation, to whatever fate that awaited you.

Terminal Island lay just across the channel. I often took the Vincent Thomas Bridge from San Pedro to Terminal Island in order to get to Long Beach where magical places like Acres of Books and The Book Treasury awaited my perusal. Terminal Island attracted my interest because it was a manmade island, made up mostly of wood pulp and the like, and constituted a major engineering nightmare because it was slowly rotting from the inside out. No one could figure out how to rectify the situation. I saw it as a particularly ferocious strain of mold or dry rot, just below the surface, hidden from view, spreading until finally the whole damned thing would cave-in on itself. Why this was enticing to me, I cannot say. Perhaps it was because it intimated that everything around me, the bookstore, San Pedro, all was just as corrupt, all of it rotting from the inside, all of it about to come crumbling down on my head.

Passing across the bridge one saw the *Princess Louise* moored below with its restaurant, gift shop, nightclub and wedding chapel, complete with an authentic Irish priest. The priest, with his charming, melodious brogue, had performed the service for my wedding in the chapel aboard the ship, and yet in a heavy-handed and ostentatious move so typical of fate, the ship eventually had to be towed out to sea whereupon it broke its mooring lines and sank, thus offering, I suppose, what amounted to a befitting testimonial to our marriage.

My wife, daughter and I shared a one-bedroom apartment in a classic 1920s bungalow on the several square-block patch of ground aptly called Land's End. The bluffs faced the ocean, and through the curtain of smog and mists, Santa Catalina Island lay twenty miles in the distance, looking for all the world like an enormous sea monster risen from the dark and gloomy depths. We were lulled to sleep each night by the mournful cry of the lighthouse foghorn singing out its monotonous sad refrain. Its persistent voice was a reassuring nightly lullaby; a melancholy but steadfast presence, whose single tone rang in my ears: "Woe" it sang, filling the night with its long, drawn-out cry, in a note I took pains to determine was a B flat, likely out of tune. "Woe!"—the sad lament of the ghost of a shipwrecked sailor stranded upon this desolate, forsaken shore.

3

Age Before Beauty

The world trickled past the bookstore windows while I took every opportunity to sneak out to hunt down more books. Instead of answering questions concerning authors and titles, I daily informed the curious and incredulous that my daughter lying in the crib in the window was indeed real and not a doll. People might come to buy or sell me books but they were shoved aside by those who flocked to the window to peer at the baby in the window; they stood amused, fogging up the glass, wiping at it to get a better view, entertained by her antics, oohing and ahing as they watched her sleep or philosophize in an uninterrupted stream of verbiage, one tiny emphatic finger raised in the air.

It wasn't uncommon for several elderly ladies to stand gawking, come in and ask a few questions, remark how sweet and beautiful a child I had, and then march away without so much as looking at, much less buying, a single book or magazine.

"Perhaps we should charge admission," I suggested to my wife. "A two or three dollar fee for the privilege of viewing our child in repose."

"No way," she said. "I won't have my daughter treated like a freak." Frankly it was difficult to be harsh or even angry with people who continuously told me what a lucky father I was to have so wondrous, bright, sweet and attractive a child.

My father popped by to survey the results of his new business venture.

"Are you working hard?" he asked.

"I'm working."

"Work harder. You don't seem to be doing much. Just sitting on your can all day." He sniffed around. "You need more people in here. There are only one or two customers back there."

I suggested he stand outside and be the barker to draw people into the shop.

"Beast which wants discourse of reason," he snarled. "Do you have any idea how hard I worked when I was your age? Get your sorry ass in gear. Hire some high school students to spread flyers. You've got a kid to support."

As if I needed any reminders.

I also listened to hysteric reports of Bukowski's occasional savagery, told by those who had heard about an incident that they swore up and down had occurred to a friend of a friend of theirs. There were rare instances reported by one who had actually chanced to meet him and had survived the encounter.

"He called me every name in the book!" one explained. "He flicked a lit cigarette and spit at me," said another. "I thought he was gonna rip me a new asshole!" complained a third.

The man they painted was an ogre, a beast, a creature who practiced vile, unnatural acts, and performed feats of public crudity with staggering regularity. They assured me he would just as soon bite your head off or piss on your shoes as look at you.

Whenever Hank did appear, however, I saw a softspoken man who shied away from overeager strangers raring to accost him. Instead of loud arrogance, the typical calling attention to oneself, which so many obviously felt was part and parcel to being a writer, I saw a humble, reticent man. He was shy, and seemed genuinely surprised that he had a following of devoted fans who thought he was the end-all-be-all of a great poet. He made it clear that he didn't think so highly of his own writing. "Ahh, it's nothing," he'd say, referring to his poetry. "I do what I do. I don't give a damn whether anyone likes it or not." I never once heard him brag, but he was always quick to give a nod to the Great Ones, the writers he admired and respected: Celine, Dostoyevsky, Fante, Hemingway. And though later, I would be guilty of unspeakable and unpardonable crimes against the man, not once did he ever attempt to pee on my shoes (although taking my head off was altogether a different matter).

Hank was older than anyone I'd ever seen, older than the Romanian, older than God, even, and that's saying something. Why, I'd heard it on good authority that if you only caught sight of the merest glint of the antiquity smoldering in God's eyes, it could shrivel your skin and cause your toes to shrink down to stubs. But Bukowski had it over God by a year or two at the very least.

I knew about God because my good friend Moses lived and breathed just a few blocks away on Pacific Ave, behind the counter of his bookstore. A wizened, whitehaired, whitebearded, wiry old man with the voice of a prophet and a gleam and glint in his eyes that could burn words in stone, eyes that spoke volumes. Moses was a man of impeccable tastes, who didn't much cotton to the superficial, the trivial, the trite. He cared not one whit for profit. He spent much of his time pondering the eternal question of why God had bothered to spare the human race. If his ire were raised, Moses would shoot you a look to make you wither. Whenever he spoke, even his sentences stood up straight, and had that biblical stamp, that aura proclaiming: This is The Law! You always expected to hear thunderbolts or see lightning flash whenever he spoke, but it wasn't put on, wasn't an act he assumed, it came quite naturally.

Bukowski was old in a different way; old like the very stones of Jericho or Babylon, like the smoldering embers of Sodom and Gomorrah; you knew with a glance that this man had lived through more hard living, self-abuse and depravity than any one man could possibly survive and live to tell about; eons and ages smoldered in his eyes. He was the essence of sin and violence—every vileness known to man emanated from each of his pores. But Bukowski didn't possess the visionary eyebrows or the lean jowls that belonged to Moses.

Then there was John Fante, Bukowski's God. Bukowski had long ago chanced upon a copy of *Ask the Dust* in the shelves of Los Angeles Public Library, a discovery like finding the finest of pearls amongst the most mediocre of swine and swill. But, of course, Fante was now dead and Bukowski wasn't, at least not yet, though the doctors would work overtime to find something that would kill him.

If Fante was older it was only by sheer weight of talent, of exuberance, an everyouthful verve, which is why his best work will never tire or become dated. Older, perhaps, but younger, too. Just try reading Fante and suddenly so much writing out there becomes difficult to stomach. Fante's particular phrasing, using the same tried and true words, the very same language everyone else used, but utilized in such a novel way; reading it had to be similar to what 16th century Portugal experienced after so many centuries of bland, tasteless food, suddenly discovering all the myriad foods and spices brought back from South and Central America and from South East Asia (imagine the face of someone tasting a cup of cocoa or experiencing nutmeg for the very first time), after Vasco da Gama finally reached India, and Pedro Álvares Cabral first landed in Brazil.

Find me another author whose writing is as word-perfect and fresh, as smart and vibrant as a first kiss.

And there I was the youngest of the young. A pure babe in swaddling clothes, peering out at the world, my eyes brimming with naiveté, expectation, and hope.

I did my time in the bookstore, watched the days turn into weeks, the weeks into months, and so on, waiting for the howling winds and rains, the deluge that would make up for the years of drought, and looked forward to settin' eyes on ol' man Noah floating by in his ark when the time came. I even had a special bookcase that I was certain would float. I loaded it up with my favorite books. If and when the floods did come I'd drift until the waters receded, find the first woman survivor and begin work to repopulate the planet at once.

I giggled and carried on like a blithering idiot at the thought of my non-book buying neighbors drowning like rats. And then the thought of restarting the human race wasn't so bad either. Oh, the changes I would make! The whole human institution would have to start out fresh on an entirely new track. Imagine, from humble bookseller to founder of a new race. Hordes of children, each my own offspring. Ah, the stories I would invent. Me, the happy patriarch. What would I tell them, that I came from a far and distant universe to set up a colony? Possibly. The choices were endless. "There was a far-flung island, children, which I left. I sailed without direction, for many weeks, drifting aimlessly, to wash up on the strip of beach we now call Leo Carrillo. And here I made my home."

It was thoughts like this that kept me going through the darkest hours of the Little Big Bookshop, my nose in a copy of *Ask the Dust* or *The Short Stories of Saki*.

The store appeared very modest from the outside, but once you stepped inside it wound on and on just this side of forever, as I was wont to say. Now and then I stumbled upon new nooks and corners of the store, which always startled me. "This wasn't here before," I'd exclaim, touching the books and the shelves on which they sat, wondering how this came to be here. In part, this was due to the fact that one never went through the bookstore in a straight line. You had to turn this way or that, wind your way around obstacles to find a path, a hallway, a space between shelves, if you were to make it from one end of the store to the other. I don't think I ever came back by the exact same route I had gone either. The apparent helter-skelter maze of shelves and rooms made it inevitable that you'd become confused and lose your bearings, or forget that this section was here and not somewhere else.

It was a public safety nightmare waiting for disaster to strike, and I have no idea how or why the fire marshal didn't have the business shut down on the spot as the most notorious firetrap he'd ever seen. I nursed a suspicion that the officials never ventured inside the shop, perhaps fearful they would not make it out again.

Trying to tell someone how to get to a particular section was a feat in itself, nearly impossible to explain. You could give them directions, but it was like instructing someone on how to find love, or better yet, how to find their way back out of love if they'd chanced to find themselves stranded upon that blessed yet maddening shore. Invariably, patrons returned to the counter exhausted and bewildered, as if they'd just been through an enormous house of mirrors and were amazed to have made it out again.

Those who tried to find their own way but failed, and who could somehow find their way back to the front counter, might ask for assistance.

"Say, I couldn't find the biography section."

"Come with me. I'll show you." I gestured for them to follow my lead, grabbed a torch and led each poor unsuspecting victim through the dim narrow passageways that wound their way in a labyrinth, much like the sewers of Paris.

"I'm Charon," I'd explain—not the cause or the instrument of their fate—I merely ushered them from one bank to the other. Whether they were escaping a threatening menace and had come seeking refuge in the bowels of the store, or were being consigned to confinement in a secret dungeon, where they were to suffer unspeakable tortures, I neither knew, nor cared. The rows and stacks of books stood mute sentinels to the comings and goings, representative of the legions of dead souls who had paused momentarily in life's long shuffle to pour a bit of themselves onto those pages. It was mind-boggling, the pantheon of authors and titles since the beginnings of written history, the lives each of those books represented, from the famous and the popular to the obscure, the unknown; all those countless dead and forgotten voiceless nobodies long-silenced by the cloak of oblivion. It was humbling to say the least.

The bookstore was in a large two-storied building built in the twenties. It had survived the Long Beach earthquake in 1933. We were unable to determine precisely what the square footage of the structure was, but we figured it was approximately twenty-eight hundred, give or take a few hundred feet. It was split level in the back, behind a false wall. And every single inch of space was piled, stacked and crammed with books, new, old and ancient, magazines, sheets of illustrations and engravings removed from timeworn volumes. Countless stacks of boxes of books that hadn't been gone through in God only knew how long, all reaching up to the ceiling.

We had hopes and dreams of doing a flourishing trade, supplying the people of San Pedro with glorious reading material. We had no aspirations of building an empire, a chain of bookstores, or of making a fortune. It was, after all, a noble if unappreciated profession, and our goal was to provide variety while introducing quality, an alternative to the run-of-the-mill, certainly to the sterile uniformity of what one found at Crown Books, B. Dalton's, and the other chain stores.

I'd been reared on the sure knowledge that hard work and persistence were all one needed to succeed, to compete with the other guy and hold one's own. In other words, I was as naïve, as untried and as innocent as the one-and-a-half-year-old in the window.

We were going to fill these shelves with all the books we could find: the rare and unusual, every genre, every subject, the recently published, groundbreaking new writers, experimental writers, the foreign and the domestic, the popular and the classics.

Family and friends stopped by to see the bookstore, including some I hadn't seen in years, many expecting free books. They had a look around San Pedro, 6th Street, the shop.

"Heard you had yourself a store," they said. "Yeah, this is where you belong. This is perfect. This place was made for you. Good luck."

I wasn't sure what they meant. This was my kind of place? Where I belonged? Were they speaking of the bookstore or San Pedro, or both? There was too much delight in their voices, a tone similar to someone who's heard you've fallen off the wagon again and though they'd be loathe to admit it, is secretly thrilled by the news, simply because misery does love its company, especially when the guy next to you is a notch lower; even the gutter has its hierarchy. It sounded too much as if I were being condemned and sentenced. And why good luck? Did they know something I didn't? Besides, it was hard to miss the fact that none of them bothered to buy a book. Don't think it didn't occur to me to wonder what that might portend.

"How is business?" they asked. "How are sales?"

"Fine, just fine," I said, pumping my legs as I spun the grindstone on which I sharpened my reason to a fine, sharp edge. "Couldn't be better."

They provided me with various opinions on what I should or shouldn't do, how to improve the bookstore: "You might want to open up a section where you can serve coffee, tea and bagels, that kind of thing, bring more people into the store. You could make a killing." Be sure to be nice to the customers, they suggested, smile, remember the customer is always right, specialize, sell textbooks, students need books for their classes; cut your prices.

I nodded my head and filed away their sage advice for safekeeping.

"Sure," I said, "yeah, yeah, yeah." If I charged any less for books, I'd have to pay people to take them.

"Hey, baby. How're things goin'?" Bukowski popped in to ask.

"Well, quite frankly..." I proceeded to mention that recurrence of twenty or thirty dollar days did not bode well for our future, nor did it escape me that had I been charging all those people to stare at my daughter I would have made more off her than I had made off the books. I was beginning to tire of the situation. After all, what effect might all these people staring at her in her crib day after day have on her future state of mind? Might being on exhibition turn my child into some third-rate carny performer?

"Hang in there, baby," Hank said. He shuffled off to go fight off his fanatical admirers, and compose a poem about a ridiculous punk kid pretending to be an adult and attempting to run a bookstore.

Friends who knew the true state of affairs told me not to get discouraged: "Business is always tough at first. Things will improve. You just have to stick it out through the rough times, like a marriage." As if I needed to be reminded of that!

Various locals dropped by to give me the benefit of their wisdom. A representative of San Pedro's Serbo-Croatian population, in answer to my idea of serving the community by ordering books written in their language, replied:

"Look, don't bother. Serbo-Croatians don't read."

Others popped in for a quick peek and an assessment of the scene of impending ruin.

"Books!" they cried, as if they had never dreamed of finding such a thing in this town. "Good luck. Don't you know people in this town don't read?"

Clearly this was far more than what people said was my having to face an uphill struggle, or having my work cut out for me. That would have been a cinch. I liked a challenge as much as the next schmuck, even more. After all, I'd pretty much been weaned since day one on my father's words: "Suffering is good for the soul." And, hey, I wanted to improve my soul as much as anyone, but at this particular point, I wasn't even sure that that flabby, deflated thing that fluttered and flopped around was indeed a soul, or just a matter of indigestion.

I began to see things in a new light. I drove up to the heights of Palos Verdes and gazed out over the seething world below: Los Angeles, as I saw it, was the result of some unholy union between Hollywood and Disneyland, which had spilled out over their borders and boundaries and spread like the plague. All these people came blinded, year after year believing with every last ounce of faith they had: yes, child, this is the land of dreams, where miracles do happen: Flying elephants, Never-Never Land and Eden, too, why, your very own Prince on his White Horse is just around that corner, and yes, Virginia, there really is a film director and a producer with your name in their eyes all lit-up in neon or floodlights, like the God-damned Hollywood sign itself; this was the celluloid Baghdad or, a 20th century techno-recreation of a Middle Eastern bazaar, where anything and everyone was for sale, a land where the air was so thick you could build your very own dream castle upon it; where each and every fresh-faced wanna-be star or starlet had a shelf life shorter than the latest model of nifty computer to hit the showroom floors; and what I was doing was trying to convince these people that this Blight was in fact the Promised Land, and not this mirage-infested desert-land with its unending beaches and beautiful blond-haired, bronze-skinned, bikini-clad sun-worshippers; the mythological California they desired just as fervently as the old conquistadors who searched the teeming jungles of South America for El Dorado, the City of Gold.

I might just as well have gone round trying to convince these people to put aside their bibles, their houses of worship and religious leaders and go back to worshiping the ancient deities instead. "Oh, Zeus, looking down from the heights of Mount Olympus; Thor, let me hear your thunder's roar; Venus, show me your lovely nymphs." Perhaps I would have had more success.

Still, I assured myself, people are capable of changing, places can remake themselves, societies can awaken from their deep slumber. The Dark Ages had come to an end, never mind that it took centuries. One has to hang on to whatever shred of hope he can manage to scrape together. Reality be damned. Valhalla, the Promised Land, Success lay just over the next ridge. All I needed were more books, better books, greater variety. I began contacting publishers and ordered a selective array of brand-new titles, and searched farther and farther to tap new sources of used books. I had discovered the Marvelous World of Credit.

4

Flotsam & Jetsam

The Father made his presence known, came nosing around to check on our progress. He tallied the sales for the day and frowned.

"Not so good. We should be doing better than this." He shot me a dirty look, indicating it was my fault we were doing so poorly. Surely, I was doing something wrong. He poked through several stack of books I hadn't yet put on the shelves. "No books signed by the author?" he asked. I shook my head. "No first editions?"

"Nothing valuable," I said. "Just run of the mill stuff."

An old man came up to the register with a weathered copy of a Max Brand western. It had a cover price of fifty cents. I charged him a quarter

"Why so little?" the Father asked.

"They're used," I explained. "Half the cover price, unless I mark them up, because it's out of print, or something special. But a ratty, tatty old book like that, hell, I feel guilty charging what I did."

The Father grunted. "There's no way you're going to make it at this rate."

I thanked him for his eye-opening words—as if I needed more encouragement.

The poor man deflated, sagged, and drooped. Success was what uplifted him. It was aspirational, a dream of people coming in droves, buying books, and money pouring through the till.

He parted with his usual admonition to work harder. "It's all in what you put into it," he said. "Think of something that will get people to buy. You have to make it worth their while."

In the beginning I bought anything that came my way. Well, not quite anything, for I found that for the most part what people brought to sell were ragged, torn, waterstained paperbacks they had pulled out of the garbage, or moldy hardcovers found in thrift shops, or their attics and basements. They had apparently looked far and wide to seek out and deliver boxes of Reader's Digest condensed books, and long out-of-date textbooks—I mean thirty or forty years out of date. And if they were covered with cobwebs or had silverfish running through the pages, it was only because these literary treasures had been preserved from some long-lost age.

"I can't use this," I explained, refusing box after box filled to the brim with useless waste, books tattered beyond recognition, missing covers and/or pages.

"Why not?"

"I need current titles, quality books, resalable merchandise, not books in horrid condition, not books which nobody any longer reads, or which fall apart at the merest touch."

"What do I do with it?" they asked.

"Take it back to the thrift stores, donate it to a nursing home, build a bonfire, just take it away, please."

What I did want they wanted the world for. "It's old," they said, grabbing one of the ancient tomes by its dangling cover, which hung by a mere thread or two. "It's a first edition, isn't it? An antique?" Never mind that its dust jacket was a ruin or missing, that they had spilled that morning's coffee on the book, or that some rat had gnawed through half of it.

Patiently, calmly, by rote. "My good man, not all books which are first editions are worth money. Not all old books are collectible. It must be a desirable book. It must be in decent shape; it cannot stink of cat piss."

They couldn't get over the fact that I paid less for books I then turned around and sold at a higher price. I offered free lessons in economics, supply and demand, capitalism, going so far as to point out that I was in business to turn a profit, not to lose my shirt. They stared at me as if I were one of those people who cleaned senior citizens out of their life's savings with the promise of a good return on their investments, a swampland with a view.

"I'm trying to make a living," I explained. "I've got a family to house and feed."

They walked out muttering about crooks, insisting the country was going to ruins, as they lugged their boxes of books back to their cars with an air of self-satisfaction, of someone not about to be bested, not to be taken advantage of; content to keep their irreplaceable literary heirlooms for themselves or throw them into the garbage, damn it, rather than getting screwed.

"That's right," I said as a parting shot. "Corporate bailouts, savings and loan disasters, and arms for the Contras you don't squawk about, but a couple of dollars for a book is highway robbery."

There seemed no end to the depths to which these people would go, as was made evident by the artifacts they dredged up and carried through my doors: library books which still had the due date stamped right there for all to see; art books missing the art, books underlined in ink, or highlighted in bright phosphorescent pink, orange or green, books, which if there truly were a merciful god in heaven, would never, ever have been published in the first place.

Book club editions and twenty-year-old books on economics appeared by the truckloads. I did some quick computing. If I had but a dollar for each and every useless volume that crossed the threshold of the store, I could retire a rich man, filthy rich, stinking rich, like all those fat devils who lived up on the hill: the terraced gardens of Rolling Hills Estates, the horse trails that wound through Rancho Palos Verdes, the manicured gardens, the houses in which our whole apartment could easily fit in just one of their bathrooms.

I itched and scratched at my nether regions while I awaited the rarities and first editions that would thrill my father, the classics and art books people had inherited: valuable old volumes people had found stashed away from their childhood, or among their grandparents' belongings. But I saw no family heirlooms, no carefully preserved copies of *The Adventures of Huckleberry Finn* or *The Wonderful Wizard of Oz*. Instead, I saw mutilated, moldy dreck, better suited to lining a litter box than a bookcase.

I saw copy after copy of thirty and forty-year-old literary horror-pieces by the likes of Frank Yerby and Frank G. Slaughter. There were some good writers, but invariably passé, old, no longer in vogue. John Galsworthy, Booth Tarkington, John O'Hara. Many I never turned away, Sherwood Anderson, for example, I didn't care how many damned copies I had. I stockpiled them for the re-edification and re-education of the human race, for that time when books would no longer be published and printed.

People brought in piles of the most ancient of romance novels, shopping bags full of them, none more recent than the Carter administration, and for which they wanted cash or to trade for all the current $5.00 and $6.00 paperbacks.

I grit my teeth and prayed when customers came in asking for a book.

"Is it fiction?" I asked.

"No, it's a novel."

Or, if I asked them if it was a novel, they said no, it was made up, or seemed utterly perplexed by the question and simply shrugged, saying, "I don't know." A book, after all, was a book.

Each day before opening the shop, my daughter and I breakfasted at Adriano's Café, an exclusive little club where many of San Pedro's oddballs congregated and sipped their weak coffee—a colorful cadre of perhaps the foulest mouths, outcasts and misfits, the world ever had to offer. Freddy the Fruit, the selfproclaimed, longretired king of all dragqueens of San Pedro, was their inimitable leader. I myself never saw Freddy wear a dress, thank God, and I don't know for certain that he ever did don one, but Freddy sure enjoyed talking about the matter, if only to scare customers away.

Freddy always informed new customers that Adriano's food was poisoned. "How can you eat that crap?" he'd ask, going up to an unsuspecting woman's table, or some couple who'd just crossed the bridge and were unused to the peculiar ways of San Pedro's more celebrated inhabitants. "That'll kill you, honey. I never eat this food. The coffee's bad enough." He followed this caution by making faces, sticking out his tongue.

Freddy was a veritable encyclopedia of minutiae culled over many long years of active participation in San Pedro's seamier history. He provided a multitude of names of those who had been maimed or killed, as well as the often strange, violent ways in which they had met their maker. He was also wellversed in who was screwing whom, and exhibited a thorough knowledge of a broad variety of illegal activities, which he claimed went on right under everyone's noses. "Everybody's screwing someone behind somebody's back," he liked to say, a malicious gleam twinkling like a faulty light in his eyes, waving around his toothpick for emphasis. Freddy's ragtag group of cronies were always on hand, looking more like grave robbers than anything else, urging him to recount the numerous racy and often bizarre stories from the good ol' days—he could rattle off the names of every prostitute to ever work San Pedro's streets, every suicide, every murder that ever took place.

Freddy's unusual appearance belied the incessant stream of garbage he spewed, the rough manner in which he acted. He was a short, squat man, more round than anything, and faintly amphibian, like something straight out of *Alice in Wonderland*. He usually wore a fedora, and was a rather natty dresser, often in a gray suit. He gave the aura of being a junior Italiano mobster of the old school. He drove around in an immaculate early 1950s green Cadillac, gave money to many of the poor elderly folk around town, was frequently seen pushing bills into the hands of drunks and the homeless. He was also the last person who you'd think would go about calling himself Freddy the Fruit. But that was the moniker by which he was known.

I took notes on the ludicrous colorful stream of obscenities that flowed ceaselessly from Freddy's mouth, and shook my head wondering how he had received his nickname, and how he had managed to stay alive all these years.

When my daughter was still a baby I'd set her Moses Carrier down on the table while I read, or spooned applesauce into her mouth, but now she'd hold my finger and together we walked there. It was just down the street. She sat beside me and pored through a couple of books we'd brought with us.

Freddy and the others were in fine form, doing their best to scare everybody off.

"I'm going to sue," Freddy said to the cook, with his usual flair for melodrama. "This is the last time you'll get away with poisoning me!" Sometimes he just up and walked out: "I'm leaving. Don't expect to see me again. I'm not eating in this dump anymore!"

The wise child beside me spoke: "Daddy, Freddy's a bad man."

"Yes, he is, grasshopper. 'Tis sad but true."

"Ah, look, the little squirt loves me," Freddy said.

Up went the girl's forefinger into the air. "Eat or be eaten."

Freddy stared at her, his lower lip quivering, fear in his eyes. Little did he know it was one of the child's favorite phrases.

Freddy decided that a young and unwary couple of innocents at the table next to his would be easier to frighten than my daughter. "D'ya'll remember Jim the flint?" he said, loudly, winking at his confederates.

"Sure, ol' Jim," they chimed in, deftly picking up their cue. "What about him?"

And here Freddy displayed his imaginative genius, or, who knows, perhaps every word was true, as he insisted, "I heard that he was shackin' up with some floozie named, Bertie. She milked him dry, and then he came to find out that the woman he was pokin' was his own mother!"

There were gasps and guffaws galore from Freddy's cronies. "Whatever happened to him?" they asked.

"Nothing," Freddy said, turning round to face the customers, smiling as he delivered the last line, his coup-de-grace: "He put a gun in his mouth and blew his brains out."

By now those sitting in the next booth had turned several shades of green, moved to another booth, or decided they weren't hungry after all and left the coffee shop, never to return.

I would sit close by, scribbling in my notebook, trying to catch each and every word that was said by Freddy and his cronies, planning to write a book about San Pedro's notorious underside.

"D'ya hear about what happened to Phil?"

"Phil? Phil who?

"Phil the Pearl. You know the bookie."

"Yeah, what happened?"

"Lost his head," Freddy said, snickering.

"His head?"

"Yeah, I mean literally. Car plowed into a semi. Head snapped right off."

"Wasn't he—?"

"Yeah, doing Old Man Steiver's wife. Apparently his breaks went out on him." Freddy winked, and then stuck his tongue out at my daughter who summed up her thoughts and feelings for the man.

"Freddy is a goof."

If ever a day went by when Freddy didn't show up it was unsettling, Adriano's wasn't the same. People could sense something wrong, a tension in the air, as they felt his absence, the empty hole that his presence should have filled. It was too quiet, too peaceful; no one could concentrate on his or her meal, which suddenly tasted bland, the coffee more bitter than it usually was.

"Where's Freddy the Fruit?" people asked, tentatively, ambivalently, as though they half-feared the mention of his name would conjure him. But those days were few and far between.

The waitresses somehow ignored Freddy, and tried to reassure the customers. "Don't listen to him, he's the resident lunatic," Betty or Tina would say. If people looked like they were about to panic or take flight, she'd try to calm their fears. "He's harmless, really, just ignore him. I've been eating this food for years."

"Yeah," Freddy shouted. "Just look at her. She may look sixty-five, but she's really only twenty-five. Why do you think she looks like that?"

Freddy teased the waitresses far beyond what anyone in their right mind would or should have taken from him. "I'll come by your place tonight, when your husband's gone, okay, Betty? Just like last week, eh?"

"Yeah, Freddy, I'll be waiting for you. With a cleaver."

His cronies laughed it up. "She likes you, Freddy."

"Yeah, women always find me irresistible," he'd say with winking at any female who happened to be close by. "They can't seem to stay away from me."

Meanwhile, I spooned cottage cheese into my daughter's mouth, and ate my eggs and toast. The food wasn't good, really. Cheap, but I mean how bad are you if you can't cook eggs and potatoes without ruining them? I certainly didn't eat there because of the food. No, it was force of habit and the charming company that brought me back time and again.

I sat and listened to these old gents' high-blown conversations, their jokes, bad-mouthing whichever of them happened to be absent that day, arguing about who was a woman dressed as a man, and who was really a man dressed up like a woman, who was having sex with whom, who was a killer, who had vanished without a trace, endless exploits and adventures, drunkenness, run-ins with the cops, fights amongst themselves: the good old days.

There were characters like Mabel—or was it Mavis, I can't remember which—from New Orleans, who always smiled and had a dear heart, but had a life not fit for a dog, filled as it was with more disappointments, letdowns and failings than any one person had a right to experience. But through it all she somehow managed to maintain her sense of humor, her raucous laughter, which I often heard as she told me stories about her life in Louisiana.

I found myself making up stories or exaggerating incidents into something a bit more interesting, just so I could hear another chapter from her life, for just as some people seem to have all the luck in the world, some have nothing but bad, and it's a lot easier to listen to someone's misfortunes than another's constant successes.

"Almost had a fire in the kitchen this morning," I said. "Whole apartment could have burned down."

She grunted. "See these scars?" She showed me marks on her arms, pulled up her pant legs to show me more gouges and scars on her legs, which were by no means a pretty sight. "I lived in a real fine house, the only one I ever owned outright, back when I had money. I let this friend of mine stay there, 'cause he was broke and had no place to sleep. One night he burst into flames in his bed, burned the whole house to the ground, along with everything I owned."

"He died?" I asked.

"Fried to a crisp, nothing left but ashes. Police said it was spontaneous combustion. Unfortunately, I hadn't renewed my fire insurance."

"Well, there was the time I just missed a car crash," I said. "People in the other car almost killed me. Tore off like a bat out of hell. Didn't even stop."

"I still have tire tracks on my backside," she said, "from when I got in the way of some bank robbers' get away car. They were being chased by the police and drove their car right over me. I was in the hospital for six weeks."

No matter what hard luck story you had to tell, Mavis or Mabel could do you one better, and put yours to shame.

She was the kind of woman who would pay for your coffee no matter how much you hollered and screamed, and who, if you weren't careful, might take you home with her to fatten you up, because everybody was too skinny as far as she was concerned. She patted your back, pinched your arms, and ruffled your hair. No matter how bad things were she'd find someone to mother; she could never turn away a stray, man, child, or beast.

She was large and loud. Her clothes were mismatched, worn, and faded, bought at the thrift stores in town. She was missing a few teeth. I searched her bright blue eyes for a sign of something attractive; was there a ghost of beauty hidden away deep inside? I wondered, had she been beautiful in her youth, a sweet, frail Southern belle? I doubted it. She was no beauty. Like Bukowski, she carried all the scars and ravages of time and a hard life, and yet there was something about her, some quality that made you like her and even find her pleasant to look at. Perhaps it was the way she always called me "sugar" or "honey child," "sweetness," or "baby doll," or how she still managed to smile and laugh in spite of everything.

Adriano's was a San Pedro landmark. I didn't know how they stayed in business with the likes of Freddy maligning them every day, or why the owners tolerated him. Not once did I see them toss him out on his ear, which anyone in their right mind would have done.

Moses sat there, coffee cup in hand, wondering how the hell God could turn His back on him and consign him to such an unholy wasteland, a place where Philistines had ransacked and ravaged everything good and decent and tasteful. I knew that God would have one hell of a lot of explaining to do, once Moses made it up there. The thought of the row the two of them would have made me almost wish I could be there to see it.

"San Pedro's intelligentsia," Moses would say with a gesture at Freddy the Fruit's table.

Moses stopped by the Little Big Bookshop every week and usually left with a nice stack of books. He invariably argued about the price, insisting on a twenty-per-cent discount, but because the previous day he had given me a stack of books at half-price, I'd want to give him fifty or sixty-per-cent off the price. Typically we'd split the difference, or he'd toss the money on the counter and storm off, while I swore that I'd return the favor next time I visited his store. We had a running battle to see who could give the other the most books without charging for them.

He often brought my daughter a book or two from his store. "She's too smart," he'd say. "She'll have a hard time of it." He called her "the tyrant" for even then she exhibited a capacity for giving orders, pointing her finger at you and screwing up her tiny mouth into an accusatory snarl, as if she knew better and was ready to argue the point until she was blue in the face to prove it.

Leaving Adriano's, my daughter and I walked back up 6th Street, while I surveyed the sad landscape of closed-down storefronts, of shops trying to make a go of it, and kept a sharp lookout for Hank Chinaski.

I thought about all the revitalization work the city was constantly promising would come, the new money that would flood the town, and transform all the vacant lots and boarded-up buildings into large hotels and new businesses that would bloom along the blighted streets, all helping out the bookstore where we awaited these changes of fortune, when Reagan's beloved Trickle Down Theory would finally reach us and bestow its sweet rewards.

5

The Shoals of Lust

People came into the store and found my wife seated behind the counter brooding, looking for all the world like she was trying to will herself to disappear.

"Smile," they said. "Why so glum?" But she wouldn't smile; she had nothing to smile about. No, sir. Joy, contentment, happiness, they were far-off distant things, shimmering like stars and planets far beyond reach, for she keenly felt the resignation that only the wife of a Kastinovich could know.

Her hobby was to count the various misfortunes that might befall her: all the thousand and one things that could possibly go wrong in life. She made lists. Sure, she had a marriage, but marriages often ended in divorce, or turned miserable. She had a husband, but husbands could leave you, could cheat on you or abuse you, or die on you, leaving you with nothing but debts. She had a child, but something could happen to the child, or she might not be able to take care of it, she might fail at motherhood. There was a long litany of things that could happen. She could become homeless, a bag lady, or she might be stricken with some incurable disease. Hell, for all she knew that selfsame tidal wave I envisioned could come and sweep all of San Pedro into the sea. Some women say the rosary; she counted disasters, which loomed ever threatening on the horizon.

Sometimes she knitted. Customers would approach but she wouldn't want anything to do with them. Maybe she expected the baby to handle the paying customers—what few there were when I wasn't around—I don't know. Her eyes remained fixed upon her work, the needles clashing together doing things to the yarn, putting it through all manner of contortions, but with a peculiar malice, as if she were knitting a choker or noose for someone she was all too happy to see hanged, or as if the two needles were swords fighting some to-the-death battle. The customer would try to get her attention but it would dawn on him that this was someone he probably didn't want to disturb after all. He'd think better of it, and either leave or go off to search for himself.

I was struck by the cast of characters that made their way through the doors of our bookstore: old ladies who came in day after day, who spent a half hour or an hour looking, but always left without buying a single title. Sometimes I saw people leave the bookstore, who I hadn't seen enter, and some entered who I never saw leave.

I began conducting interviews: "May I help you?"

"No."

"Are you searching for a particular title or subject?"

"Not really."

"Can I point you in the right direction?"

"I'm not sure."

Perhaps they hadn't actually intended to enter a bookstore, but had made a wrong turn somewhere and were too embarrassed to simply turn around and walk out. Maybe they felt they should appear interested, pretend they were where they belonged, where they intended to be, have a look before scrambling out the doors again, never to return.

If only I could size up potential customers, discern who might spend money, and who were just gawkers killing time.

I made the rounds of the store to keep an eye on things, to make sure people weren't slipping in and tunneling to a safe in the next building or the bank down the block. Perhaps all those stories of secret tunnels running under the streets of San Pedro really were true. Walking down the aisles it was eerily silent, far too quiet. I peered into every room, wound my way through the store several times, my heart beating wildly. It was as if I were the lone caretaker of an ancient manor house, in which strange goings-on were purported to occur, a house of mystery—likely haunted—and one that no one had dared to adequately explore. I'm not sure what I expected, exactly, but whatever it was, it left an indelible presence lingering in the atmosphere, the hint of something malevolent: a corpse or a ghoul, or some bizarre, if vague, act of depravity occurring to one or more members of my clientele.

Some folks spent nearly the entire day hidden away in the innermost depths of the shop, where time apparently gave them the slip. It was impossible for me to keep track of everybody, and the bookstore itself seemed to make things even more difficult in that regard. There were, after all, a lot of nooks and crannies in a twenty-eight hundred square-foot haphazardly arranged bookshop.

Inevitably, I forgot someone, only to discover that person after locking the doors. Others were heard muttering, laughing, and chattering to invisible companions. A few would leave wearing broad, satisfied, almost beatific smiles, as if they had just witnessed a glorious revelation or experienced an epiphany of staggering proportion, or had had every secret desire satisfied in an instant.

I frequently went through the aisles, not only during business hours, but before opening and after closing too, when I could take my time inspecting the walls and floors, to see for myself whether this brother or sister to the pyramids or Sphinx or Templar's castle housed some terrible secret; but I could find no trace of hidden passages and secret rooms; there were only the old wooden shelves and stacks of books that offered nothing extraordinary, nothing out of the ordinary, as mute as the stone statues on Easter Island.

The bookstore was far too large and far too understaffed to ever keep neat and orderly, but one of the activities the habitués practiced was removing books from one section and taking them to another, which certainly didn't help matters. Why they felt this was necessary, I don't know, but books on sex and sexuality constantly found their way to business and self-help, books on war gathered in the child care section, books on abnormal psychology gathered in gardening, and so on. Perhaps there was a kind of logic to their madness, or some purpose that was served, but if there was, it was beyond me.

During all of this my life was in continual crisis. I hung by a thin thread to life, limb and property. The ship of matrimony was fast sinking and there were no lifeboats to be found. A beautiful young woman ever on the verge of bursting with radiance all along her seamless, faultless body lured me, enticed me farther and farther from my wife, who retreated behind a wall of silences and frowns. Now and again she showed up, the way a man adrift in a rickety boat might suddenly land upon an island oasis. Katherine was her name, and I adored it, mouthing it over and over again, loving it as I had loved no other name I'd ever heard. Everything about her made my head swim: her enigmatic smiles, her gestures, her clothes, the very words she spoke, so lovely, so enchanting and delectable.

She was a siren, one who had left the sea behind, at least for the time being, who appeared to my astonished and bedazzled eyes, perhaps in order to save me, to provide a mate in anticipation of the flood to come. I knew it to be true, because every time she appeared, wisps of sea foam, grains of sand, a breath of ocean air, and spray touched and wet my parched lips.

Meanwhile, the bookstore was ever on the verge of going under, and the pressure of trying to keep everything and everyone afloat was giving me one hell of a royal pain.

Still, in the midst of creditors calling and solicitors soliciting, I marveled how no one used their mouths to speak quite the way Katherine did. No one pursed her lips to take a drink from a bottle of Dr. Pepper or Seven-up quite like Katherine. No one stood or walked or spoke...my

God, it was getting out of hand.

She was the type of woman with whom you are always waiting for the bubble to burst, for her to start laughing and people to rush out of hiding and proclaim it was all a joke, a cruel hoax, for everyone to have a good laugh at your expense. She was too good, someone you discover you have longed for and dreamt about all your life without ever truly believing she existed, asking yourself repeatedly, "What is she doing with the likes of me?"

But the rub of it was that so far she wasn't with me. She was a woman, or lover, on the periphery. She appeared on occasion, nearly causing me to lose control of my normal functions. She hovered and fluttered around my head, filled my dreams with fantasies that kept me awake at night.

I wrote out a page-and-a-half of only the words: What if? Then I did the same with: If only.

Sure, my marriage was floundering. And Katherine, well, she was simply gorgeous, desirable in every way. A woman who adored Twain, and not just Huck Finn, but who read and treasured books like, *A Pen Warmed Up In Hell*, and *Letters From The Earth*. I introduced her to John Fante and she fell in love; how could I not fall in love with her?

I watched the way she fondled my books, the way she caressed the covers with her fingertips, held a book in the palm of one hand, carefully lifted the cover and turned the pages with a majestic sweep of her hand. She would never ever dog-ear a page, never write in a book, or lay a book open, face down. The way she handled the books was how I wanted to be handled by her. I watched Katherine while "I want to be your book," screamed in my head.

I observed how she swept her hair behind her ear, or cocked her hips in a cool casual way, and had to pinch myself hard in order to prevent myself from leaping over the counter and lunging at her.

Furthermore, it is my humble belief that smell is the most underrated, understudied and under-appreciated sense we possess. People don't realize its profound significance. Scent, I was sure, had made and unmade empires and fortunes. It was the secret stuff of legend. And the scent Katherine exuded kept me sniffing the air long after her departure, set my heart and head reeling. If our hands touched, I kept that hand near my face for the rest of the day and night, sniffing it every chance I got.

God alone knew what perfume she wore. But indeed she didn't, it was just her own natural essence, her fragrance, and I could only hope and pray that I smelled it again and soon. Her voice, too, had just the right timbre, frequency, tone and pitch to make me break out in a cold sweat.

"Do you have any short stories by Eudora Welty?" she emerged from the mists to ask me.

Did you hear that? I was so stunned I had to ask her to repeat herself. Turns out I had heard correctly. And curses and hellfire that I happened to be out of Welty collections at the moment. Not a single one.

"I could order that for you," I promptly informed her, panting like a puppy. "I've been meaning to order some."

"How long will it take?"

"A week, two at the most."

"Okay." And then the sweet pleasure of taking down her name and phone number, as if this was destiny calling, telling her I'd telephone her just as soon as the book came in, which meant, of course, that I would indeed see her again. Jesus! Maybe I'd call her in the meantime to let her know that it was on its way, traversing the country state by state, and perhaps again to inform her it was nearly there, any day now. Just to hear her voice once more. I knew what crystal felt like right as it reached the point when a pitch was about to shatter it.

A couple of days later, as I worked, I caught a stray whiff of Katherine. It hit me unexpectedly, and I sniffed the air to follow it, but it was gone, though days later, I occasionally smelled it for a moment here, there. It was the foil to the sight of Bukowski, who passed by my door, or down the street with the slow wave, "Hey, baby," there and gone, checking up on me as if he suspected I would disappear in the dark of night. He resisted the urge to pat my head, and would merely ask how things were, then make his way across the street to sit in silent communion with the Cyclops.

My brain sizzled with the simple aspects of Katherine that appealed to me: her naïve yet beguiling lips, her skin, the way she opened and closed her eyelids in a manner that made me feel as if I was being lovingly caressed. the way her clothes fit, as if made for her alone, made on her body, rendering them unwearable for anyone else, whereas on her they bounced and shimmied with a life of their own; it was as if she were all lit up, the choice of lighting most intriguing and sensuous, enhancing and showing off her best features. Indeed, like Ingrid Bergman, Katherine didn't need lights or make-up—she exuded her own luminescence.

While my wife was thoroughly convinced that each and every misfortune, every bad day, was something I had personally wrought and fashioned in order to ruin her life, as if to make her miserable was my sole occupation, Katherine blew in and out of my world, fresh as rain, and as delightful as a baby's laughter.

The act of repeated resistance was in itself exhausting. If I declined farther, perhaps if I selfinflicted that scar I so often dreamt about, women, meaning Katherine, would start throwing themselves at my feet. Maybe if I poked out one of my eyes, I could kill two birds with one injury and have both the woman and the prestige and respect that would surely come from wearing a patch over my eye. Hank wouldn't likely forget me then.

Women, too, would then surely look at me in a different light.

"What happened to you?" I could hear them ask. "Why do you have that patch on your eye?"

"Oh, that," I'd say, "Well, you see I used to sail. Where? Why, all over the world. Been in every port. Got in this fight once, however—in Algiers, it was—took on five thugs who were beating a onearmed man, well, yes, and one of these had a hook, you see, and took out me eye.

"What? Why, yes, it was a miracle I survived. I couldn't see but with one eye, but I still managed to maim most of the gang, before they scattered to the winds.

"The one-armed man? He offered me everything; house, his only daughter, wealth. I took the daughter, but left him with the house and his wealth, for I knew that if I didn't take something, if I'd refused, he'd have been insulted by the man who had saved his life, and he'd consider me his enemy for the rest of his days. I don't like to make enemies unnecessarily, you see?

"What happened to the daughter? Don't ask. It's a long terrible story. Suffice it to say that that chapter of my life is closed forever. No, don't try and persuade me to talk. I'll carry that secret with me to my grave.

"What? Yes, very sad. Of course, her life was utterly destroyed. Poor thing. There was nothing I could do for her, though I tried my damnedest. There, I've said too much already. I won't say another word about it. I've tried to put all that beyond me, to forget."

My wife, when things were really good and on the mend, sent me love letters signed by her alter ego, Syn Sobriquet, letters with which she attempted to get me embroiled in some sordid love affair with this mysterious, yet alluring doppelganger. And while I must admit I liked this other persona much better than her normal self, I still did my best to resist. Things were difficult enough. Besides, one never did know when or where the alter ego would come or go. She could snarl at me, tell me what an inconsiderate louse I was one minute, and drag me to the bed the next, demanding that I satisfy her. If only she could decide on one or the other; inconstancy always makes for one miserable headache.

Our state of matrimony could adequately be summed up the way Dickens summed up the era of *A Tale of Two Cities*: the best of times and the worst of times. Clearly, I preferred the best. Therefore it seemed reasonable to me that when I was on the outs with my wife, I could balance that ordeal with the best of times that was Katherine's presence. And by the same token, when things were hunky-dory with the wife, they'd be made even better with Katherine there as well. I tried my best to make my wife happy, but knew, too, that it was a losing battle; I longed to run off with Katherine, for I knew instinctively that the two of us were aligned in some indefinable way, that together we would have lit the world on fire, or at least left some nice skid marks.

My wife wasn't a terrible person. She just didn't appear to believe in conversation, and often liked to be alone, *really* alone, as if she didn't even want to be with herself. Not only that, but she apparently had inherited a manual for affection and sex that the Nazis might have devised, and from which she would never deviate. No, strictly by the book here—there was a time and place and manner for everything. What was acceptable, and where, when, and how. Everything else was *verboten*.

If we went to a party she would enter and leave without a word, and while there she'd somehow disappear. No one would see her. People would come up to me, "Hey, you come alone? Where's your wife?"

"Trust me, she's here."

"We've looked. *Everywhere*. What'd she do, make herself invisible?"

Eventually, she'd be found hidden in a tucked-away corner, sitting as still as a sculpture. Those searching for her would say, "Hey, wallflower, come join the party." She would ignore them and instead continue murmuring in the ear of some unsuspecting youngster she somehow corralled, telling him about the endless misery of her life, trapped in a loveless, pitiless, abusive marriage. The young man would shoot me a dirty look, and I'd cringe in guilt, nearly believing her sad tale myself, so convincing was she.

I'd take her home, gnaw my lip, and say to myself, look, all you have to do is make her happy, and it stands to reason she will make you happy. Compromise, give in a little. Let her have her way. And while she sat in the bedroom, surrounded by all the paraphernalia of what looked to me like voodoo, mumbling and muttering prayers or perhaps curses upon my head, retreating farther into herself, practicing a vow of silence, lighting incense and gazing into crystals, I did the only thing I could do, and left to go take a walk.

I hung around the bookstore at night, crawled on all fours down to the harbor, and stared at the inscrutable slick surface of the water. I listened to the sea and the creaking of the boats, while the waves gently lapped, murmured and whispered, "I won't let you down. I'll take you away from all this."

I chewed on the idea of stealing one of the boats, a dingy even; just a few planks of wood, the sea, and myself. "Escape," the waves hissed softly. "Es-cape." Combined with the Bb of the foghor,n and the wind whistling through the stays of the boats, it was a symphony of longing and yearning that reverberated through every fiber of my being.

I inhaled the pungent smell of the harbor, took in the birds scurrying for pieces of dead fish, and the motion of the sailboats, huge cradles rocking their crews to sleep. How easy it would have been to simply untie one, climb aboard, hoist a sail or two and be off in the night, into the Pacific Ocean, dreaming of Wynken, Blynken, & Nod, letting the winds and waves carry me where they would.

I envisioned a remote island paradise, some South Pacific atoll, or the distant shores of the Azores in the Atlantic, where I could bring Katherine, but instead, the gnarled image of Hank Chinaski rose from the oily depths of the water, scarred and ruined—the personification of life lived to the extreme—grinning at me and whispering that all my turmoil and troubles were just so much nothingness, reminding me that one could be beaten, but that others had survived far worse.

"Come out swinging," Hank whispered. "Don't let the bastards get you down."

The image faded and I was left there with only the wharf rats, the birds and shadows for company. I peered around me. Had Bukowski followed me down to the harbor? Was that his presence I sensed? Did he like the serenity and the ripe smells of the waterfront, too, or was he going for a bit of atmosphere, local color, for another of his stories? Was it possible I had become one of his protagonists, one of his hapless characters? I worried how he might use or misuse me as a subject.

I peered over my shoulder now and again and kept my eye on the vague figures that lurked in the shadows, as I crept back home. I returned without the satisfaction of having seduced Katherine, without having escaped from my troubles, without even a decent scar to show for my pains, but armed with the idea that I would take whatever punches, kicks, scratches and bites were to come my way, like some punch-drunk pugilist, I would stand my ground. I'd go down in a blaze of glory with my boots on, swinging.

I'd show Hank Chinaski I could take it.

The very next day I bought myself a machete at the hardware store. At least I'd be able to take a few heads with me if and when it came my turn to be taken down. All I needed now was a whetstone. There I'd hover day after day, nodding my head and drooling, as I sharpened my blade to a fine edge.

I wasn't going to go down easily or quietly. Not if I had anything to say about it.

I thumbed through Hank's most recent collection of poetry, searching for the character of a crazed bookseller, to identify myself among his oddballs, misfits, and whack jobs.

6

Seekers, Escapees, Dementia

Running the bookstore, was being caught in a slowly churning whirlpool, incrementally sucked down to the lowest rung of Dante's Inferno. It consumed my every hour, even my sleep. I needed more books, better books, but at the same time I desperately needed to sell those same books.

When the incoming used books were far and few between, I panicked. Night after night I was jarred awake by terrifying visions of near-empty bookshelves. To compensate I placed orders for new books, quality literature, fine poetry, essays. There was a particular joy I found in going through the alphabet, selecting books by Kobo Abe to Brigid Brophy, Dickens to Dostoyevsky to George Orwell, Voltaire to Oscar Wilde, and so on.

A bright, attractive student from the junior college entered the bookstore. I spotted her right off. She wore a halo of intelligence. Ah ha! Someone who reads! A young woman—perhaps a literature or history major—looking to stimulate her mind, her creativity. I waltzed over to her, all smiles and joviality, eager to provide assistance, ready to cater to her every wish.

She opened her mouth to speak. Come, come, out with it, young lady! Don't be shy. How may I serve you? Are you looking for Stevenson, Conrad or Melville, perchance? Speak to me.

"Do you have the new Barbara Cartland book?"

And with that my heart sank low. Crushed, I ushered her to the romance section where insatiable women young and old competed for the latest in sultry, steamy sub-literate titillation, the likes of which no human being alive or dead has ever experienced in reality. These poor souls hungered for the least spark of *True Romance*, à la the white knight on the white charger, sweeping her off her feet, the steamy glances and breathless kisses, eyes undressing the inexperienced lover, the ravishing delights!

I watched her scour the shelves. Girl, are you ever going to be disappointed, I thought. Here, you're reading about soaring lofty idyllic passionate lovemaking, and as Eliose May Gunther once said, you'll find out it's really only an all-too-brief interlude of pleasure ending in a wet, sticky mess.

A welldressed, rather sophisticated middle-aged woman came into the store, tried ordering a book, some insipid author not worth remembering.

"So many of the books I like are out of print," she whined, as if I had personally managed this irksome outcome just for the sake of annoying her.

"That's nothing, lady," I said. "Most everybody I like is long dead." She looked like she'd just put something in her mouth she couldn't possibly swallow. "In fact, my best friends, the people I like the most, have been dead the longest, with only one or two notable exceptions." She eased her way out of the store, smiling ever so faintly.

I thought of Hank. Most of his friends were dead. There were no heroes in today's world to take the place of the Great Ones. No modern-day equivalents of Shakespeare or Baudelaire, any more than a 20th century Mozart or Leonardo was wandering the streets of Wilmington or San Pedro.

"So, we do have something in common, after all, eh, Hank?" I muttered to myself. I frequently spoke to people who weren't there. They didn't very often answer, but that was okay, too. I knew they would reply in their own sweet time. I also waited for ravens to show up, croaking something ridiculous like "Nevermore."

People drifted in and looked about with a stunned expression, their mouths hanging open, as if they had intended to enter a bridal shop and never saw such a strange and mysterious thing as a bookstore before.

Where am I? How'd I get here? What is this?

They pirouetted, gazing in wonder at objects on the shelves, while I watched warily. They reached out and touched the books ever so gingerly, as if to make sure that what they saw wasn't a mirage. They rifled through books and magazines in dumbstruck awe, seeming to fear that what they held in their hands might at any moment take flight, vanish before their eyes, or transform those who held them into some other being or to another realm, or perhaps burst into flames.

I observed these people with a fair amount of apprehension, for I hadn't the slightest clue as to what they were capable of, or what they might do; whether they were going to run off with a book, throw it to the ground and stomp on it, or kiss the holy relic.

There were those who simply had never been instructed on how to properly handle a book. They grabbed hold of a precious volume, bent the covers and tore dust jackets as if they were just so much superfluous wrappings. I gasped and felt my knees buckle whenever they took a book and proceeded to bend the covers so far that they broke the spine. I felt my own spine snap in sympathy, as they destroyed a book they had carelessly picked, which I could now no longer sell, and for which they had no intention to pay.

"Where do you get these books?" one older, overly dressed gentleman in a coat and tie and shiny leather shoes, with thin slicked-back hair asked, sticking his nose behind the counter. I counted to ten, and resisted the temptation to grab a ruler and rap his knuckles. Instead, I moved and blocked his way, preventing him from reaching further into restricted territory. "*Well?*"

If ever there was a question from hell, this was it. I gazed up toward heaven and bit my lip in order to resist saying something truly flippant, like, "They felleth from the sky."

"Here and there," I said, hoping that might satisfy his burning curiosity.

"You buy them?"

I could say I stole them, or that I printed them in a cellar each night, so that I could avoid paying royalties to the poor authors who had written these books, but usually it was more like: "Houdini didn't tell his secrets, I don't tell mine," or, "They come to me, I don't go find them." Nothing like an air of mystery, to keep them guessing. But this customer had a particularly obnoxious and insistent air, as if he were some federal investigator. So, I just said, "Yeah, sometimes."

"What do you pay?"

"Depends on the book. As well as the condition. Not to mention the author."

His expression changed, as he chewed something bitter. "Give me some idea."

"Anywhere from fifty cents, to a thousand dollars. Does that help?"

"How do you know how much it's worth?"

"It's my business to know."

I simply adored this cagey routine. People who wanted information for nothing, perhaps thinking of going into business for themselves, so that they too would have nothing to do but sit around and read books all day, and they thought that I was here to supply them with whatever knowledge they happened to desire.

This particular gentleman was more persistent than most. He made a beeline for some boxes of recently acquired books that I had piled up off to the side, and covered with a tarp, which he lifted, peering underneath.

"Excuse me," I said. "Those books haven't been priced yet."

He acted as if he hadn't heard me, and kept digging around.

"Excuse me," I repeated, coming out from behind the counter. "You can't go through these boxes. These books aren't for sale."

He looked at me with a supercilious air, that I'm-about-to-make-a-total-ass-of-myself attitude so many people hold in reserve for clerks or waitresses. "Why are they here, then?"

He leveled a smirk as though he'd just cornered me in his verbal trap.

"Because they have yet to be gone through, priced, and sorted.

Because I don't have room anywhere else to put them."

"Can't I just look through them?"

"No." I closed the boxes back up.

"You have all these books sitting here, and no one can touch them?"

"That's right."

Even then he continued to try to open a box, the contents of which he wanted explore, as if he might stumble upon some biblical find meant for his eyes and no one else's. Or perhaps he was merely one of those people who go out of their way to get denied service or kicked out of shops just so they can tell their handful of friends how they are constantly victimized by ruthless storekeepers.

I shooed him away from another stack he was making for. "Leave those alone."

"I don't see why I can't just look through them." Petulant as all get out.

"For starters, because I asked you not to." He started to say something again, but I cut him off. "Look, you're going to have to leave."

He harrumphed or some such thing. "I'll be sure not to bring my business here again." He made for the door and stormed out.

"Don't do me any favors."

I received a phone call a couple of hours later. A very irate gentleman asked to speak to the owner. "Speaking," I said. He proceeded to relate bit by bit everything that had transpired earlier, how a rude and disagreeable employee had prevented him from looking at books he wished to look at, and treated him with an unruly disrespect.

"I want you to do something about this ruffian. He's obviously never been properly instructed on how to treat customers."

"You want me to fire him?"

"Yes."

"I'm sorry," I said, "But I simply will not fire myself. Besides, you were the one acting rude and disagreeable. You were told they weren't for sale, you were asked to stay out of the boxes, and you refused."

"That was you, then?" he asked.

"Right-o. Just so happens you were dealing with the owner when you were here earlier."

"I see." Gone was the attitude, all his arrogance dissipated with the realization that he wasn't pulling the wool over anyone's eyes, and he wasn't going to get me to fire my best employee, as he'd hoped. "Well, whatever happened to the concept 'the customer is always right'?"

"Not here, not when you act like a first-rate schmuck, not in my store."

Countless shadowy figures drifted into the store, blown hither by the unpredictable bursts of a capricious wind. Accompanying them were dry leaves and dust, twigs, bits of paper. I spent an inordinate amount of time sweeping up this detritus that accumulated as if we had a stationary tornado in front of the shop.

These vagabonds glanced around as if they found nothing more distasteful, nothing more repulsive than books. Hats or shoes, fine glazed pottery, yes, but books? Books were those things in which people who had no life, in fact those who escaped life, took refuge.

They strolled twenty feet into the store and no more. "Where are the prices of these books?" they asked, pointing as if they were afraid of laying their hands upon something used.

"They're priced on the upper right-hand corner of the first blank page."

I watched as they opened one or two books with a roughness that bordered on the criminal. I wondered if they would treat a painting or a vase they found in an antique shop so ruthlessly. What did people have against books, against repositories of plotlines and dialogue, of knowledge and ideas? Suddenly stricken with near-sightedness, they peered at the prices, their expressions showing even more disgust than before. They burrowed their faces between the covers of the book and stared at what was neatly penciled on the page as if the price might lower itself if only they stared at it long enough. And after they left, empty-handed, I banged my bruised head on the cash register. "Why? Why, God? Am I missing something?"

I wasn't sitting out on the street corner with an out-stretched hand, waiting for some passer-by to grease my palm. There were Hare-Krishnas down at the airport accosting passengers for money. I wasn't begging. I was merely trying to sell books for a trifle more than I had paid.

It boggled my mind that these people wouldn't ever venture farther into the shop. "You've only just scratched the surface," I tried to tell them. I made signs, arrows, gave them every clue I could think of. A banner: More Books In Here!

I stopped people as they walked out, "Wait, you haven't seen the rest of the store. Don't you want to see what we have in the back?" They were leaving behind whole unexplored realms.

They mumbled, muttered, shook their heads, as if nothing could coax them into that inferno, that din of iniquity, the horror that lurked in the very heart of the Little Big Bookshop.

Some nameless wideeyed stranger—glancing around and twitching nervously, as if someone or something stalked him with an interest in procuring his soul—informed me that he never read books. A man walks into my store and informs me—a bookseller—that he never reads books. Furthermore, he says it with a smug pride; am I supposed to beg and plead for an explanation? Or is he telling me this in order to save me from what he perceives as a sacrilegious activity? After all, people banned Twain and Salinger, boycotted the sale of *Playboy* magazines, and others of the sex trade. He says it in so a boastful way, as if to say, I've outgrown all that, I no longer need books; I know all I need to know.

"They're full of lies," he said. "They're not true." I nodded and let him go on, confiding in me what he obviously needed to get off his chest, while I ruminated over the possibility of serving alcohol, a combination bookstore/bar. Maybe if I got the customers drunk enough I could convince them to buy bags full of books. Buy ten books and we'll throw in a fifth of Scotch for free.

"I used to read," he continued, "but I found that all books were full of lies." He sounded every bit like the former sinner or drug addict, shamed by his past behavior. I told him the store was full of nonfiction that he could read to his heart's content. "They're the worst," he shrieked. "Pick up a book on Astronomy. One says there are 400 billion stars in the universe, another that there are 250 billion. Every year they change the number of moons in the solar system. They don't know anything. How can they write books claiming to know what they don't know? It's all lies!"

And here I thought *I* was paranoid! All these books with their erroneous facts were all part of some elaborate conspiracy by the powers that be to mislead the unsuspecting American public. But before I could explain to him the various shades and kinds of truth, how knowledge was never absolute but was written and rewritten with the goal of updating and refining, of seeing the larger reality; how Newton sufficed for the truth of his day and age, only to be replaced centuries later by Einstein's much truer schematic of reality; how truth was dependent upon one's perspective; before I could ask him what had made him enter the premises of a bookstore given his attitude toward books, he wandered off, presumably to go converse with shadows and howl at the moon.

I tallied up the sales on the cash register at regular intervals and shuddered. Occasionally I sold something: a dollar, fifty cents, twenty-five cents, a dollar fifty. What did these people do? Did they go through the stacks and rows of books until they found the absolute cheapest books we possessed? Was this how I was going to pay my bills? I debated raising all the prices. We were living in the 1980s, not the 1950s. Nothing sold for a quarter or fifty cents anymore.

A singular type of individual came in simply because they had it on their minds to discuss books and writers: "Have you read Nabokov?" they said breathlessly. They would express disbelief when I informed them in the negative. "You must. Nabokov is superior." These folks wanted to tell me who was better than whom, who stank, what the inspiration was for this book or that. They were sometimes interesting at least, and occasionally fun. Perhaps they had just discovered Hawthorne, or were interested in listening to my comparing and contrasting the Great Russian writers with the Magic Realism of Latin America. We held forth protracted arguments and discussions. They never bought anything, instead they got all their books from the library or from the junior college bookstore, but for some reason they liked to habituate used bookstores, a place for socializing, and testing their theories.

Maybe they were lonely. Maybe no one they knew would listen to them. I confess I frequently ignored them myself, as I went about my work, nodding and shaking my head, occasionally saying, "Hm hm, yeah, sure," and the like, as I straightened things, sorted books, used lighter fluid to remove the old price stickers off the new arrivals, and priced the books before shelving them. After all, it wasn't as if I had nothing to do. I let them ramble on, holding extensive conversations with themselves.

Maybe I should have kicked them out, but sometimes these were as close as I got to seeing real live customers, and besides maybe if people saw others frequenting the bookstore, they might get curious and come see for themselves, the way people followed crowds.

Meanwhile, I received inquiries over the phone as to whether I rented or loaned books out. "That's called a library," I informed them. "This is a bookstore." Some called up to ask me the population of Sauk City, Wisconsin, or the distance in miles of the circumference of the sun.

I also fielded calls asking for diaries, blank books, pens, notepads, calendars, rulers, post cards, greeting cards—almost anything but real honest to goodness books, the kind you can't put down, and can barely resist peeking to find what happens in the end; the kind you stay awake late into the night reading, unable to stop, just one more page.

I received numerous calls by people who were surprised that the store was here. "Where is the store located?" Invariably these were people born and raised in San Pedro. What did they do, drive down 6th Street wearing blinders, or did they simply avoid the street altogether?

Some found fault with the exorbitant prices I charged, incensed at my pricegouging.

"I don't get books for free," I explained. "A dollar or two for a used book isn't a whole lot to ask."

Often I had to test my precognitive powers. A customer—or so I assumed by his or her presence in my establishment—sidled up to the counter. A guilty look, if ever I saw, like someone about to buy condoms for the first time.

"Can I help you?"

"Yeah. I'm looking for a book."

A book? Be still my heart!

"What book?" I asked.

"I don't know. It had a green cover. I think."

Or, "I can't remember the title but I saw it here, last month."

Or, "I heard about a book on the radio, but didn't write down the name of the author or the title."

We're talking years before computerized inventories, yet, they expressed shock that I couldn't tell them every title in the shop. And when I knew I didn't have a particular book, no amount of explaining could make them understand why it was I didn't have the particular title they needed.

"I've got to have that book," they pleaded, as if my stock were somehow contingent upon their needs and desires.

"Well, I'll see what I can do," I answered. "Let me have your number. I'll call you if it comes in." Anything to get rid of them, but leave them with a sense of hope.

Reassured, they walked out, mollified, at peace in heart and mind, convinced that I was focusing all my capabilities on locating their precious tome, whether it be *The Survivalist's Handbook*, or *The Love Life of Bruno Schultz*.

More and more I learned not to explain. They never accepted my explanations anyway, but looked at me like I was Nixon saying, "I'm not a crook!" But for a while, I had to try. I told them I sold used books that people brought to my shop to sell to me.

"I don't telepathize with them," I explained, "saying bring me such and such a book. Books are printed, they go in print and out-of-print, and out-of-print books can be difficult and expensive to locate."

Telling them you'd do your best, and taking their name and number, seemed to satisfy most. It was only the ones who felt you were in effect saying you would call them in a week or two with the book in your hand, who managed to sometimes make a nuisance of themselves, repeatedly calling back or stopping by to see if the book had appeared yet, as if I merely had to run home where I kept every book ever published locked up awaiting such requests.

But hell, I would gladly endure a thousand of these folks just to have one Katherine. I called to inform her that her collection of Eudora Welty stories had come in that very morning. I was holding it for her behind the counter, keeping it warm in my hot little hands.

She sailed into the store as poised and graceful as Aphrodite, sure of herself and most likely sure of the servitude and the adoration of those who waited on her. I handed her the book.

"Thank you," she said, smiling deliciously. "I can't wait to read this."

I showed her that I had gotten two copies. "I thought I'd read it too," I said. "I've always liked Eudora Welty."

"That's great," she said. "Maybe we can compare notes and talk sometime about the stories."

I nodded like an idiot, like one of those toy dogs you used to see on car dashboards whose head is attached to the body by a spring, sending the head bouncing this way and that with any movement. There was an admirable twinkle in her eyes, and I heard Bukowski's words: "There is always one woman to save you from another, and as that woman saves you she makes ready to destroy."

Nah, nah, nah, I thought. Not this one. And if destroy she would, well, I could think of no better way to go.

I was unable to form a coherent reply and watched her leave, painful though it was. I had to hold myself back, and grabbed the chair to prevent myself from flying after her.

While I read the stories I had no idea what I was reading. I couldn't follow plots or the development of characters, for I kept busy weaving my own plots with Katherine. I read with the thought in mind that she too was reading these very same stories, that we proceeded in union she and I, perhaps even sharing the very same thoughts and feelings. I imagined her lying in bed, in some exceedingly thin, sheer nightie, her head on the pillow, the covers pulled up to her waist.

Her enchanting eyes gazed upon the very words I read, and as I beheld her lying in her bed, I began to fall down a bottomless precipice, spiraling head over heels down a gulf without end.

7

Balancing the Books

The waves continued to carve away at the bluffs at our Land's End apartment. I kept a wary eye on the ocean. Wasn't the water a few inches higher than it had been the week before, and the month before that?

I examined the flooring in all areas of the bookstore certain that there was a trapdoor somewhere that led to a tunnel or cavern below. People simply could not vanish without there being an egress. Meanwhile, my wife made vague references to my "strange ways," though I had no idea to what she referred.

An elusive balance was critical in running the business successfully. One wanted to bring in new and varied titles, to dazzle the customers' eyes with an ever-changing display, while at the same time selling off the old stock. One didn't want too many books going out and nothing coming in, or too many coming in and not enough being sold. Problem was there was nearly always far more arriving and too little going out.

Some days I was taken by surprise and we'd be slammed. We made huge sales. I didn't know why, but I wasn't about to complain. It was intoxicating, ringing up purchase after purchase and wondering how long it would last. If the Father happened to be there he'd rub his hands together.

"Yes. Now this is more like it," he'd say, looking over the cash register tally every fifteen minutes, his voice cracking with glee. "Keep this up." As if it had had anything to do with me.

The best days were, naturally, around the holidays, when hundreds and hundreds of volumes, including some quite expensive art books and Bukowski signed/limited editions would sell. I'd sell a good number of Fante titles, too, for I seemed to have an unnatural talent for convincing people they should buy his books.

If we happened to be in a slump, my wife would again find gainful employment so there'd be money to pay the rent on the store, and our apartment, to say nothing of food, but also so I could continue to stock the shelves.

I answered ads in the paper, visited the homes of people who had accumulated thousands of books, or who had inherited their parents' or their favorite uncle's collection, which they now wished to sell off, having themselves no interest in books. I was telephoned and lured to people's homes by promises of great books: "No junk, no, no textbooks either, no book club editions, but a wide assortment of high-quality books, I assure you."

The effect of going through shelf after shelf, each laden with all manner of titles, to perhaps finally pick a meager two or three that were worth barely buying, only because you couldn't bear to leave with nothing for your efforts, was not only discouraging and disheartening, it sucked the life out of me. It was a mortifying experience that filled me with unanswerable questions and a forlorn queasiness in my gut. How could somebody accumulate so many bad books, and only bad books? It simply boggled the mind. Books by A.J. Cronin, Lloyd Douglas and John Marquand were somewhat on the way out, and nobody was clamoring for long-forgotten love stories or adventure sagas from the 1930's. No one but no one bought this stuff anymore.

Sometimes a newspaper ad mentioned "treasures" or "antiques" which naturally piqued my interest, because the store was saturated with the ordinary and could use the boost that collectibles would give it. But when I arrived—my heart palpitating wildly and my bowels contorting with anticipation—I found nothing more than the run-of-the-mill garbage: old diet books, biographies of sports figures, readers digest, political musings by some right-wing pundit, World War II books by the score; it forced me to reflect how one man's meat was definitely another man's poison.

On rare occasions there was something good, or at least something salable, only it had been ruined by being left out in the rain, or chewed by a dog. I pointed out to some older customer's doubtful eyes, how a particular book, which he thought was so much trash, how if it had been in fine condition, could be worth over a hundred dollars.

"For this, a lousy paperback?" he said, in disbelief. "How could that be worth anything?" All he saw was the original price of ten cents.

A book-reading, book-buying gentleman came into the shop looking for first editions by Faulkner; he'd read everything by Faulkner, loved the man to distraction, would read his shopping lists if he could. I, on the other hand, couldn't bear to read Faulkner, and wouldn't do it, not for love or money—Nick Kastinovich read the writings of a man who referred to Twain as a hack? A man whose own writing was as muddied as the mighty Mississippi? And here this gent was devoting his life to this one writer as if there were no other.

Just to endear myself to the man, whose soliloquy, quite frankly, was preventing me from getting any work done, I stood him in front of a copy of *Erections, Ejaculations, Exhibitions and General Tales of Ordinary Madness*, by Charles Bukowski.

"Here, if you think Faulkner is great, read a few lines of this. It's sure to warm the cockles of your heart," I said, knowing that action would speak far more eloquently than any words I could say.

"Bukowski?" he said. "Never heard of him."

"Read on, read on" I said, certain that the fact that this Faulknerian had never heard of Bukowski wouldn't have troubled Hank in the slightest. In a matter of moments he began having convulsions, gasping, and shaking uncontrollably, right before my eyes. He huffed and puffed and made some strange inarticulate sounds, as if he were gagging or choking on something. Finally, he stammered, "This...this is filth!"

With a title like that what did he expect, "The Book of Psalms?" Or, the love poems of Elizabeth Barrett Browning?

Okay now, pay attention! This is clue number one:

People stopped me, pulled me aside. "What are you doing?"

"What, me?"

"You're alienating your customers, the very people you want to come in and buy books."

"What do you mean?" I asked.

"You can't insult them, or badger them, and expect them to come back for more. You want to bring customers in, not chase them out."

It was true. I wasn't exactly acting my usual meek and mild self. "Must be the store," I said. "It's affecting me." It was as if I became a different person when inside the shop. Get me away for a couple days and I returned to my old self, but the more time I spent inside the book store the more it seemed to work its unholy forces of corruption upon me. I thought, felt and acted differently.

A mysterious gentleman named Mike Hodel, a man with a voice that clearly should have been preserved and tapped for only special purposes, showed up once. He ran a radio program called "Hour Twenty Five: the hour that stretches." We talked some about books and authors, in particular Sir Arthur Conan Doyle. Afterwards, he explored the deep chambers of the store. Then he departed. It was soon afterwards—mere days—that I learned he had passed away.

I tried to remember whether I had said something, anything at all that might have brought on this sudden, wholly unexpected calamity. Was it the bookstore, those very depths that he had plumbed, as if he sought something, shall we say, very particular? Had he gone too far, too deep? Perhaps a rare title that someone had told him I possessed? Why else would he have come so far, and mentioning, in that classic madefortheair voice of his, Sherlock Holmes, Aleister Crowley, Jack the Ripper, and others? A man meets me and days later is dead. It was an ominous sign.

I'd purchased a huge amount of material (three cars loads) from a woman in Hermosa Beach, who was closing down an antique stall, and who took me aside and informed me she was a witch. I don't know, perhaps she was one. She sold me all manner of ephemera: photos, etchings, newspapers, train memorabilia, postcards, ship menus, as well as books, much of it dating from the pervious century. There was a lot of material on magic and the occult.

She must have been a witch for why else would I have let her silver tongue get the best of me, and talk me into this deal I could ill afford? I had thoughtlessly piled up all the boxes, making a false wall in front of the back wall of the shop, which was already a false wall that hid a second story, which I had conveniently filled up with boxes of books and magazines, so there was no more room up there. I supposed that Hodel had stumbled upon some of these newly arrived boxes, and in them discovered something likely intended for me. Some tome on which the witch had cast an evil spell.

I tuned in to his Hour-25 radio program and found some idiot guru for positivism named David Brin proclaiming that there was a new renaissance in full bloom, signs evident all around us. I turned it off. A renaissance, huh? Death and decadence, the advent of videos and chain stores, Reagan and Bush in office, and he's talking renaissance? What the hell planet was this guy living on? Just flick on the radio and listen to the crap being played on the airwaves. Come down to San Pedro, Mr. Brin, where there is more litter and trash gravitating up and down the sidewalks than people, and where businesses open and close down again faster than you can spell the word renaissance!

I mourned Hodel's passing, and walked up 6th Street, Pacific Avenue, Gaffey St., 8th and 9th Streets, as far as 10th and 11th, with a keen sense of survivor guilt. I surveyed the impending prospects of construction down as far as Front St. Ah, sweet rejuvenation. Everywhere I witnessed the burgeoning signs of The Great Enlightenment with my own eyes: prophets who spoke on the curbside and gutters so as to be close to the common man, reaching out to the lowest of the low, as opposed to those who isolated themselves in the ivory towers of Academia, far removed from reality.

I observed the small but tightly knit groups of young men and women others might see as unruly teenagers out to intimidate, waiting for the slightest pretext to cause trouble, but who I recognized as freedom fighters, seeking only the dissemination of information, the exchange of ideas, eager to express themselves as distinct individuals, shaving their heads, piercing and/or tattooing their flesh so as to stand out above the crowd. They embraced a diversity of cultures. They represented the future. Like Bukowski and the Romanian, they too spoke mainly in grunts and monosyllables; perhaps these were the next generation of poets. Rejoice America, Art isn't dead!

Shakespeare, Shelley, Lord Byron and Dickinson had all been pulled down to the level of anyone who could string a few lousy words together. Art was democratized, anyone could do it, there was no genius, no good or bad, it was all the same. Just a matter of opinion if you thought one was better than the other.

Making my way down Pacific Avenue I heard heated conversations, among an older crowd, which to the ear sounded much like cursing and arguing over trivialities such as which of them was the toughest, the meanest, the nastiest, who had staked the most pussy, but which I knew were really discussions of the deepest and highest intellectual content. These were clearly San Pedro's philosophers. Behind all the swagger and bravado, the contests to see who could drink the most, and the jokes of an emasculating nature, the threats and sneers directed at women, there was some serious male-bonding and extemporizing on the finer points of life and death. Don't be fooled by the drink, the spit, the smoking, the violence, the raw sex of the notch-on-the-belt variety, or the mob mentality. That's merely looking on the dark side. And as David Brin had sounded the clarion call, the herald of Positivism, let us look instead on the unsullied side. If you bothered to scratch below the surface of grime, sweat and oafishness, you would find a wealth of meaningful life-philosophy. Had they only been taught to read and write perhaps they would have put all their combined wisdom to paper to be preserved for posterity. Besides, who needs the complexities of literature, of poetry, when you can swear like a cabbie and speak in rhyme?

Hordes marched up and down the streets, overflowing the sidewalks. They only appeared to be scrambling in search of a cut-rate deal in clothing, or the latest hard-to-find doll or toy that was being promoted as something their children obviously must have—after all, you want your kid to be the only one on his or her block to do without?—these weren't the mindless rabble, the vacuous consumers some might see them as; they were, in fact, the seekers, the journeymen for truth, people who ached and yearned and were starved for culture, bereft of the music, poetry, literature, philosophy and fine arts they sought and which they mistook for the pornographic comic books they bought instead.

"Hallelujah!" I shouted. "The time has come at last! Yea! Good-bye to the Dark Ages, the sun doth shine once again. Adios ignorance. Hark and rejoice, the Renaissance is here at last!"

8

Titties for Tattles

My wife sought Mr. Right in her personal crusade for not just love, but Ultimate Love, the Big One. She sent out carefully worded letters composed by her alter ego to people she didn't know, while I immersed myself in the complexities of the bookstore, and kept one finger on San Pedro's at best weak and erratic pulse.

"What ever happened to romance?" my wife wrote. "I want real love, passion. I want to be adored." She sat waiting in her quiet corner for Prince Charming to show his errant face.

My best moments were when I looked up to see Katherine standing before me in the flesh. I reached out and touched her arm, her shoulder, or her hand. Steady, my boy! I gauged her enigmatic smile and couldn't help but forget all my troubles, happily reassured that the mirage before my eyes had substance.

God—the thought inescapably entered my mind—the things I could do with her.

For some painfully delicious few moments she chatted with me, then pored over a display of books, her fingertips tracing invisible designs on the dust jackets, asked if I had read this or if I liked that particular book, while she allowed me the glorious pleasure of gazing at her or standing beside her. She exhaled the very breath of life, which I greedily breathed in, growing lightheaded in the process.

She had an unmistakable regal bearing, not of someone acting a part, but someone born to it, subtle, not overdone. It was a feeling of supreme confidence; she was completely comfortable inside her own skin, self-possessed, imperious in her every gesture.

The casual way she entered and left, even the way she looked at me made me think she must enjoy this. Did she smile as she left, walking out with her back turned to me, knowing my eyes were trained on that too-perfect rear end, which as it moved created swirls and eddies, threatened to pull me forward, knock me off balance? Let's see the physicists try to explain that!

To glimpse Katherine's face, her incomparable ass, her breasts, but even the sight of her legs, a bare arm, her ears, her exquisite neck, to have her words rattle around the inside of my head; it did inexplicable things to a man.

I rushed to offer her poetry collections by Pablo Neruda, and then watched open-mouthed while she read the titles aloud in a voice that to my ears sounded as if she were saying, "I love you, I want you, I must have you."

In my spare moments I read Voltaire, an essay or two by Montaigne, tried to ignore my urges by immersing myself in reading, but it was difficult to drag my mind away from the shimmering after-image of Katherine, which left me as contorted as Quasimodo. The proof of the deleterious effects on my judgment was that as I pored over piles of catalogues and Publishers' Weekly, instead of ordering the top ten, the big blockbusters which were announced with full page, in-your-face advertisements, or even the standard fare popular authors, I found myself ordering things like *The Collected Works* by Ambrose Bierce, or the Plays and Short Stories by Oscar Wilde, short story collections by Dostoyevsky, *Gogol's Wife and Other Stories* by Tommaso Landolfi—books that sparked in me something I couldn't explain, or resist.

In some strange way, these odd books I bought were some sort of substitution for Katherine; a pale, weak substitution, perhaps, but, though

I couldn't have put it into words or even cogent thoughts at the time, I knew they were to some degree one and the same thing, even if merely figuratively.

I chased dreamily after these lingering images of Katherine and resolved to write a serious treatise on this phenomenon. I felt it hadn't been given its due, but was casually dismissed as yet another example of male macho absurdity, a manifestation of the single-track mind of masculinity. Perhaps. Yet perhaps, too, it transcended the excretions of testosterone my glands were manufacturing to no good avail. And something as potent as hunger or thirst, as ingrained as jealousy, I felt, deserved some serious consideration. At the very least this was the stuff about which the poets should write. I perused Bukowski's books, tried to find a poem dedicated to the subject, but instead found: "everything is so sweetly awful, so continuously sweetly awful: the art of consummation: life eating life."

Nature being in an apparently playful mood, I glanced over to see Bukowski seated across the street at the Ka-bob place with the crazy Romanian, perhaps sharing a flask of rotgut whiskey. The two of them smoking and cursing the ceaseless passage of time.

"Youth of today," I could almost hear them mutter. "What do they know? These young punks. Soft. They don't make 'em like us anymore. I could do more with one finger than most of them can do with their whole bodies. Even at my age, I could show them a thing or two!"

I peered out my window at the Sphinx and the Cyclops. Would they understand? Perhaps those two were beyond the afflictions that troubled me. Maybe that was what made Bukowski so different from me, why he looked at me as you would a babe lost in the woods. It worried me. Does Bukowski appreciate beauty? He must. He had his lovely wife, Linda. I wondered if Hank would gaze upon Katherine and register no reaction? Or would he see her only in a sexual light; a nicely proportioned woman in her mid-twenties? Could he possibly overlook her other aspects, those that made her stand out, that made her so singular to me?

I eyed my enormous shelf loaded with multiple copies of Shakespeare's plays and sonnets. I needed to get my mind off of Katherine, and my problems both with my wife and with the store/customers. I decided to read the entire Shakespeare canon. I pored over psychology, and remembered how I had once promised myself that I would read all of Freud's writings. Everything by Dostoyevsky, by Twain and Dickens. *The Golden Bough* from cover to cover. The same with the Oxford Dictionary, the Encyclopedia Britannica.

Books leaped out at me as I searched the shelves looking for titles my customers were interested in. *The Structure of Evil* by Ernest Becker, while hunting up a copy of *Your Erroneous Zones,* which some poor deluded woman had been convinced to buy by her allegedly-enlightened boyfriend.

It was too bad psychology was dead. No longer could aspiring minds find volunteers to give electric shocks to their study partners, to see how often and with what intensity the shocks would be given. No more could volunteers be assigned roles as prisoner and prison guards. What invaluable lessons were we missing by playing it safe? What with the folk running loose in San Pedro and some creative assistants I could arrange to have the upstairs converted into a laboratory for psychological research, getting these people off the streets and into some productive kind of work, something that would benefit mankind.

9

Don't Peek Behind that Curtain

Clue number two: Over the months people stopped in or called and asked for Joe.

"Joe? You're mistaken," I explained. "There's no Joe here. Just me, our baby girl, yes, sometimes my wife. But no Joe."

"Look, I don't want to deal with you. You don't know what I like. Joe does. Where's the old man?"

They didn't wish to deal with me? Hell, I was the owner of the damned place, wasn't I, even if technically speaking it was the Father? Still, I ran the joint.

This was peculiar, most strange. Were they talking about a different store, perhaps; had they gotten their towns and villages mixed up? Or was someone going around, sneaking into my shop and selling people books behind my back? Someone might have a spare key, open the doors at night (when I wasn't inside hiding) and run God only knows what kind of operation. It could explain why sometimes there were books that hadn't been there before, and others that were missing, disappeared into the strange invisible vortex that was the heart of the bookstore.

"What old man?" I asked these persistent people.

"The book guy," they said.

The book guy. The old man. Why was I completely in the dark

about all of this? I tried to explain. "Look, I took over the store from a woman. There was no old man, no Joe. Who is this guy?"

I gathered bits and pieces, one clue at a time, over many months. "Joe knows what is good," and, "Joe is the expert on books."

One or two described the old fellow, and I finally made phone calls to someone whose number I had, a person who used to do some occasional part-time on-call work in the bookstore years before, under the previous owner.

This guy, Joe Melkert, it turns out, was a real character, a guy who loved books, and who studied and read everything, but who also had some street smarts, some moxie. He drank and rag-tagged with the best and the worst of San Pedro. He was irascible, known to be an ornery codger, a crotchety, hot-tempered, though charming old coot. But he knew his books, and writers; he could rattle off titles in any subject. He was said to have encyclopedic knowledge, the bastard. He could sift all the crap from the mediocre, the gems from the rest. He could tell you a thing or two about rare books.

The more I learned the more fascinated I became, and the more familiar he seemed to me, like a favorite uncle you hadn't seen but once or twice. He had raised Arabian horses. He'd been an actor on the stage, Broadway, no less, even if it was just bit parts. Rumor was he had also written a number of books under a pseudonym. He had gone to fight in the Spanish Civil War, because he felt that it was the right thing to do. Naturally, I wondered if he had bumped into Hemingway, perhaps even tromped, camped, and drank alongside old Papa.

But he had died years before my sojourn at the Little Big Bookshop had begun. It was quite eerie to have people show up years after the old man had died and ask for him, as if they had talked just last week. I felt his presence in the store, sensed him lurking about, haunting the aisles.

After closing and before opening, I knew the bookstore was his, was Joe's. It may have been run by my wife and me, and may have been the Father's legally speaking, but in reality it was still Joe's. The building had that special quality one found in a cathedral or museum, if not some ancient Egyptian tomb. I stared up and down the aisles, at the rows and rows of books. I wanted to stay here, like this. I didn't want to leave. I didn't want to open the doors. I wanted to be alone with the books. I had to summon all the will I could muster to turn on the lights and open the shop, or lock up and leave the building.

10

Babylon Revisited

I attempted to assemble some scrap of sanity in my life by choosing to ignore my wife for the moment and write love letters instead to her alter ego. I was careful not to bad-mouth the woman to whom I was married, but made it perfectly clear in my missives that I preferred her alter ego any day of the week. "Dear Syn Sobriquet (her chosen pseudonym), I cannot keep quiet any longer! You are a precious jewel, nay, a rare flower. To sit back and watch you wilt and wither under the untender merciless harshness of your marriage is more than I can bear! You are deserving of being well-loved, of being adored, and yet, it seems to me, that while your husband may be a fine upstanding person, he isn't doing you right, now is he? A blind man could tell that you are starved for love, and (quite frankly) I have loved you long and hard, and have affection in abundance. I could easily love you for an eternity. If you are interested in allowing me to demonstrate this, pray, let me know, and I shall begin at once. Yours, Daniel Kashmiri (my pseudonym). P.S. If you wish to meet me face to face, merely name the place and I shall be there with a rat-a-tat heart and adulation in mine eyes."

Who knows, perhaps things would come to a boil and her alter ego would take over permanently, and then I'd finally enjoy companionship and affection once again; if only we could somehow lock her real self out, and trick her into remaining a shut-in, cloistered in a quiet refuge. In the meantime, I enjoyed romancing her alter ego every bit as much as I had once done her true self, and awaited the outcome with anticipation and high hopes, for we had once been as wild and insatiable a pair of lovers as you could ever hope to find.

Even now, I sometimes encountered her desire for me, but only when we were both asleep. It was the only time we made love, the only time she let me touch her, the only time she gave me the time of day.

Perhaps that was because it was the realm Syn Sobriquet ruled over her.

I awoke, heard her mumbling, was aware of her body pressing against me. I could either lie still, could move away from her, or press even more against her body. Of course, I chose the latter. She groaned, grabbing at me, and we made love. I wondered, was it possible to love another only when asleep? Was sleep an aphrodisiac for her? What did this mean when a woman showed no sign of desire for you when awake, and yet desired you when she was unconscious, a somnambulistic lover?

When I referenced her renewed sexual desires the next morning, she denied it. "You dreamt it," she said.

I scrambled through medical dictionaries and psychological texts attempting to find a term for this condition, this somnambulistic gratification, this narcoleptic-amorous state, whereas in her waking state she avoided me like the proverbial plague.

"Hey, what gives?" I implored the devil-may-care-Universe, God, the whole enchilada. After all, she a modern woman, unfettered by the unspeakable neuroses of her forebears; not someone who had to fear the light of day, who had to practice sex with all the lights off, under a blanket, with a sense of duty that forbade pleasure.

I returned to the scene of untold crimes, Adriano's coffee shop with daughter in tow, and visited my old friends. I scowled at the familiar faces and ordered breakfast for the two of us. The kid sat and looked at a picture book and made faces at Freddy.

"You look terrible," Betty the waitress said, as she brought me my coffee. "You'd better take care of yourself."

I grunted. More and more I was beginning to resemble Moses, sure as I was that He was what the future held for me, what I would become in a few years. The two of us would likely be put somewhere safe, a home for former booksellers, perhaps, where pretty nurses would come and read us bedtime stories:

"Tonight gentlemen, we have selections from *Tales of the Arabian Nights*, but only if you two are well-behaved. That means no pinching!"

"Come here and sit on my lap, won't you?" Moses would suggest, with a wink.

"Need I remind you gentlemen of the punishment for unruly behavior?" That kept our tongues in check and our hands at our sides. The head nurse, while being a looker, also had a mean streak worse than Nurse Ratched. Her favorite punishment was prolonged readings of Judith Krantz or Sidney Sheldon.

But if we were really good and quiet, and she happened to be in a rare good mood, Nurse just might let us snuggle up as she read, while we pretended to doze off, and pressed our faces against her breasts, one of us on either side.

This vision of the future faded as I gazed round the coffee shop. Why didn't these people ever come and shop for books? Our store was just a few doors down the block. It was clear: A person had to eat, but no one died from not reading. Still, there was death, and then there was *death*. They cared not one whit when it came to food for the soul.

Everything I did to drum up a little business seemed to work counter to my intentions, to say nothing of my intuitions, whether I put a larger ad in the yellow pages, or ran a special in the newspaper.

The Jews I knew, and those I encountered, looked at me with shame and embarrassment. Some Jew, they huffed and wheezed. Their deflated expressions, their sad, downturned mouths summed up my pitiable state, as they sadly shook their heads. Jews were supposed to be successful. What kind of Jew was this who couldn't make money? They blamed my failure on the fact that I was only half-Jewish, an example of what dilution produced, and of course my being a Kastinovich.

Paranoid survivalists who bought books on building bomb shelters before heading out to the desert to await the coming race wars kept telling us that not only were all Jews rich, but that they controlled the country, in fact the entire world. A conspiracy of Jews ran the whole show, and yet I had nothing. No money, no power, a pariah amongst my own people.

Nothing is so bad as a failed Jew, as any Kastinovich could tell you.

Moses was one of my best customers and I was one of his, but this didn't exactly fill me with hope. San Pedro had seen the shipyards and the canneries close down, but if they lost the used bookstores it would spell doom. It would cease being a town and be a mere suburb of that great sprawling mess called L.A., which the good people of San Pedro resented, always quick to point out to the ignorant that San Pedro wasn't L.A., but a proper separate town of its own. Well, not without a used bookstore or two, friends.

When I could get away I took solace in Moses' bookstore. I bought poetry by Octavio Paz and Neruda, plays by George Bernard Shaw, stories by Evan S. Connell and Gabriel Garcia Márquez. It didn't matter if I already had these books. It didn't matter if Moses had purchased them from me. Hell, somebody had to buy them. At the same time I brought Moses the occasional gems that I had found: a copy of *Closing Time*, by Norman O. Brown, *The Night Visitor and other Stories*, by B. Traven. But no sooner would I bestow such a gift upon him, then he would reach under his counter-top, such as it was (Moses didn't have a cash register or the other usual paraphernalia that one might associate with running a store, a business. Prices were tallied up with a pencil and paper, God bless him!), and present me with a copy of *The Golden Ass*, by Apuleius, or *This Quiet Dust and other Writings*, by William Styron.

Moses' shop was always filled with the sounds of symphonies, of sonatas and concertos, recordings of Mozart, Beethoven, Brahms, Corelli, Mendelssohn, Haydn, Schubert, Bach, and many, many others. Music resonated among the bookshelves, the rows and stacks of unshelved books. It was an oasis in the midst of a wasteland, and the people of San Pedro had no idea how lucky they were to have it right there under their noses. Old friends and loyal customers came from outside the area, even a traveler now and then from some far-off land who stumbled upon the shop, to be pleasantly rewarded by his discovery. They could come in at will and listen to music, gaze upon wondrous books, while Moses conducted the London Philharmonic, or side by side with Leonard Bernstein conducting the New York Philharmonic Orchestra, or Vladimir Ashkenazy and the Boston Symphony. Moses lived and breathed this music; it was as much his life as the blood and air, which coursed through his body.

Nothing was more inspiring than the sight of Moses standing at his podium, waving his arms about. There was a simple explanation, you see: Passion, Music, Poetry—for if it happened to be Pablo Neruda Day, he'd be there reading or reciting the works of one of the greatest poets of this century. Or it might be Robinson Jeffers Day, or Johann Sebastian Bach Day.

Moses also wrote reviews, both literary and musical, composed his column of definitions in the spirit of Ambrose Bierce, and wrote poetry, which he published under a pseudonym in the local papers. His bookstore was a haven, a sanctuary from 6th Street and the lunacy, mystery, and misery of my own store.

I returned to my own shop and played each of Beethoven's symphonies, one after the other on my stereo. I sat behind the counter, where I sharpened my machete and pored over voluminous books like *Crowds and Power,* by Elias Canetti, *Extraordinary Popular Delusions and the Madness of Crowds*, by Charles Mackay, and *Myth and Guilt,* by Theodor Reik. I combed the pages of these books, seeking an answer and possible solution to my problems, hints as to how to handle my wife, Katherine, and those I wished to entice into reading books. I listened to Beethoven's Seventh for the umpteenth time, the volume cranked up—there was nothing like Beethoven for a troubled mind.

11

Hey, buddy, get back on
your own side of the Looking Glass!

For a spell of some four or five days my wife and her alter ego jointly retreated behind a veil of impenetrable silence. For a period of just under a week she didn't speak to me. No words passed her tightly drawn lips. I wasn't informed as to why she had made this move. Perhaps it was an experiment, the way some people put on a blindfold to try and see how it is to be blind.

I knew she had been on some kind of spiritual quest, because she made a point of repeatedly telling me so. "I'd like to go to a retreat," she said. "I could live in an ashram for a while." I envisioned her in a quiet little temple. Nuns took vows of silence, so she'd fit right in. She became more and more of a shadow; she slipped in, and slipped out, sat quietly, all alone, like a mouse. I consulted books by specialists. Was this typical? Did every married couple go through this? It was puzzling. If men were traditionally reluctant to get married was it because they sensed the secret potentials that I found in my marriage?

I wished I could converse with Hank about this. What would Bukowski tell me? I'm sure there was something in his vast repertoire of experience that would lend aid to a fellow man afflicted as I was.

My wife and I came and went, entered the house, left the house, ate, took care of the kid, visited the bathroom, shared the same bed, but through it all she ignored my words, my entreaties.

"Aren't you going to say anything? Aren't you going to talk?"

Silence.

A different approach, a joke or two, to ease the tension.

"Cat got your tongue? I heard you speaking in your sleep, so I know you can talk."

Silence.

I was a mariner adrift on the vast ocean, like Columbus searching for some lost shore, or Noah looking for a piece of dry land, any place to escape the awful stench of all those animals. Nah, I was more the old man in "The Rime of the Ancient Mariner," guilty of some terrible crime, even if I was ignorant of precisely what that crime was.

How best to respond? Proffer silence with silence, or lay down and play dead, let her use me for a doormat until she grew tired of it?

It was getting harder to bear up. Even Bukowski seemed to sense the way the wind blew and couldn't be found to be asked his opinion on these thorny issues.

If she was anything she was stubborn. It was a matter of pride, self-righteousness. She could sit it out for longer than I could, that was for certain. And any punishment or retribution I could conceive of would, in the end, hurt me far more than it could ever hurt her.

I picked apart our relationship like a scab, pondered the imponderables, and knowing what Hamlet went through in his predicament; perception was a slippery item, reality difficult to pin down with precision. When to cut one's losses and walk away, when to trust one's ears and eyes, and the words of that little voice inside you, saying, "Get out while the getting's good," while denial is drowning out everything with boisterous proclamations of, "Take it easy; everything's all right! Quit making a big something out of a big nothing. Go on, stick your head back under the sand." And before Common Sense can come out with, "Yeah, but..." another voice (Conscience? That inner reservoir of dark fears, longings, loneliness, the haunting image of a child of a broken home) interjects with, "This too shall pass. Things will improve. Tomorrow is another day. Just ignore this."

Then again, I was a Kastinovich and as such I knew this was my lot in life.

Because these questions and thoughts jumbled and jangled in my already mangled brain, and because being around her in this state was so disconcerting, and it occurred to me that it was possible she might perpetrate some act of vengeance in my sleep, I began spending my nights at the bookstore. Apart from the sensation that I was never alone—the unceasing noises, the strange sounds, the groans and squeaks, movements that sounded exactly like footsteps and things being moved about, to say nothing of whispers and murmurs, all of which gave me chills and caused me to rise numerous times in order to explore and determine the source and cause of the noises—this was my favorite time in the store.

To sit alone (so I kept telling myself) with all those books; to have the time and the solitude to think my thoughts, to pick up whatever I wished to read, lose myself in a story; to jot down some notes, or pick up my guitar and bay like a wounded coyote. It was a blessed few hours of reprieve, a furlough from the tense unpleasantries, an asylum in my time of need.

Here, the unbearable burden of my marriage was a thousand miles away. Here, I picked up *The Sea Wolf*, an unabridged version of *Les Miserables, Alice Through the Looking-Glass*. Here, I took it upon myself to be Chief Justice of the World Court. And in my warped sojourn through the nocturnal landscape of the Little Big Bookshop—so different from what it was during the day, as if Salvador Dali had come in after closing and painted his otherworld over everything—I held court pointing the finger of incrimination at those wrongdoers the world over. My friend Moses was the executioner. The bookstore, like a plaza in the heyday of the Inquisition, was bathed in blood, while Moses beheaded those who were responsible for all the ills of society, the guilty. The typical objects of Moses' most scathing attacks, as prodigious as swarms of locusts, were morally bankrupt politicians, corporate CEOs, money-hungry, power-hungry religious leaders. Not surprisingly, many of our fellow business owners were there facing retribution for banding together, boycotting our store, for their unspoken prejudice against newcomers, whom they viewed with xenophobic fervor.

I spent many strange nights alone in the store. More and more I found myself thinking about Joe Melkert, the old man who had worked in the back. People continued to seek him out now and then. He remained an integral part of the shop, even if he was dead. Perhaps he too had spent his nights there as I now did. Some essence of him lingered, and he and I held many a strange conversation as he told me of the many things he'd seen over the years.

"The landing at the beaches of Normandy was a cakewalk compared with the Battle of the Bulge, my boy. The sights, sounds and stench from that stayed with everyone who was there."

"Hemingway was there, no?" I asked.

"Bah, sure from a safe distance. Now, Salinger, he was in the thick of it. Still, writing like a fiend. Typing like a madman even while the bombs fell all around us."

Each night I read myself to sleep. The way you sometimes hear the sound of your name spoken into your ear as you sink deeper, nearer to the realm of slumber, so too did I hear words now and then, words I wouldn't exactly remember the next morning, and thus casually disregarded, ascribed to dreams or imagination, or the regular creaks and groans of the bookstore, though it seemed so much more than that at the time: words of import, messages of a disturbing, troubling nature, like deep cold water currents running beneath a warm sea; currents which could pull you under or carry you far out into even deeper waters.

The Father made an appearance, marched in and sniffed around, like a border inspector seeking contraband. "What have you bought, what have you sold, what's in this box over here?"

He gave it the once over, pulled out an old copy of "Death of a Salesman."

"Arthur Miller," he said, in reverential tones. Since I knew full damn well what was coming, I tried to avoid it, or at least delay it by feigning I had to use the bathroom, adding that there was something I desperately needed from the other side of the store. "Did I ever tell you I saw Lee J. Cobb in *Death of a Salesman*?" he said. "Fantastic! The only time I ever saw grown men cry, men weeping like babies. He was great. Nobody could do what he did. I've seen Broderick Crawford, and others, but it wasn't the same. Lee J. Cobb took soldiers, lawyers, businessmen, hard men with hearts of stone, and reduced them to a group of blubbering babes. A whole audience in tears!"

He paused for a moment, gathering up his wherewithal to make a speech, and then let loose: "I am not a dime a dozen! I am Willy Loman, and you are Biff Loman…you vengeful, spiteful mutt!"

If he found a copy of Macbeth or Hamlet: "When shall we three meet again? In thunder, lightning, or in rain? When the hurlyburly's done, When the battle's lost and won…" on and on, gesturing, playing to an imaginary audience. "I, Teresias, old man with wrinkled dugs, who foresaw the scene and foretold the rest."

Like Reagan, who so often spoke in film quips, the Father couldn't resist quoting from a play or song or book, or the "The Love Song of J. Alfred Prufrock."

"Dare I eat a peach?" he asked, imploring, gazing at the ceiling, as if he expected a response from above. Potential customers roamed the shop, listening to this madman. He didn't care. Not the slightest hint of self-consciousness. He was a hell of an exhibitionist, a man who couldn't help but make a spectacle of himself.

He'd eventually tire of his soliloquies and continue peering round, nosing here and there.

"Where are the goodies?"

"Goodies? What goodies?"

Poking into boxes, the shelves behind the counter. "Come on, you know, the good stuff. The first editions."

"First editions?"

"People in this town don't care about first editions." I said. "They hardly care for any type of book, at all."

"Once they see you have a special section, they will come. You'll see. If we put them on one shelf, and mark them first editions, then we can price them higher."

I shrugged. "Go at it then."

He immediately set himself the task of going through the shelves and finding all the first editions. He picked a special shelf with a sign to display the valuables. And whenever a Somerset Maugham, or John Steinbeck, or any other first edition entered the shop up on the shelf it went.

"Remember, you've got to pick a pocket or two, son. You've got to pick a pocket or two."

Some people enjoyed looking at them, riffling through the pages, and balking at the prices. On rare occasions, someone from out of town even asked where we kept our first editions, but ours were usually not the first editions they sought or preferred. These were serious collectors; they bought first editions and only first editions, and sometimes only first editions that were first books by certain authors. With dust jacket in pristine condition, nary a crease or tear, and preferably signed by the author, and if with an advance slip laid in so much the better.

Did they ever read these books they valued so highly, or was it the mere possession of the object that gave them such a thrill? For the tiniest tear, or a chip, a small smudge would send them into a tizzy; they wanted mint condition; a book which had never before been read, or opened. They were after nothing less than biblio-virgins for their collection.

"See this specimen here in the glass case, gentlemen? It's never been touched by a human hand, never been soiled or deflowered, but is as pure as the day it rolled off the printing press."

The ones who were really far gone, and in desperate need of some twelve-step program at the very least, were those who sought proofs and galleys, because these preceded the actual first edition hard cover printing of a book. There was such a thing as taking something too far. Why not bottle the author's inspiration that had set him or her to writing a particular book in the first place? It was like collecting an artist's notepad or sketches. Never mind the painting itself. Give me the doodlings that preceded it instead.

It was yet another exercise in futility. Selling first editions in San Pedro made about as much sense as trying to sell original Matisses and Monets to punks who spent their nights spray-painting graffiti and sucking up the fumes.

Usually after an intense barrage of advertising, two or three new customers came strolling into the shop, though I hard-headedly kept preparing for an onslaught of the multitudes. Against all the obvious economic indicators I still expected crowds to swarm through the doors, if for no other reason than to get a discount, even if it was for something as useless as a book; still, I wasn't in a position to turn anyone away.

A middle-aged gentleman showed up. He was dressed in expensive clothes, that couldn't conceal his air of a shyster. He looked like a lawyer. "I need a book," he said, looking around as if he were in some hurry.

"What kind of book?"

"Oh, I don't know. Something good."

Well, that was a good start anyway. "There are tens of thousands of books in here," I said. "I'm sure we can find you something good."

He grunted, picked up a title impatiently, put it back down, picked up another, and flipped through the pages without looking at them, as if—were it a good book—it would whisper, "I'm the book you should buy." Obviously, this wasn't the one, because he put it back down, too, and so on. I wanted to tell him, this isn't the way to find a decent book, that this method of his was really no better than eeny meeny miny moe, but instead I tried a different tactic. "Do you like classic literature, adventure, science fiction, humorous tales, mystery, or biography, perhaps?"

"I'm not sure." He put down the last title he had picked up. They might as well have been written in a foreign language for all the attention he paid to the text itself. What was he trying to glean from its cover, his fingertips brushing against the pages? I offered him salvation by handing him a copy of *Ask the Dust*, by John Fante. "It doesn't get any better than this," I said.

He didn't even thumb through this one, but put it back down. "Look," he said breathlessly, "I don't have time for this. I've got to go."

He started walking out. "I've got some great books on this table over here," I said, trying to catch him before he walked out the door, before I lost him for good.

"You don't have what I need." He was gone, out the door like a bullet.

I sat at the counter, my reasoning capabilities having sunk down to the level of my equal in the window—the child, that is. "What just happened?" I spoke to no one and no one answered. It was as if all the books in the store were oozing fog, or maybe it was the building itself, excreting some substance that transformed the atmosphere and everyone in it, turning the bookstore into a gigantic aquarium, distorting every-thing within and without.

What had he been searching for? Was he really looking for a book, or was this just his way of killing time before going in for a root canal? Maybe he was looking for porn, but was too embarrassed to come right out and ask.

A woman in her early forties showed up, dressed in bright colors, a forgiving smile, a book in hand. I greeted her, fully prepared to fulfill her literary needs.

"I bought this here, but it turns out it was the wrong book," she said. "Can I exchange it?"

I looked the book over, a nice copy of Dante's *Inferno*. I made sure it was in good condition, that she hadn't gone through and highlighted half the pages.

"Sure, no problem," I told her. "You can trade it for the right book."

A few moments later she came back with a manual on how to soup-up your hot-rod, the title she had been after when she had taken home Dante's *Inferno*, a common enough mistake, one I'm sure anyone could have made.

I nodded, quietly slipped the book into a bag and bid her adieu.

Amidst all this I received a note, penned by none other than Bukowski: "The track runs until the 21st, sorry I missed you. Bukowski." Beside his name he had scribbled a little man with a bottle.

I held the note, read and reread it. What was this? What did this cryptic note portend?

My wife reminded me that evening that she had written him asking if he would help us out by doing a book signing.

"Oh, my God, he's taking you up on it? He must want to do it, then. Unless, of course, he was sorry I wasn't here so he could rearrange my face, for daring to pester him."

"Don't be silly," my wife said. "He obviously cares, since we're a San Pedro store."

By now the weekend had come and gone, and the storm over my marriage had passed. Suddenly everything was light and clear, brilliant and beautiful. Somehow I had been transformed from the Master of Darkness to a loving, kind, marriageable human being, full of redeeming qualities. This disturbed me to no end; being a beast, I could handle. Even being Mr. Wonderful wasn't so bad, but this back and forth business every other week was wreaking havoc, and giving me a personality crisis. "Make up your mind," I wanted to tell the little lady. "Or minds. Pick one or the other." But, then perhaps it was more complicated than that. If she reviled me, and her alter ego loved me, what else could she do but vacillate? She too was split down the middle. See how easily one person's problems can become another's?

I decided in the interest of peace and quiet, to go along with it, to take advantage of the good times while they lasted, for who knew when the tide would turn again?

I imagined myself among the trenches on the front lines of World War II Germany or Italy, the ceaseless fighting, the battles, mortar-fire, grenades, death and destruction, wholesale carnage. And one day amidst countless days of this bloodbath, the troops from both sides come together, put down their weapons, embrace, make endearing toasts to one another, drink and eat side-by-side, buddy it up, laugh and joke like there was no tomorrow, for tomorrow, of course, everything would return to normal: the fighting, the bloodshed, the hatred, the violence.

This same thing happened on rare moments with us: a day when we went about as if we were still in love, as if a referee had blown a whistle instantly changing what had been a heavyweight bout into a love-fest, only I never heard the whistle and so never knew whether to duck, take a swing, or pucker my lips.

The caliber of the acting was incredible, not merely the lines spoken, but the body language, the expressions, the glances. I don't know who we were trying to convince the most, ourselves or the world around us.

We were suddenly at ease around each other. We said all the right things. "Now I remember why I married you," she said, dreamily. "We have to keep these things in mind. We can't forget. It's so good, when it's like this, isn't it?"

"Yes, yes," the little puddy dog said, tongue lolling, head bobbing up and down.

"Let's do this more often."

There we were, arm in arm, a kiss here and there, an embrace or touch of the hand; gone were all the recriminations and resentments, shuffled off like so much discarded clothing.

We planned it out as if it were our first date. A baby-sitter for the toddler; a fine restaurant, a concert or a movie, a romantic and tender evening alone.

We leaned on one another, sat on a friend's boat, rocking gently in a slip in the harbor, my arm around her shoulder.

This was how it should be. This is the reality, I told myself. That other stuff was merely bad dreams and nightmares creeping into our waking moments, where at any moment the White Rabbit would appear to turn everything upside down.

"Okay, my dear, where to? I shall steer this ship wherever your heart desires. Shall we sail to the Nile, or Hawaii, to South America or Indonesia?"

"We can go now?" she asked, innocently. "On this boat?"

"But, of course. I've instructed the crew to prepare at a moment's notice, destination unknown."

"Anywhere?"

"My dear, just name the place."

"I'm sorry I've been such an idiot," she said. "I don't know what got into me."

Careful now, don't rock the boat. Let it glide snugly out of the slip. "That's all right. I didn't exactly behave sensibly either."

"Would you still marry me if we had it to do over again?"

"Of course I would. You love me still?"

"Yes, even more."

"You still haven't named the spot."

"Oh, that's right! I know, let's go to Cabo San Lucas!"

I blew the whistle and informed the crew of our port of call. Then I kissed her like we hadn't kissed in many months. Cabo San Lucas was where we had honeymooned.

12

Hunting For Chinaski

I held my breath and waited for Bukowski to show up, wondering what that would mean to life, limb, and property. I'd seen too many allegedly good things come and reveal themselves to be anything but, for me to gaze dreamy-eyed at what Hank's presence might bring me.

Every week one or two far-ranging road-weary souls straggled in, on the last leg of completing their long difficult pilgrimage to find Hank Chinaski. Sometimes they came right out with what they wanted. Others fawned over his books, talked about how much they loved his stories and poems, recounted tales they had heard thirdhand relating to his various infamous misdeeds, before blurting out, "Oh, by the way, do you happen to know where Bukowski lives?"

I received phone calls from the city council's office: "Someone just arrived in town, flew in from Germany, that's right, says she's Bukowski's long-lost cousin, once or twice removed, on his mother's side, trying to locate him, could you help her out, give her his phone number or his address?"

My god, but they were persistent, and devious, too. German, French, Dutch, all looking for Hank Chinaski, writer extraordinaire, raconteur, boozer, fighter, racetrack aficionado.

His disciples were often not at all what you'd expect, either. They ran the range from the unclean and malodorous to well-dressed, educated sometimes men, but mostly women; likely models, actresses, smart (at least in appearance), sophisticated, good-looking and oozing enough sexuality to transform a monastery into a seething horde of mad rapists—they apparently found the old boy irresistible. Why should it surprise me? There were women out there who flocked to killers, wrote love-letters to incarcerated murderers, and women who were turned on by ugliness, the physically repellent, just as there were men who placed personal ads seeking physically deformed women. Variety is defined by what is considered attractive, a turn-on, which on the human scale runs the whole gamut. And if someone found the dives and bars, the flop houses and coffee shops of Los Angeles, the beaches, and racetracks, the sex shops, and lonely streets attractive, why then wouldn't they find the personification of all that attractive?

Some of these characters clutched a photo or a picture from a magazine article that showed Hank standing in front of his home. "Do you know where this house is located?" one such desperado asked, firmly believing he was being subtle by not mentioning Bukowski by name. "It's somewhere in San Pedro."

Let me guess, a budding architect intent on studying the classic 1940's bungalow of small town North America. "Sorry," I said. "I haven't memorized every street, let alone house, in town." When I turned down their requests for his address some swore they would walk up and down all the streets of San Pedro until they recognized his house. I had no reason to doubt them. I hoped and prayed that Hank would be out there watering his lawn or hosing down his car as they did, and that he would turn the water on them as they approached so hopefully, so naively, so inconsiderately.

They all seemed to readily believe Hank would welcome them with open arms; that either they were the only ones to seek him out, or that he had an endless amount of time and patience to entertain the strangers who showed up on his doorstep.

I had stacks and stacks of Bukowski titles, everything available from

Black Sparrow Press. I cleaned them out of their stock of hardcovers, for until then the typical Bukowski customer usually bought only paperbacks, used if possible, more often than not stained with some indeterminable something, the residues of having emulated the author's lifestyle, while those with money bought the signed/limited editions.

Used Bukowski books were a rarity because they were usually put through the same excesses as the author, and face it, a paperback book just couldn't take the abuse, but would quickly fall apart.

People thumbed through copies of *Post Office*, *Women*, *Love is a Dog From Hell*, and *Notes of a Dirty Old Man*. Some laughed or chuckled; a few were surprised, for it'd be difficult to find someone who could out-raunch Bukowski. There were the irate few who felt I should ban Hank's books from my shelves. "He's a sexist; he constantly denigrates women," I heard repeatedly. "He's sick. He glorifies drunkenness, violence. He's disgusting." None of which I was about to argue with except: "First of all," I informed them. "I like the old boy, and second, if you don't like it don't read it, and third, if I was to ban anything it'd be books by creeps like Nixon, William F. Buckley, Jr., Charlton Heston, and their ilk."

The bookstore was already marked by several local community groups as a dispenser of evil, in cahoots with the devil, protested by rightwing religious groups for selling Playboy magazines, and possibly for my close association with Moses down the street, who repeatedly received threats in response to the vitriolic, political articles he wrote. Obviously, people like us stood for the moral degradation of San Pedro's unsullied populace.

Just when things got so bad that we could see no way out of our plight, just when we were about to hang it up and walk away from it all, we were saved. And our savior was none other than Charles Bukowski.

He phoned up, spoke to my wife, and set a date to do a book signing at the Little Big Bookshop. Shocked and stunned though we were, we instantly began to spread the word, and advertised the event that would put us back in the black and save the bookstore from oblivion.

People were incredulous. "How did you get Bukowski to do a signing?" they asked.

"I have no idea," I explained, "other than my wife wrote to him and asked if he'd do a book signing, against my advice, no less." Of course I hadn't forgotten the many and varied reports concerning his unpredictable temper, his dislike for doing signings, or being pestered, and I had no desire to get on his bad side; and yet, Hank responded favorably, said he'd be glad to help out.

John Martin, Hank's publisher at Black Sparrow, told me, in hushed tones of disbelief: "Bukowski *never* does signings." Clearly, he too was impressed, perhaps amazed. He had absolutely no idea what mysterious powers of persuasion I had brought to bear upon his most famous, if not notorious, writer. Who knows, maybe my wife had sent Hank one of her alter ego's cryptically worded love letters—perhaps that's what enticed him to do the signing. If so, her efforts had finally borne fruit, as I certainly wasn't the only putz to receive her suggestive missives.

I faced the event with more than a little apprehension. Why had he agreed? I fretted. Was it a trap? Was there some dark purpose hidden behind the smiles and urbanity? Did he mean to thwart me, and the Little Big Bookshop by canceling at the last minute? Perhaps my wife had complained to him of my evil ways, my abuses and neglect. After all, I hadn't read the letter she had sent him. Perhaps she had sung him a sad song about our sorry relationship that had touched his crusty old heart. Bukowski's agreement to do a book signing could well be nothing more than a guise for him to rescue her from my clutches. Bookstore Wife Saved by Bukowski, I could see the headlines scream.

I jumped every time the phone rang, was spooked again and again by people who merely opened the door. I suspected that Red Stodolsky, the owner of Baroque Books, in Hollywood, the premier long-time Bukowski dealer, known far and wide, the man who sold Bukowski books back when people wouldn't touch him with gloves and disinfectant, would come gunning for me. Word on the street was he was pissed off. Why wasn't Bukowski doing a signing at his shop? After all, Bukowski was *his*, what right had I to think I could request Hank make an appearance at our shop? I thought of emblazoning a sign above the cash register, informing any and all that the idea was my wife's and not mine. Let her be responsible for whatever disasters might befall us with the arrival of Charles Bukowski. If Red Stodalsky were only half as old and half as vicious as Hank it could prove ugly for me.

We printed up flyers, plastered them everywhere, had kids go to parking lots and place them on car windshields. Contacted the local media. We prepared as best as we were able for the event.

Hank arrived at the store accompanied by his lovely wife, Linda. He smiled and was pleasant, gracious even. He sat at the small table we had set up for him, and drank six-pack after six-pack of Heineken, which was all he had requested, when we'd asked what he would like to have.

I looked over the crowd that grew until it reached beyond the doors and down several storefronts.

People marveled at finding themselves face to face with their hero, Bukowski. He was, after all, a sweet old guy, whose humility and generous nature I couldn't help but admire. He bantered with a few of the more eloquent fans. Several brought him copies of their own work, which he accepted without tearing a single copy to shreds.

"Keep them coming," Hank said, though I wasn't sure whether he was talking about the people or the booze. We supplied him with an entire case, plus one six-pack, on this lovely Saturday between the hours of 2:00 and 6:00 p.m. as he sat and drank and smoked and signed books for the approximately five hundred people who stopped by to have a look at their hero.

He didn't snarl or swear or threaten to rearrange anyone's face, though many lingered, hoping to see a show; he didn't hit anyone, or throw anything, didn't so much as chew a single person's head off; he signed, scribbled, laughed and joked, the very picture of urbanity. He took the bottle of wine a French woman brought with her when she flew for the second time in as many months from Europe just to see him. Another woman from Germany also made a second appearance, and brought him a bottle of something special. Others brought him flowers. He enjoyed the festive atmosphere, Linda, was charming and sweet, and clearly enjoyed all the fuss Hank received.

Bukowski beamed, perched in our most comfortable chair behind the table with his beer and cigarettes. "I'll be here as long as there are books to sign, baby," he said, as I attempted damage control, keeping my eyes on the crowd that at any moment could turn unruly. I waved at Hank, thinking, thank you, thank you, knowing there'd likely be a riot if he stopped. People kept arriving, including finally, one local newsman. I'd expected and hoped for more.

I peered outside. This was unbelievable. We were actually making money. Some of our fellow shop owners stood on the sidewalk and stared in disbelief. Who were all these people, and where did they come from? Hadn't they heard about the boycott? I laughed and called out to these supporters of ours. "Pretty good crowd, eh?"

"They're buying books?" they asked, unable to mask the incredulity in their voices.

"Oh yeah, today Charles Bukowski is in there signing his books. We're selling like crazy."

"Charles who?"

"Bukowski. Famous writer. They just did a film of his. *Barfly*. Bestseller in Europe."

"Never heard of him."

Now, just imagine that. None of these luminary members of the local business community had ever heard of Hank?

"Well, you have now. By the way, how's business down your way?"

"Okay." I gathered that was why they were spending the afternoon sweeping down the sidewalks. I went back inside and watched as the books from the table we'd devoted exclusively to Bukowski titles disappeared.

Hours later, when it finally quieted down, Hank looked up.

"Is that all?" he said. I looked down the street. No one else was coming. I nodded. "Well, we did all right, eh, baby?" Hank winked and grinned like a boy who'd just made the winning pitch.

I didn't know whether I was more amazed by Bukowski's staying power, at the wondrous capacity of his bladder, as he only got up to pee once, and then only toward the end of the four hours he spent signing books, or by the unparalleled success we'd just experienced, the number of people who had come and gone, leaving us stunned in their wake.

It was quite an event. And we did very well. I noted with satisfaction and relief that we came through it unscathed. The signing had come and gone, and though the newspapers and radio for the most part ignored the event, busy as they were with reporting the daily petty crimes plaguing San Pedro, we still had a good turn out, and I promptly reordered a large amount of new Bukowski titles, sure as I was that now the bookstore was to become known far and wide to Bukowski aficionados the world over.

Perhaps more people would fly from Europe to have their pictures taken in the book store where Hank Chinaski had recently appeared. I wished I'd had the presence of mind to have been photographed with Chinaski when he did the signing, but I'd been far too busy looking out for trouble.

13

Heads or Tails

It was important to keep an eye on the drunks, as well as the inhabitants of the several halfway houses that adorned the neighborhood, who now and then forgot to take their medication or had taken too much, and had wandered into the bookstore. I'm not sure if the drunks believed I was hiding a bar in the back, or if they just desired a nice quiet place to down the distilled juices they carried on their person. Or maybe they had merely taken a wrong turn. It wouldn't have surprised me to learn there had once been a bar or speakeasy here before the bookstore. I quietly ushered these tottering folk back onto the sidewalk as best I could, and pointed them in the direction of the nearest bar, just around the corner and across the street—a mere dozen or so stumbles from my door.

Those from the halfway homes were mostly a harmless sort, like Manuel Costa, who, for whatever reason, unbeknownst to myself, happened to love being around books, though I couldn't swear that he ever read a single one of them; he found unbridled joy in simply flipping their pages, first one way then the other, staring at the pretty covers, and trying to make sense of the pages of words. He could be sweet and mild as pudding, but when he went off the deep end, he stormed in and out of the shop like some comic Keystone Cops parody, raving, ranting, flailing his arms about, with his face contorted as he shouted and cursed those unfriendly faces he observed in the ceiling and floor.

Sometimes I heard Manuel coming down the street, yelling at the top of his voice, holding the same arguments he'd apparently been conducting for years. I'd meet him at the door and bar the entrance, "Keep going, Manuel. Not today." But far too often, he slipped in silently, and once in a back room, began having it out with his unseen adversaries. Then I'd have to go and retrieve him, warily, for I never knew if he was going to take it upon himself to bite my nose off.

"Go on, Manuel, take it outside," I'd say, urging him toward the door. He'd storm off, snarling and muttering under his breath as he left the building.

On occasion the patients from the halfway houses came in droves. Their day out. There was nothing like being overwhelmed or besieged, only why couldn't it be with paying customers? "Dear God," I cried, "if you are going to send me people to pass through these doors, at least do me a favor and make them literate. And if that's asking too much at least give them spending money." Truth is I often couldn't tell these people from many of the regular San Pedroans who entered the bookstore. I never knew who or what I was dealing with. Who was friend, who was foe? Sometimes I tossed someone out of the store to later learn they were perfectly normal. I also let people inside, offered to assist them, only to find out too late that they were heavily sedated and let out of their cage for a lark. These were the type who ordered twenty-four copies of the same book—and an expensive book at that—you'd assume for a class they taught, that they were a teacher, only they weren't, and had no intention of picking up, let alone paying for those twenty-four books.

As for the more questionable people, like Manuel Costa, the drunks, and the assortment of others who frequented the establishment, my wife was frightened by their erratic and neurotic ways. They appeared deranged, deformed, and dangerous. Every other one, she was sure, would attack her, the baby or me.

"They might pull a knife," she said. "How do I know they won't become violent?" She spoke as though she feared they might bare fangs. It was good that she only spent weekends at the store. My daughter, on the other hand, found most everybody amusing. She sat and practiced her vocabulary out on these people: "despicable, nauseating, hideous, repulsive, suffer!" She even on occasion took it upon herself to order troublemakers out of the store; at one-and-a-half the girl had more backbone, more chutzpah, than her mother or I had.

Now and then my wife complained about our daughter spending so much time in the store. "What better place to raise a child?" I said. "This is beautiful. With her papa, no baby-sitters. Surrounded by books."

"I just don't think she should be exposed to all this."

"Not to worry," I said. "I'm right here. Nothing can happen. Besides, she's learning all sorts of things." And to prove it I asked my daughter to name the planets, which she did with gusto, each and every one, and in the correct order.

"You're turning her into a parrot, or a monkey," my wife said.

"Hold your tongue," I answered. "This girl has brains. She's sharper than a pickaxe. Watch. Ask the child what Republicans are. Go on."

"What are Republicans?" my wife asked, wearily.

"Scum of the earth, and scourge of the cosmos!" the kid said, pointing her finger in the air for emphasis.

"Great," my wife said. "Most of our customers are probably Republicans."

I ignored her. Clearly the kid was brilliant. What did her mother know? This kid said Dostoyevsky with such enthusiasm, here where many of the adults couldn't even pronounce the name correctly. True, she hadn't yet read *Crime and Punishment* or *The Brothers Karamazov*, but she was already familiar with his shorter works like, "The Dream of a Ridiculous Man," and "The Double".

My wife didn't much care for having to deal with customers. She found it particularly difficult to buy books. If the person in any way appealed to her, she offered far too much money, and if she didn't like them, she might turn down their books altogether, even if they were unusually good. Furthermore, if she offered a dollar for a book and the person griped and bitched and said she should pay two; she generally went along with it. And if they had crap to sell, which, of course, was usually the case—book club editions and the like—she often purchased it, whether to help out someone who needed the money, or to hasten our destruction, or to spite me, I couldn't say.

"You have to be tougher," I explained. "At this rate they'll clean us out. They can sense weakness. They can smell it if you're soft, and they'll go straight for the jugular."

"Look at them," she said. "They obviously needed the money."

"Yeah, well so do we. At this rate we'll soon be out on the streets with them, and I doubt if they'll be offering to share with us when that happens."

"Don't be so mean."

"I'm not being mean. You want to feel sorry for someone, feel sorry for us."

I walked a tightrope, had to watch my every step, my every word and the tone in which I spoke. If I went overboard and spoke too harshly, criticized too adamantly, there would be hell to pay.

"What is it now? What have I done?"

"You know what you've done."

"No, really, did I say something I shouldn't have?"

Silence, as deep and impenetrable as death. She stood and glared at me with the full force of her accusations, the manifold sins of Nicholas Kastinovich.

"Come on, how can I apologize or avoid repeating when I don't know what it is I did?"

"I can't live like this. I'm tired of being treated like dirt."

"Whoa, treated like dirt, living like this? Am I allowed to know what crimes I am guilty of, or do we just summon the executioner?"

Out would come the ledger. 8 1/2 by 11 inches of yellow notepaper upon which she had conveniently listed all the injustices, all the offenses I had caused her to bear. Neatly recorded in sequence of severity, my misdeeds and abuses, the terrible grievances she was forced to endure with such saintly fortitude. She had an uncanny memory, too, for in an instant she'd dredge up things I had said and things I had done months or a year ago. Usually, these were things she had mentioned a number of times before, and yet there were always one or two which I had never heard, as if she had saved up these especially choice salvos for just such a moment to toss my unsuspecting way.

I glanced it over. It was an impressive list, to be sure. Long, too. Each item numbered, written in black ink, an indictment of every single one of my transgressions against her. It was complete, all right. She had been careful to leave nothing out: what I thought of her, slanders and libels, defamatory language, unfair accusations I had leveled against her, even the vague and insubstantial, such as "He has no faith in me." I read through the list. There were horrible things, cruel things listed, but none of it was more than gross exaggerations, and distortions. I shouted after her, "If Jimmy Carter could lust in his heart, then surely I cannot be condemned for actions which I have failed to act upon!"

But she made no answer, having already slammed the bedroom door behind her, retreating into our bedroom to beat the pillows senseless, which she did with alarming regularity.

14

The Wandering Jew in the Sahara of the Bozart

There were increasingly dangerous times at the bookstore, moments when the doors were bolted and I waited inside until it was time to open up, moments when I had the bookstore to myself, when I sat in the quiet, semi-darkness—the lights switched off—and watched the traffic go past the windows, the occasional pedestrian stagger by.

"Don't open the doors," a voice whispered like an unoiled hinge down the darkened corridors. "Stay inside, refuse to let anyone in." I spun round looking for the source of those words, but saw no one there. The thought occurred to me that I might remain holed up in the store, my hideout, read a few more books, tackle something momentous like *Moby Dick* or *War and Peace*, something to keep me engrossed for a good six months. Here, I could find some peace of mind, dream wild dreams, and keep the nightmares at bay. I'd allow no one but Katherine inside. This would be our sanctuary, our little love nest.

I regularly tested myself: how long could I stay shut-in, keep the doors locked? I watched the clock tick, one minute late, two, three... How long before people demanded I open up, let them inside? Could I prolong it, remain locked inside for days, weeks even, before the authorities were called in to investigate?

These fantasies lasted precious few moments, until the phone rang, or someone jangled the steel gate outside the doors, wanting to buy a copy of the TV guide or *The Enquirer,* or some other pointless distraction brought me out of my thoughts.

I opened the doors with only the faint hope that Katherine might show up to sustain me.

Instead, people marched in and barked at me: "What happened to the shop next door? There was a nice furniture shop there," or, "What used to be here? I can't remember?" or "How long has this bookstore been here, anyway?"

I answered their questions and grew heavier in spirit. A bookstore, an information kiosk, what the hell was the difference?

"Years, lady, years."

"Funny, I never noticed it before."

I shrugged. "Why would anyone notice a bookstore? What is it but a repository for useless information? A warehouse, no, a tomb full of dead letters, the words of dead men and women, forgotten words," I intoned in a voice remarkably like the one I heard in the bookstore at night.

I went through the charade of selling books, when in fact what I sold were Cliff Notes to teens and adults alike, people who didn't want to waste the time reading the actual book. I invariably tried to convince them nonetheless.

"Why, when I can just read this? Saves time."

Why indeed? Why not ask a friend or a neighbor what the book was about, get your information for free and without having to read a single word? Or better yet go see the movie.

The cheapitude people exhibited worried and annoyed me. The media of course encouraged and promoted this: get it for next to nothing, lowest prices ever, bargain discounts, etc. That was all that mattered. Get your stuff for less, even if you had to drive two hours to get it.

We had no shortage of people who wandered in asking for money or a job, too. "Yeah, I always thought about working in a bookstore," they said. "To have all that time to sit around and read all those great books."

Why they thought I'd hire someone who just wanted to sit around reading all day long was beyond me, but many people thought this was the ideal life. How could I break it to them that the only time I had to read a genuine book was when I stayed after hours to avoid going home to a wife or a nun-in-training who regarded me as her sworn enemy? How could I explain that otherwise the only reading I did involved bills and statements, *Publisher's Weekly*, and zillions of publisher catalogs?

I let them find their way back to the door and wished I had Moses' staff and his inclination to smite the sorry sons-of-bitches on the backside. Moses knew how to handle undesirables. He dealt with them expertly; a mere turn of phrase, a few well-chosen words like, "Get the hell out of here," sufficed, spoken in that biblical voice of his, which left them stammering and gasping for air, rushing out of his store never to return. Or, eschewing words, he'd simply raise the axe he kept behind the counter. And good-riddance. The terrified looks on their faces, "I only asked him if he'd go lower on the price," they said weakly, in self-defense. They looked at me in appeal, sought consolation and solidarity, but I shook my head, condemned them for their thoughtless act. This wasn't a used car dealership. Moses charged less than anybody for books. You don't go there thinking to haggle over the prices, not when you are getting quality like that. No, buddy, you blew it.

There were requests for an entire genre of the Awaken-the-Slumbering-Goddess-Within-You, and the Develop-Your-Own-God-Like-Powers, etc., etc., ad nauseam. Become a Superbeing! or Tap Your Latent Genius!

Everyone was a potential psychic, a potential artist, a genius-in-waiting. It said so, right there in all those books, in black and white -- must be true. Isn't it clear when you look at the world around you, your neighbors, your teachers, your boss, your co-workers, family member, friends—each of them fairly bursting with all that potential?

"Ah, yes, the Psycho-babblers," Moses said. "Watch out for them, my boy, they are prolific in number." And as an antidote he gave me a copy of *The Three Christs of Ypsilanti*, by Milton Rokeach, one of the obvious inspirations for the play "The Ruling Class," and a fantastic book about three patients in an institution who each claim to be Christ, and how they face the if-I'm-Christ-how-can you-be-Christ issue when brought all together.

"That's where you and I will end up," Moses prophesied. "In some home for the incurably insane. I'll be Ambrose Bierce and you'll be Poe. The two of us locked up together for the remainder of our un-natural lives."

My eye twitched like mad, and I scratched an incurable itch that made the rounds of my flesh. "Say, did I ever tell you I married my cousin?" I asked Moses.

"Ed*gar*!" he said, flashing me his infamous grin.

People stopped by or phoned asking for Bibles, or books on astrology, the powers of gemstones and tarot, and the wisdom of the Druids. I mused over this problem. How had humans survived and not driven themselves off a precipice like lemmings? Had we as a species progressed one iota since our infancy? Was society, after hundreds of thousands of years of history and culture, no better off than the primitives whose beliefs were infused with fear and superstition? I searched through my catalogs. I found much needed ammunition in Prometheus Press. I ordered copies of *Christian Science*, by Mark Twain; *A Skeptic's Handbook of Parapsychology*, *Science Confronts the Paranormal*, *Flim-Flam!*, *The Gemini Syndrome: A Scientific Evaluation of Astrology*, and other titles, with which to battle against these adherents to the Cult of Atavism, all those who want to keep people cowering in the dark, afraid of shadows, those who keep the species in an eternal adolescence. I ordered everything I could find by Carl Sagan.

I took polls and was nothing short of flabbergasted when I found that most people believed in anything but reality. Every kind of phenomenon imaginable: ghosts, heaven, hell, UFOs, devils, angels, psychics, and reincarnation—you name it! To make it worse, everyone polled also believed they knew 76 to 87% of everything there was to know. How was this possible?

I devoted an entire table to all of John Fante's books, both paperback and hardcover, some of which Black Sparrow had seen fit to republish, either out-of-print since the nineteenthirties, or published for the very first time.

I brought out beautiful art books and wonderful non-fiction, like a reissue of Norman O. Brown's *Life Against Death*, the works of John Sanford—yet another neglected American writer, the author of *A More Goodly Country*, *A Walk in the Fire*, *The Winters of that Country*—and H.L. Mencken, Ernest Becker, books, I might add, which during the final days of the bookstore I couldn't even give away. There they lay discarded, tossed aside like obsolete volumes written in a dead language, of interest to nobody.

Now and then a few souls dropped by in search of an actual book. Older women and young girls combed through the stacks looking for romance novels; little old ladies asked for the latest in truelife serial murderer case studies; weathered old men in search of a sizzling Western by Louis L'Amour or Luke Short.

Could I cater doggerel like this? People warned me I was cutting my own throat. "Let them read Shakespeare or Dostoyevsky," I said. "If it's variety they want, hell, I've got Amado, Borges and Marquez, Poe and Twain, Dickens and Fowles, Peter Beagle, Shirley Jackson, Gerald Kersh, Charles Beaumont, Angela Carter, Stanley Ellin, John Collier, Bukowski and Fante, for Christ's sake. We've got books from Cervantes to Saki, Aristophanes to Voltaire. What more do these schmucks want?"

It wasn't that I objected to people reading bestsellers or popular fiction. Had they been tattooed, wellmuscled biker women buying true-crime books to do some fond remembrance thing about their abusive step-fathers, or their former boyfriends or girlfriends, now stuck doing hard time in maximum security, I assure you I could have lived with it. But to see harmless, sweet, little old ladies lap up murder in a Pavlovian feeding frenzy, was more than I could bear. To see their kindly eager faces and their fragile bodies fairly shaking with anticipation as they begged me for more, the latest in serial killers, ax-murderers, dismemberments, while their leaky little old lady eyes swam round and round not in visions of sugar plum fairies, but of knives dripping with blood and gore, of strangulations and rape filled me with dismay.

If there had been some balance, say, one or two each day to set off the vast numbers who were buying the really wretched stuff, I might have been able to stomach the whole sordid affair. But as it was, that person who came in looking for something above mediocrity was better than a minor miracle, and just as rare, usually only occurring when a big ship came to town or a film crew were setting up a shoot. What irked me even more was that time and time again I saw how those who bought the godawful dreck never bought anything else. They often picked out one or two authors and would wait until they put out a new book, rather than find something else to read. They seemed to have an aversion to someone new, to someone different, someone they'd never heard of before.

But like some deranged zealot trying to find converts to Judaism in the midst of Nazi Germany, I did my best, thrusting books at these people, "Here, read this Machado de Assis novel. Go on, it won't bite." Their faces betrayed mistrust, fear.

"I don't know," they responded, vacillating. "What is it?"

"It's hilarious, great characters, well-written, you'll like it, trust me." But whether it was Machado or Charles Portis, perhaps they thought the Nazis might catch wind of their conversion, the thought police might catch them with outlawed reading materials and gas them for their crimes. Perhaps someone had teased them when they were youngsters, called them ninnies, or smarty-pants or something because she had found them reading a book, heaven forbid. Still, I cajoled them, "Go on, take the book, hide it, if need be, read a few pages when no one is looking."

Perhaps book lovers would have to unite and create a Reader's Protection League to swoop down on those thugs who harassed readers.

But the vast majority of these people I tried to reach were untouchable, unbendable. Those San Pedro cowboys who read Luke Short and

Louis L'Amour read that and only that. The women who read romance read nothing but romance. And of course those on a diet of crime and murder couldn't wean themselves of the taste for blood; perhaps they would graduate to reading about cases of genocide throughout history, the history of torture and other delicacies concocted by a species with a genius for depravity and violence.

What surprised many with whom I discussed the matter was the fact that our best customers were those burly, tattooed souls who worked on the cargo ships, the tankers, and the fishermen who stank of sweat, oil, and fish. They came in and bought sacks of paperbacks to read during the long sea voyages, and quality stuff, at that. They were the few who actually bought and read Twain, Jack London, Jane Austen, Joseph Conrad, H.G. Wells, the Brontes, and Rudyard Kipling. Sailors, abalone fishermen, and divers came and bought piles of good novels and short story collections, brightening my day and lifting my spirits in the process, permitting me to grant a temporary stay in my utter damnation of the human race, condemning it to a speedy annihilation at the hand of Moses down the street. Only problem was there just weren't enough of them.

Maybe the people who lived up on the hill with the fancy cars, the big homes and the degrees from the very best schools were too busy raking in the money, too busy counting that money and building up extravagant interests on that money, and making sure all the world knew. They had no time left over to read literature. If they read anything it was market analysis, the stock exchange, *Forbes* and the _Wall Street Journal_, something that gave them an indication of their own worth, as opposed to the triviality, say of reading Jonathan Swift or George Orwell.

I observed a familiar-looking chap, typical of the streets and the late-night meanderings through town. He was shabbily dressed and unkempt. He was lean as a pork chop and tall, or at least appeared so, perhaps more than anything due to a lack of sustenance.

I left the store and followed him at a short distance, even crossed the street and quickened my pace to get a better look at him. He was thin, all right; he looked like a figure who'd been whittled with a sharp knife.

Whoever his maker was he had done a rush job, or at least was distracted during his work, paying little attention to finery or aesthetics. He had been carved so that there was no smoothness to his features, a haggard, haunted look as if he had been a man hunted and punished by his fellow beings, a man who had suffered years of abuse, neglect and want.

"Raskolnikov," I said in a choked-back whisper, as soon as I saw his haunted ruin of a face.

This ashen-faced specter then turned toward me, but I don't believe he saw me. He had eyes that didn't appear to focus or discern anything. My heart beat rapidly, and adrenaline pumped overtime. To get him into the store to tell his tale, now *that* would be a feat. I watched him enter what looked like a cheap boarding home on 9th Street and made a mental note to try and make contact with this fellow, buy him a few drinks, loosen his tongue, get him to tell me the story of his life.

I envisioned the Little Big Bookshop as a place where Raskolnikov, and others—a young Huck Finn, maybe a Dorothy Parker, or even a Holden Caulfield or two—could come and have a platform, a place where they could be heard.

I tried to imagine a young Mark Twain trying to sell his books, struggling to get read and published in today's market, until I nearly choked on my laughter. He too would likely be wandering the streets, or forced by today's harsh reality to a life of crime, or else become a real estate salesman.

I took copious notes and planned out scenarios featuring my famous guests, the introductions I would give each of them. We could pass a hat around as opposed to charging at the door, for those in the audience would likely be as poor and downtrodden as the guests themselves.

Let regular bookstores have poetry readings and signings by second and third-rate poets who wrote mainly about how mommy or daddy or their teachers didn't understand them, or about the first time they got laid. I'd close up my shop and go out in search of Arturo Bandini, John Fante's alter ego, and I'd come back only if and when I found him and got him to agree to amuse the crowds with his wit and pathos.

"Don't hold your breath folks. No telling how long it might take to find the elusive Bandini, miracle wonder-worker of a turn of phrase in the English language, last seen tromping through the fields of Wilmington. But, I'll be back, as soon as I catch him, I assure you. Never say never. I have only just begun to fight. Only the good die young! Onward!"

15

Miracles, Saints and Refugees

I manned the fort armed with my loyal one-and-a-half-year-old foot soldier. People still loved to come and stare at her while she played in her pen, or wandered through the byways of the bookstore raiding the children's book section, or shed every stitch of clothing in the front window for all the world to see.

My wife kept her secretarial job, since she was the only one of us with actual marketable skills. With regular income coming in I could still afford to buy books now and then.

Even still, once in a blue moon, there did occur the blessed miracles, the answer to my prayers; the kind I spent hours hoping and praying for: paying customers. And I would have to restrain myself to keep from kissing the ground at their feet, refrain from lavishing too much praise and adulation their way, from salivating too much.

Our usual mailman was replaced for a couple of weeks by another who became a regular customer. Not only that, but he brought his wife and daughter in too. They bought books, read books, recommended books, and I would have given all I had for the ability to clone them, to be able to replicate this ideal pair of customers a thousandfold. We would meet for dinner, and watch old films like "The Awful Truth," and "You Can't Take it With You," as well as foreign and independent films.

Then a film producer and his wife, John and Barbara Cutts, un-abashedly, unashamedly entered the store looking for literature. I noted a British accent. "Say," I said. "Being from England, have you heard of Gerald Kersh?"

"Why, yes, indeed. As a matter of fact I collect Gerald Kersh," the noble man, the saintly, learned fellow professed.

"What about Peter Barnes?" I asked. "He wrote the play 'The Ruling Class?'"

"He's a good friend of mine." This was too good to be true. I wanted desperately for the two of them to take me home with them, to have them keep me as an adopted son.

We chatted about the film *The Ruling Class* that was adopted from Peter Barnes' play, and he mentioned *The Three Christs of Ypsilanti*, which I had coincidentally been reading; the dear woman to whom the gentleman was married promised to send me an album (yes, folks, a genuine vinyl LP), of the music to *The Ruling Class,* which she did, and which I treasured ever after, playing it now and then at the bookstore to delight the crowds. We discussed other writers, as well: Simon Raven and H.E. Bates among them.

They later told me they had stumbled on the store by accident; they had merely been looking for a place to eat. But that didn't change my opinion or my feelings for them. Upon seeing a bookstore, even with empty stomachs, they boldly entered and graced me with the lexicon of lettered, cultured folk, for which I was most grateful. John had an uncanny memory, and any time I mentioned a writer or actor, Richard Harris or Dustin Hoffman, Kathryn Hepburn or Beau Bridges he would have me in hysterics with anecdotes featuring the person.

They gave me their phone number and invited me to their home. There I saw for myself that wonderful feast of books, books from floor to ceiling, good ones, too, not junk, but a treasure trove of quality titles, which dazzled my culture-starved eyes.

Unfortunately, this couple were last seen some months later sailing off to some nether part of the world to join a film production, having been assigned producer of some movie of gigantic proportions, something about the Casbah, or India. What did it matter where? Again, I was alone in the world. Fate had seen fit to bring these wondrous people to me, to show me, yes, my son, the people you seek do exist in this world, and then promptly sent them halfway around the world. What could I do, pack up my books, buy some rickety pull cart and drag my wares after them? A traveling bookstore. Now, why hadn't I thought of that before? Have books will travel! Low overhead, mobility. I could go to my customers as opposed to waiting for them to come to me. I could partner with Cyclops at the Kabob shop. The two of us traveling as we hawked our merchandise. If only we could convince the Sphinx to join in—the three of us roaming the countryside, Bukowski penning poems we could sell as leaflets or chapbooks.

There were others, too, now and then, blown in by an errant breeze: Oddballs, misfits, black sheep; people who read and appreciated books, customers with whom I laughed and conversed, people who also liked good music and old films. We swapped authors and titles, dispelling—at least momentarily—the sensation that the people who entered my establishment and I were not of the same race.

Katherine, with her shoulder-length blondish halo, the very woman who was the cause of my sleepless nights, appeared regularly to knock me off balance and play havoc with my equilibrium. In her presence I gasped for air, my mouth became a desert and I was unable to bear the pounding in my ears, my head, my chest, as my heart bruised the inside of my ribcage. I couldn't stand straight and walked off kilter. I had to steady myself as I went along, groping for ballast, as if at sea.

To be in the bookstore, lost amid the ruins, the shadows, reading a story by Ian McEwan, or a poem by Carlos Drummond de Andrade, and hear Katherine say my name—not Nick, which was what everyone called me, but Nicholas, which she preferred—and said as if the fellow she addressed was someone she would devour, annunciating all three syllables with relish—to look up and see her standing before me was so startling and thrilling an experience comparable only to perhaps a shipwrecked sailor suddenly seeing land before his disbelieving eyes.

Like some half-mad devotee making an offering at the feet of his favorite god, I handed her a copy of *Love's Body* by Norman O. Brown, which I had put aside, able only to say, "Here."

A wood nymph concocting a bit of magic, she turned the pages, until those eyes that tickled my soul settled on a page. "'To be stuck; stuck together in eternal coitus; wedlock as deadlock; coitus and covenant; stuck together in the social compact, bound by their oath, the waters of the River Styx that freeze a man and make him stiff.'"

She stopped reading and I gulped. Her finger delved deeper into the book.

"'Porphery says that souls proceeding into generation are nymphs ready for marriage; the pleasure of sex is the honey in the bowl by which they are seduced and fall into the world of generation.'"

I felt myself go red in the face. "Looks interesting," she said, with a causal smile, before she turned around and left me staring at the glory of her retreating derriere.

After work Katherine and I met for dinner. We sat together, just the two of us, in a restaurant that overlooked the L.A. harbor. She sipped white wine, as poised as only a wood nymph could possibly be, while I fought to keep my hands to myself. Every blessed cell of her body called to mine. Her divine teeth, the cutest little sliver of ears, her eyes, and lips, her button nose. She had it all!

She was saying something about remaining friends. Oh, but when I breathed in the air she exhaled, smelled her scent, when she reached out and touched my arm I knew it could never work. Her voice alone was every bit as intoxicating as the best champagne cognac. I trembled at the sight of the nape of her neck.

The woman positively left me with the shakes.

This is it, I thought. If there is going to be an earthquake or something, please, God, strike now. If the rains and floods are to happen, do it this moment, don't wait. Let me go out on a high note, with her by my side. With luck, this entire restaurant will break off and float away. Who knows, maybe we'd sail off to Hawaii, or the South Pacific. That would be a choice place from whence to start repopulating the planet.

"Nicholas," she said. "I like you a lot, but what is happening, you know, as far as you and your wife are concerned?" I knew my vacillating had left her confused and frustrated, but not one 100th of what I experienced, I guarantee.

"I don't know," I said. "Honestly. But let's not talk about her, please."

We drank our wine, nibbled at the food, and gazed into each other's eyes. "Are you writing any songs?"

"Yes, well, a bit. Seems my mind is preoccupied of late."

"Of the bookstore?"

The bookstore. No, silly. "Of you, Katherine. You've been traipsing through my dreams, to say nothing of my every waking hour."

"Oh, come on."

"It's true. I can no longer think, can't remember chords, notes fritter away like cockroaches scurrying into the woodwork." I took a deep breath before continuing. "You're magnificent, Katherine. You must know I love you."

She reached out her arm, and rested her hand on mine. That gesture caused me more pain and grief than just about anything else until that point.

She smiled her Mona Lisa smile that left me musing for hours wondering what she had been thinking. She steered the conversation away from her and on to books and authors. And then it was over. All too soon she left, and I returned to the bookstore happy in a sort of I'm-bleeding-out-from-a hundred-wounds, yet she touched me way, light yet heavy of heart.

16

The Torture Never Stops

A friend now and then met me for lunch, or coffee. It wasn't as though we *had* to shout that there was a fire, that the building was going down in flames in order to clear the building. We were usually the only ones there. We merely shouted fire to determine whether there was anyone lurking in the remote corners of the store, before locking up and marching down to Adriano's.

I warned my friend of the theatricalities of Freddy the Fruit and his Merry Band of Outlaws.

"Not to worry," I said. "If the food really was poisoned I'd be long dead."

We sat down, and ate sandwiches, while I filled him in on the goings-on in the book business.

"I'm getting to the point," I said, "where I'm starting to mistrust books."

"What do you mean mistrust?"

"I'm certain that right at this moment, since we've turned our backs on them, left them alone—thousands and thousands of books—that there are strange things going on back there. Perhaps books aren't really the inanimate objects we take them for. It could be a charade, the way they sit there without stirring, but behind closed doors, who knows what might be occurring?"

"Really?" He shot me a look, his Look-bub-I've-known-you-since-the-third-grade-and-I-know-better-than-anyone-else-that-you-are-nuts look.

"Yes," I said. "Sometimes I come into the store and find things moved all around, right? Or sometimes, sitting there with the lights off, no one in the store, I hear sounds. I get up, turn on the lights, have a look, and find books that have fallen from a table or a shelf lying on the floor. It's friggin' spooky."

"Sounds serious. Maybe you need a vacation, time away from the bookstore? Have you thought of early retirement?"

I thought of telling him how the pressures of the store had gotten to me, how I had succumbed, how I'd been led to say things I never would have ordinarily said, how my life might come to a quick and sudden end. But I didn't want to say aloud what I secretly feared, lest I summon the forces of the universe to bring about a self-fulfilling prophecy, forces which always seemed so willing and eager to bring disaster upon one's head.

"If anything happens to me," I said, instead, "my records are yours."

"Really? Thanks! Could I have your Bukowski books, too?"

"Yeah, sure." So much for any concern over my wellbeing. He would reap the benefits of my demise. And this from a trusted long-time friend.

"You don't seem to understand," I said, restraining myself from grabbing him by the scruff of the neck. "The more books there are the more mischief they can do. There is something that two or three books together can do that one book cannot."

"Replicate?"

"Perhaps, but at least form a catalyst, spark trouble."

My friend nodded, and murmured, "No, really, I do understand, all right."

Freddy the Fruit, several tables down from us, muttered something about being a degenerate, a pervert, a very sick man.

"They should lock me up and throw away the key." He stuck his tongue out.

"Daddy, the bad man is sticking out his tongue at me," my daughter said, pointing at Freddy.

"Do the same to him," I told her. She proceeded to do so.

"Kids love me," Freddy said. "Look at that. They can't resist me. I'm loveable."

"I can't get away," I told my friend. "I don't have any money, and besides I'm afraid of what might happen if I was gone. God only knows what those books would do."

"You're really becoming one with San Pedro."

"Thanks."

I returned to the store. My friend drove off down the road toward relative normality, while I watched the rows of books with increasing mistrust.

Just a few streets away Moses remarked that no matter what anyone said of him the truth was ten times worse. He invited disaster, courted it as though it were a voluptuous siren. His store was quiet but for the music on the stereo. There wasn't a paying customer in sight. I noticed Moses was having another sale. All Books One Dollar!

"How's business?" I asked.

"I've sold all of three books so far today, and had an assortment of people wander in, ask me for money, and try to sell me hot watches and bibles."

"Stolen bibles?" I asked.

"They were Gideon's. All in all, though, I'm doing better than yesterday."

It seemed the entire town was spiraling downward with the highest per capita number of lunatics and misfits to be found.

I envisioned the transformation of my bookstore into some twisted version of Hermann Hesse's "Magic Theater." I planned to darken the windows and offer strange and rare delights to those who wandered in. I'd sit in a booth in semidarkness and pull out impossibletofind tomes by favorite authors; people would retire to a lit booth where they would sit and furtively read the likes of Raymond Chandler, John Kennedy Toole, or Thomas Berger to their hearts' content, laughing in soundproof anonymity; reading and rereading *To Kill a Mockingbird* until they knew each of Harper Lee's blessed words by heart; there'd be readings by homeless men and women, people who had seen something of life, in particular the dark side, but who transcended and were in themselves transformed by their experiences; survivors of concentration camps; there would also be musical performances, and nameless other acts and exhibitions of lost and forgotten arts; a modern day carny side-show.

I stayed after closing at the bookstore, hunched like Quasimodo over my ancient manual typewriter. I tried to write a poem, something that would wring the heart of whoever read it. I drank from a bottle of whiskey with savage glee—typically after two or three sips of alcohol, I'd put it aside. The stuff always made me retch. Clearly, I was no boozer, any more than I was a poet—but now, true to form, having metamorphosed into something if not someone else, the drink had no ill effects upon me. It was as though I had drunk all my life.

I watched the passersby peer in through the store windows. Who were they? What thoughts flickered through their minds? What desires? They seemed to look at the books, but did they read? Perhaps they thought of reading the way so many thought of writing their life stories, something they would eventually get around to doing. Or maybe they reminisced on those days long ago when they were forced to read at school, refusing thereafter to open another book so long as they lived.

I put off people who called me up from various firemen's associations and retired police or sheriff's associations, asking for money.

"Buy two tickets, support the children of slain officers, support children with physical handicaps. Help support the illegitimate orphans of former F.B.I. agents."

Hustlers selling ads for phone directories I had never heard of popped in for a chat. Every one of them insisted that my business was suffering by not being listed in their book.

"God, I love books," each and every one informed me. "There's nothing like sitting down to a good book."

"Really?"

"Oh, yeah, especially on a rainy day, curled up on a sofa. This is a great place you have here," they said as I wrote the check. "What a great place to work, surrounded by books."

"Yeah, why not buy some books to take home with you?"

"Oh, I will. I'll come back after I get paid, you'll see."

Needless to say I never saw any of them with a book in hand, or in pocket, let alone buy one from us.

Everybody had something or other to sell us, something I needed. Everybody had an angle. Fund for the widows of deceased ex-cons. Send in your small donation and we'll give you a free advertisement in our monthly newsletter, and we'll make sure to ask all the kiddies to include you in their nightly prayers.

Who were these devils of persuasion, of never say no? Maybe I could hire them to sell our books, to bring in customers. They began sounding familiar, the peculiar bark of their voice when I picked up the phone, their slick, Buddy-have-I-got-a-deal-for-you manner made my skin crawl.

"Hello, is the store owner or manager in?" A voice quick, clipped, no nonsense, no time to be talking to peons here, give me the boss.

"Sorry, he's out."

"Do you know when he'll be in?"

"Not for a long while, I'm afraid."

"Well, is there somebody else I can speak to about?"

"Nope, nobody here but us chickens."

"What?"

"This here store operates on its own. Even my voice is generated by the store. None of us are real. The store runs itself. Like Hal in *2001 a Space Odyssey*."

Click.

They were all alike. All sure-fire, fast-talking hucksters zeroing in for the kill, without a pause, or break or breath. Don't give them a chance to say they aren't interested. "What d'ya mean not interested, we're talking a steal, man, term life insurance, think of your family, wife, children, you want them to starve, you want them turned out on the streets should something catastrophic happen to you, God forbid? What's a few dollars a day when it comes to your family's security? Chance of a lifetime. Don't be caught unprepared, buddy, we're doing you a favor, man, there are a million other suckers out there just waiting to take advantage of what we are offering here."

I wandered up and down the unlit hallways upstairs after hours, tried the doors of the offices. Perhaps that unknown business in the one office, the person I never laid eyes on, was the person who called asking for all that money; one person running a thousand-and-one schemes? I put my ear to the door and listened. Nothing. I put tape across the doorjamb and checked the next day to find that the door had been opened. I didn't know how they were coming in and leaving without my noticing, or in what ungodly hour of the night they came and left, but it certainly did nothing to settle my nerves.

Meanwhile, I awaited a new book by Harlan Ellison, who'd promised to do a book signing at the store with the publication of his new collection, *The Essential Ellison*, a massive tome. I was sure that one more signing, promoted with decent advertising, would finally turn things around. And to prove it, in my blind optimism I hired a couple of youngsters to help out in the store. My wife may have had a soft spot for people who wanted more money than their books were worth, but I found out I had a soft spot for the vast numbers who came in asking for a job, especially if they were willing to work for books.

I justified it by insisting that it would be good for business, and what was good for business when business was bad would be even better when business was good, which it was bound to be any moment now. After all, Harlan's (Uncle Harlan to my daughter) new book would soon be out. Besides, things couldn't remain rotten forever. There had to be a point when things would turn around; eventually the pendulum had to swing to its opposite apex. It was an unwritten law of nature.

I could tough it out. I was just as thickskinned and ornery as any of them. Bukowski and his drunkenness, his barroom brawls, his wild carousing; Hemingway and his bullfights, his big game hunting. They weren't so damned tough, after all. Harlan, too. I remembered hearing him saying something about always wanting to climb Mount Kilimanjaro. I sent him off a quick note. "Dear Harlan, I'll meet you anytime you feel up to climbing Kilimanjaro. Bet I beat you to the top!"

Harlan's book was delayed and delayed. He stopped answering my letters. The man had become convinced I was some kind of deranged lunatic. I couldn't for the life of me understand how. We'd met several times. He never remembered me, anymore than Bukowski did whenever he saw me. When he did speak to me he called me, "Kid," which at least was a step up from Bukowski's "baby" though not by much. Still, we had conversed on the phone, discussed writers, etc. I applauded him for championing the likes of Fante and Frederick Prokosch, and bringing out collections of stories by B. Traven and Gerald Kersh. He was to be commended as well for fighting against the tide of stupidity, for his most scathing, unsettling and angry writings. But he gazed at me with some trepidation, the way you'd look at someone who was in the habit of biting the heads off live chickens.

I phoned the publisher. "When's the book coming out?"

"Soon," they said.

"What's wrong?"

"Delays, printers, proofers."

"Look, I need this book!"

"Give it a week or two."

"That's what you said last time."

"This is it, trust me, I promise."

The loonies came and went, the rich customers from up on the hill in Rancho Palos Verdes and Rolling Hills Estates sent their interior decorators to buy books by the yard. They didn't give a whit what the titles were, they merely wanted books to fill a shelf or two, to look as if they owned the requisite library that all good homes should have.

One year earlier I would have had them for breakfast, but now demoralized into a shadow-being no longer myself, without morals, or scruples, with neither rhyme nor reason, remembered by no one, I brought out a yardstick and happily sold dreck by the yard to the rich

customers for far less than they bought curtains, or paneling, or anything else.

I looked for Katherine but saw neither hide, hair, nor halo of her.
She didn't call either. Once or twice, returning to the store after some
venture, I sniffed the air thinking I detected a whiff of her scent. I questioned the workers I'd left in the shop.

"Who came in while I was gone?" I asked. "Anyone ask for me?"
Could she be avoiding me? I wondered. Had she left for good, given
me up for useless, decided I would never leave my wife? Not that I was
with my wife, either, for she was back to keeping her distance. I was in a
wretched never-never land, where I wasn't free, and neither was I taken.
I was a man without a home. This was limbo, purgatory.

Book scouts invaded the store like vultures eyeing a halfrotted car-
cass, circling round and round before swooping down to pick the bones
clean. They usually showed up in twos or threes, one battering you with
a constamt barrage of questions while the other scanned the shelves,
stacks, boxes, whatever they could get their hands on. They moved
quickly, like an elite military force, and looked like people who'd fence
stolen Van Goghs, and to say they tried to talk you down was a slight
understatement.

"I wouldn't pay more than ten bucks for that book."

"I guess you shan't have the book, then."

"Hmph, let me see it. I'll give you fifteen."

"Twenty or nothing."

Some of them attacked boxes which hadn't yet been gone through
and priced, or even reached behind my counter, to try and grab books I
had back there for safekeeping.

"Outta there," I said, my machete within easy reach.

Why doesn't someone write a book on how to be a better human being?
I wondered. A book on personal comportment for the new millennium?

There were bookstore dealers, of course, who were wonderful, like
those too few customers, the ones who made it all worthwhile, people
who also loved books, who appreciated great writers. They were like old

friends, whom you met once or twice a year for a reunion. They came to you or you went to them, reported the latest news: what bookstores had closed down, how so and so was doing "Gee, have you read this writer, this book?" A sense of letting someone in on secrets: "Say, Jon, you don't have any Stanley Ellin in stock, do you?" Dropping names and making purchases furtively, as if it were a guilty pleasure at which we might get caught. Exchanging information that was a thousand light years removed from the lives of the majority of this spinning dust ball's inhabitants.

Some of the best moments in the business occurred while making the rounds to some of the best bookstores in what was the sprawling mess of Los Angeles, dropping in on Moses' shop in San Pedro, Jon Gentilman in Long Beach, Andy at Other Times, in West L.A.—venerable saints of the used book trade, each attempting to maintain a foothold in the citadel of culture that the enemy threatened to annihilate. They understood. I made my way to Morrison and Kline in Santa Monica, Krown and Spellman, and Vagabond Books on Westwood in West LA, to Heritage Bookshop, places with the most amazing literary treasures to be found.

Every time we managed to ring up more than one hundred dollars in one day, we thought, this is it, things are finally turning around. We'd celebrate. I'd walk with pride outside, look up and down 6th Street.

"You haven't gotten me yet, San Pedro. Oh, don't think I don't know. I'm still here, try as you may to defeat me."

The owners of the other businesses out sweeping down the sidewalks or admiring their store window displays, would glance over and wonder how I had stuck it out for so long, when would I throw in the towel? They took bets on when our ultimate demise would occur. The mailman we'd befriended informed me that since I wasn't from San Pedro, the other businesses shunned our store. Even the cops who walked the beat, the first time they met us asked, "You go to San Pedro High?" When we said no, they shuffled off. "Oh," never to drop by again.

One day, for absolutely no reason, we were hit by droves of book buyers. One afternoon mass hysteria reared its head, affected these people simultaneously, filled them with the irresistible desire to buy books.

The day's tally soared to uncharted heights. People bought anything it seemed, just so long as it was a book, while I rushed back and forth suggesting this title or that author.

They moved into the store en masse, like a conquering army eager to plunder the spoils of war, propelled by desire for acquisition. For a few sweet hours I tasted success. And then they disappeared, just as quickly and just as inexplicably as they had appeared. I checked the calendar. It wasn't buy-a-book-day or anything. Yet something had driven these people to do just that. It was baffling, mystifying. But like any dream it left little in the way of anything but an aftertaste of regret. Like losing your virginity, you knew damned well it was never going to happen again, not in a million years.

People wandered in and congratulated us. "So, you're still here. We thought you'd closed down. We've driven past a hundred times, and never noticed you were still in business. This is great!"

Good God, how had they missed the bookstore? There were signs... Big signs. Never mind. What did it matter?

I knew what I needed. I needed sanity, fresh air. I slipped out and ran to visit Moses.

"They haven't come to take you away either, I see," he said.

"No, not yet. How are you faring?"

"Insane as ever," Moses said.

"Nah, come on, we're sane. Among the sanest. I'm sure of it."

"Anyone who would voluntarily live in this place and open a book store, of all things, is not playing with a full deck."

I couldn't argue with him there. We were doomed, and we both knew it. It was just a matter of when and how.

I returned to the shop, where I sat awaiting the end, and read Dostoyevsky to my daughter. *Notes from the Underground.* And at least she and I laughed together. She thought it was funny, an amusing situation, the silly man who said he tried to become an insect. Sure, she still liked her *Goodnight Moon* and *Winnie the Pooh*, but this Dostoyevsky was a riot. More daddy, more.

The man rumored to be my father dropped by to look over our accounts and offer sage advice. In the beginning, he'd always entered the bookstore and gazed about at the shelves and stacks, the boxes of books with his proprietary air and a look that said: today San Pedro, tomorrow the world!

"How much have we taken in?" It was always the first thing out of his mouth, and after I gave him the dismal report. "That's all? You must be doing something wrong."

I could see that the state of the store depressed him. Too much bad news. He didn't know how to face failure. He'd popped in to see if the patient could be saved.

He grunted. "This is bad. Really bad."

"I don't need you to tell me that," I said.

"You're spending too much and taking in too little," he said. "Stop buying books."

"I can't stop buying books. I'm running a bookstore. I have to buy. If I don't buy I have nothing to sell."

"What are you talking about? Look at all the books in here." He gestured at the shelves. "Look around, thousands and thousands of books."

"Yeah, but is anybody's interested in them? Most of these books have been here this side of forever. People don't like seeing the same old titles whenever they come in. They want to see something new. We've been cleaned out of anything good, anything salable."

He poked among the shelves, tried to put a row or two in alphabetical order, soon gave up, and finding a porno novel and one or two other titles, shuffled up to the front with a bowed head.

He began reciting: "'You are Old Father William, the young man said, "and your hair has become very white.'"

"Nice to see you, pops."

"There's no fool like an old fool."

"'Bye, dad."

My recurring nightmare was that my stock was dwindling down to nothing. There were fewer and fewer books. I woke up each night in a cold sweat, gasping for breath. I saw spaces widening in the shelves, then entire shelves with only one or two books, gaps growing larger; the bookstore emptying.

I'd go out to buy more books, but nobody had any books to sell. Books were disappearing, everywhere, drying up like everything else in L.A.

God, I prayed, help, won't you, I can't do anything else. This is all I know. I'd never cut it as a shepherd.

17

Down, Down, Down
the Rabbit Hole We Go!

I was a man afraid to stay in his own home, afraid to sleep, afraid of the silent shadows that lurked behind every door, under the bed, in the closets. I spied devils lying in wait, ready to spring from every corner. My own wife was Catholic, a daughter of the Inquisition. For all I knew, one of these nights, she would turn our bed into a funeral pyre, with me in it, burn that failed half-Jew Kastinovich once and for all.

I held protracted conversations with God. "You're testing me, aren't you? Trying to see how much I can take, what my breaking point is, a cat playing with a mouse, right?" I spoke to the deafening silence. "That's okay, I can see how boring it must be for you up there in heaven, surrounded by the unrelenting goodness of angels, nothing to do all day and night, millennia after millennia except to have a bit of fun with a Kastinovich now and then. Go on, enjoy. Why shouldn't you, after all? You are the supreme ruler of the universe, the all-powerful creator, while I am lower than a puny ant."

Perhaps God was punishing me for having abandoned the synagogue, for denying my religion, for residing in a country of heathens who worshipped only the dollar bill. Hell, I hadn't even stepped foot inside a synagogue since I was ten, and didn't know a *yarmulke* from a harmonica.

Penance seemed the only solution. I began giving books away. "No, no, keep your money. Just take this book, brother, may it serve you well."

"What? You mean you don't want me to pay for the book?"

"I don't wish to sully my fingers with cash, filthy lucre. Nick Kastinovich may be many things, but he's neither whore nor pimp."

"Gee, thanks."

"I offer beauty and sustenance to the masses," I proclaimed, attempting to shine a feeble torchlight into the dark, cobwebbed corners of the minds of the masses, to show them the enchanting alternate universes to be found in great books.

I grabbed people who wandered into the store, lost, confused, disheveled. *Where am I?*

They looked up and down, and wavered with uncertainty.

"Fear not, *entrez, entrez, s'il vous plaît!*"

"Bookstore?"

"Yes, yes. Correct! You win the prize. Today we are giving books away." They stood, mouths agape, tongues stammering, eyes bewildered, stunned, speechless. "Yes, it's true. We are spreading the word. Here, this is yours, a copy of *Fata Morgana*, or here, *Doctor Rat,* or *Jewel of the Moon*, all by an ingenious gnome by the name of William Kotzwinkle—you pick."

I stuck books by Faulkner, Fitzgerald and Hemingway beside those of Fante, so they might learn from the master; I put Kerouac and Salinger next to Mark Twain, hoping he might improve their books. I grouped Bellow, and Heller around Dostoyevsky and Gogol for their betterment. I blessed and kissed the books by Bernard Malamud, as well as Roth's early work. John Fowles, now there was a man who could write. Colin Wilson I excluded from the whole club, one for being a pseudointellectual of the first water, and second, for badmouthing Dostoyevsky, calling his writing flawed; he, who wasn't fit to wipe the boots of the man. Joyce Carol Oates I sent off in search of an editor and with a citation for giving up quality for quantity. For all her worldwide reputation nothing of hers excited me, thrilled me, or even moved me, except to put the book down. Once she learned to behave herself I'd put her books near Shirley Jackson's and Angela Carter's, to glean what she could from them.

I set the heavyweights of fantasy like Tolkien and Peter Beagle around their many inferiors so those lesser writers would be edified. Perhaps it will save them, I thought, as they saved me when I took a fantasy class in high school and found the fires of my imagination stoked by repeated readings of *The Last Unicorn, The Hobbit* and *The Lord of the Rings*.

Darlings of academia like Bret Easton Ellis, Tama Janowitz and Jay McInerny, I was at a loss what to do with. They were too much like the current crop of Hollywood filmmakers whose only point of reference appeared to be comic books and 1950's television. For starters I buried them under stacks of Freud and Sartre, Nietzsche, Einstein and others. Let them find fiction later, much later.

I piled up treasure-troves of Rabelais and Boccaccio and Cervantes—big, thick, massive Viking Portables which I figured would be the most eloquent and persuasive arguments to convince the Ellis', the Janowitzes and the McInernys of the world never to take up the pen again beyond writing a letter or two, for at least the next twenty years.

Brave individuals strolled in. "Can you help me? I'm looking for a book."

"Here," I said, "Take this. Read the first few pages of *The Road to Los Angeles*, or *The Brotherhood of the Grape*. They were written by a saint named John Fante. Well, not a saint exactly, but one hell of a writer. Go on. They won't harm you. Quite the contrary. If you don't love it, why, I'll gladly pay you five bucks."

"Wow, thanks."

I ordered even more Fante books from Black Sparrow, box loads of new copies. John Martin informed me that just as I had done with the Bukowski titles, I had single-handedly cleaned them out of practically every one of their hardcover copies of Fante's books.

This was it. A wholly new and revolutionary marketing approach. If the customer showed up again, I would give him or her another book, gratis. Every time they came to the bookstore, another free book. If nothing else, the shelves would empty, people would see that books were indeed things to buy and take home, and those I'd ladened with free books would begin to feel guilty and bring all their friends and families at long last to spend all their money at the Little Big Bookshop.

If guilt-tripped properly, I reasoned, perhaps they would instigate rallies in support, urge their local representatives to earmark special funds to go toward subsidizing the bookstore. Christ, one tenth of the fees collected from parking meters and the tickets they generated would have set us up for life. Anything to keep the bookstore going. I wasn't talking about lining people up, under the threat of a firing squad, forcing them to buy our books.

Of course, by this time I had a fair intimation that perhaps my name was what was behind all our wretched trials and tribulations. And for that reason I began using my wife's maiden name. After all, she had taken mine, not that she had realized what she was undertaking with that foolhardy action.

A fair number of the people I'd persuaded to take Fante books did come back and bought more, filling me with hope, and surprising me with how many were convinced by these tactics: persuasion by battery.

I thought of operating a much smaller store, a specialty shop, filled with Fante titles and nothing else. *Books By Fante*. In the meantime, I searched out magazines and anthologies in which his stories appeared, and bought all I could find.

S

"Without books," I preached from the pulpit of my counter to the ghosts and shadows that came and went, "We have no imagination no future, no hope. Unable to think, to imagine, to create, we'll become mere automatons. The feeble flicker of whatever paltry soul we do possess is being sucked out and snuffed altogether. Listen brothers, sisters, don't walk away. Look around you. We need all the ideas we can get."

I delivered sermons to those customers who I noted never ever bought fiction, who tried to tell me that only nonfiction was worth reading. They shook their heads when I tried to tell them that there was more reality and truth in good novels and poetry than in their alleged factual books. Good books tell us truths about ourselves and connect us to one another and to our past in a way that nothing else can: all the historical reading one might do on the Holocaust, for example, cannot compare with reading *The Diary of Anne Frank,* or *Night* by Elie Wiesel. Just as Huck Finn speaks volumes about nineteenth-century attitudes and views toward Blacks and slavery, the hypocrisy and stupidity of the prevailing social mores.

I had a flash of inspiration. I could bring people in and force them to read, play tapes of stories, surround them with books. A scene straight out of *A Clockwork Orange.* In the end, I'd make converts of these recalcitrant and erring folk.

I sat in the bookstore plotting the entire circus; the books I would make them read, the authors I'd introduce them to. Katherine, of course, would assist me. She could lure them in -- the lost, the weary, those without hope, the aimless. With her beauty and good will, long lines would form, like the soup kitchens of old. They would be treated to the glories of "The Man Who Corrupted Hadleyburg" and "The Celebrated Jumping Frog of Calaveras County." Once they'd gotten their feet wet, once over their initial panicky, reluctant moments, we'd introduce them to a whole world of pure delight: *Dreams From Bunker Hill* and *1933 was a Bad Year,* or *The Mysterious Stranger,* and I mean the true version, not that sanitized fraud they've been circulating for most of the past century, the one some editor altered and toned down so as not to offend anyone, never mind that Twain himself is probably still cursing so as to cause the editor's descendants' ears to burn. Imagine this inferior's unpardonable audacity, his dunderheaded attempt to "correct" Twain's prose, making it more palatable to the common man—all the Bumpkins, Boobs and Yahoos who believed that books should be filled with white lies and sweet sentiments, each with a nice happy ending, and that all others should be burned.

A twisted bit of human wreckage named Mike crawled into the store one day. He was around fifty, shorter even than myself, balding, with a huge dent on one side of his misshaped head. He exhibited a lack of control over his limbs, which twitched and flailed. He laughed a high-pitched nervous laugh. I let him hang around and read books, and stand idly by in the aisles.

I subjected him to a barrage of my current thoughts and ideas on art and social policy. Seeing as how he spent so much time there I began to harangue him with my views on writers and quality, chain stores and American commercialism, while he listened quietly, nodded, and uh-huhed.

I decided on making use of Mike, who was between jobs, and between living quarters, and who informed me that the back of the bookstore would make a lovely spot to sleep until his fortunes improved. He would be my guinea pig, my Igor, to my own Quasimodo-like self.

I made him my assistant. "You can sleep in the back," I told him, "but only on the nights when I'm not here, and provided you read everything I give you." I loaded him up with some books and bid him adieu. It worked fine. I let him out of his cage in the mornings, had him alphabetize various sections in the afternoons. After three or four days he disappeared, apparently fell off the wagon, or returned to one of the institutions. Perhaps he was an escapee, after all, who'd finally been apprehended.

I toyed with a new idea: a last refuge for the written word. Crowds would shuffle in and shuffling out the doors; inquisitive patrons of my Museum of Dead Literary Arts. I could see the little ones sitting round the dinner table. "Mommy, daddy, the school took us on a fieldtrip today."

"Oh, where did you go, dear?"

"We saw books! People used to read them."

"Really?"

They'd describe the sights they'd seen in the museum: books of all kinds, shapes and sizes, books and magazines that spanned centuries, testaments to the written word, which of course had long since fallen out of favor.

The Father couldn't understand our lack of sales. He roamed the shelves, examining the stock like a man who'd lost a Lotto ticket some-where among all those books. Perhaps he'd used it as a bookmark.

"What's wrong with these books?" he muttered, bemused. "There are plenty of good books here." And to prove it he pulled them off the shelves, showed me the Somerset Maugham, the Booth Tarkington, the Erskine Caldwell. "Here's Thomas B. Costain, Edna Ferber, Du Maurier, Pearl S. Buck."

"Nobody buys that stuff," I said.

"Why not? They're perfectly good. I used to read them. What's wrong with people?"

I shrugged. How the hell did I know? I didn't see him shelling out the cash and lugging those books home to put in his library. This was a man for whom T. S. Elliot was the last word in poets. He was content to comb through the rows and stacks of books and take home a copy of an old Playboy magazine and a book or two by Anne Morrow Lindbergh. He'd take these to bed with him where he'd allow fantasies of having Lindbergh's wife as his personal love slave run free.

"Advertise." That was the magic word. Not God's, this is true—for God was giving me the silent treatment—but the Father's forthcoming advice. "You need to advertise." He said this new favorite word of his again and again; a jingle that would make his wishes come true.

If there was one thing I admired it was people whose lives could be governed by a one to three word sound bite: *Just say no, Try harder, Sweat, Never say die, Think success, Advertise.* How simple. The answer to every-thing distilled to a neat little word or phrase.

"More people need to know you're here," he said. So we advertised. "The store is too big," he said. "Too much wasted space. You should rent out the back of the shop. Lower your overhead."

I tried that route, but couldn't find anyone to rent the space that wouldn't interfere with the operation of a bookshop, or who was willing to pay for the space.

"Maybe it's the name?" the Father suggested. Ah, now you're on the right track, I thought. "We could change the name of the shop," he said. "Call it Books By Kastinovich." I shook my head. He envisioned a large sign emblazoned in lights. Big, beautiful neon setting the San Pedro night afire. "Kastinovich's Books, Inc." He liked that, nothing finer than seeing one's name dotting the familiar landscape, as rewarding and fruitful an enterprise as leaving a large litter of children bearing your name; the beginning of an empire.

"Things are bad enough," I said. "Putting our name up on a sign would be the coup de grace. It's our name that has likely brought this ill wind which blows misfortune our way."

"What kind of name is that?" a stray customer remarked. "Kastinovich." He said it as though it left an unpleasant taste in the mouth. "Are you communists?"

"Don't you know?" I said.

"Huh? Know what?"

"Why, Kastinovich is a name most infamous, responsible for the downfall and overthrow of governments; members of our family hunted down and reviled. People have tried to exterminate us, to remove the stain of our name from society. That's why there are so few of us left."

I had them now; there was silence in the bookstore. The sound of people holding their collective breath. They listened.

"Do you remember that scene toward the end of *The Brothers Karamazov*? When Mitya, the son in prison begins ranting to his brother Ivan about Bernardos; how you couldn't trust the Bernardos, how the world is full of Bernardos, too many Bernardos, a plague of Bernardos? Well, it so happens that this Bernardo chap was none other than my great-great-grandfather, Bernardo Kastinovich. Dostoyevsky despised the man; and you would have as well had you ever met him. If Dostoyevsky hated Jews it was due to his having met up with Bernardo Kastinovich. A man reviled throughout the countryside. A man whose depraved actions caused his own family to disown him, and forced him to flee to escape an ignominious death at the hands of his fellow villagers."

The Father stood speechless—a first, believe me. "Is that true?" he finally said. "I never heard that before."

"What do you think I do here after hours with all these books? I've been doing my research, believe me. I have uncovered dark truths about our clan."

"Really?"

"Oh, the records are legion. Everywhere the Kastinoviches have settled disaster has soon followed."

He turned away, ready to leave me to my ravings. I made it clear, however, that I was not about to put my name to the bookstore, but would leave the name what it was. For good or bad.

"For the first time in my life I actually feel like a Jew," I said.

"You're no Jew," the Father replied.

"Okay, half-Jew, then."

"Half of nothing is still nothing."

"If I'm nothing, what does that make you?" I said. "For you are the bigger nothing that begat me. Besides, I'm entitled to be Jewish merely by my suffering, by the rabbis in our past. If I'm Jewish enough to have gone into Hitler's ovens, I guess I can call myself a Jew."

"Never mind all that, I've got an idea," he said, finally, panting with excitement. I awaited the results of his latest brainstorm. Here was a successful businessman. He would know what to do, what actions we should take.

"What is it?" I asked, dying of curiosity and impatience. Speak, oh wise one, Oh sage of experience.

"We could start a bordello in the back. There are all these sailors coming in off ships and boats. I'm telling you, where there are sailors and ships, there's a ready market for whores. You run the bookstore, and I'll run the back. The whorehouse will make enough to pay for keeping the bookstore, then it won't matter how much the bookstore makes. I can see it now: *Bernie's Bordello*."

Instead, we tried another sale. A big twenty-percent-off sale. We ran advertisements. Nothing. All books half-price. Nothing. We thought seriously about selling them by the pound, and I toyed more and more with the idea of *Bernie's Bordello*.

18

Where Fools Rush In

My wife challenged me whenever opportunity arose. A pretty woman would enter the bookstore, ask for something, exchange a few words with me.

"She likes you," my wife would say.

"No she doesn't."

"A woman knows when another woman likes someone. I can tell. Why don't you go for it?"

What was this? My wife was playing at matchmaker for me. She wanted me to go off and find someone else.

"No, thanks," I said. "I'm not interested in anyone else. If you can live without sex, don't think I can't, too."

But don't think I didn't seriously consider taking her up on the suggestion. I assure you it was only the rottenest luck and my refusal to be the instrument of her self-fulfilling prophecy that prevented this much-dreamt of scenario from occurring. And later when I would look at Katherine I saw only what my adopted father, played by Chief Dan George in *Little Big Man* said about a dream in which he saw a time of "Great copulation." At least the agonizing potential for it, if not the sweeter, better, but as yet still unfulfilled, reality.

I wasn't half as stupid as I appeared, for I knew it was part and parcel of my wife's great plan, urging me in her own charming way, not to be better, not toward noble deeds, but to either leave or do something which would give her a solid excuse to leave. How unbearable could she make it, in other words, before one of us finally snapped? And how long could I stay before I finally did something I might or might not regret?

I continued to spend my nights at the store. I knew I needed to be alone. People had been telling me how odd my behavior had been of late. "What do you mean? Odd how?"

"I don't know," they said. "Sometimes you say things I've never heard you say, odd choices of words now and then. Your attitude, too."

"What's so amiss with my attitude?"

They shrugged. "Can't really say," they answered. They just emphatically reiterated that it was most odd. And truth be told, I felt plenty odd. I was living in someone else's skin. Nothing fit, like in as if I was trying to be someone I wasn't.

That's right. You got it, clue number three.

During the night when I tired of reading, I dug through the caverns of the bookstore. The office was filled with boxes of papers, file cabinets stuffed with notes pertaining to the shop; stuff which the previous owner had left behind and I had never gone through. I had no idea what I was searching for, but I had to look, as if I knew there was something hidden in all that which warranted discovery.

On the third or fourth night of exploration I came across a small notebook, upon which were scribbled names and book titles: Miguel Angel Asturias, Mario de Andrade, Camilo José Cela, Federico García Lorca. There were others, many of them Latin American, but predominantly Spanish writers. I found it interesting, and kept digging away.

There were some letters and loose pages. I couldn't decide which to read first; I'd try a letter, but they were difficult to decipher. I'd picked up some of the pages, and ruffled through the notebooks.

After reading some of them, I was sure they were Joe's, the old man's writings, from before, during and after the Spanish Civil War, and they were in my hands, in the very bookstore where he had once been a partner.

There were only fragmentary bits left, but between the letters and notes were repeated references to H—, a writer, who had shown up during the Spanish Civil War. A braggart, who let it be known he was some sort of war hero, and a writer of no small fame, though the comments Joe repeatedly made clearly showed that he regarded George Orwell and Kipling as being better men, better heroes, certainly better writers, and less "show-offy" than H—. I couldn't rid myself of the certainty that H— was none other than Hemingway.

The gist of the notes indicated that H—had come barging in with a whole lot of noise, parading for all the world to see, and pissed off a lot of people who were fighting for their lives, for their homes. And there was a woman, apparently one that Joe had had an understanding with, but with whom Hemingway, attempting to prove what a great macho American he was, somehow interfered. There was, by all inferences, a hell of a lot of bad blood between the two Americans.

It galled Melkert to no end that this boisterous, arrogant ass, whom he would only derogatorily refer to as H—, was treated as though he'd been fighting on the front lines of the battle, when, in fact, he'd merely been an observer. "People," he wrote, "must have their heroes, who, more often than not, are not in the least worthy of being regarded as such. People read his writings as though they expect some of his so-called greatness to rub off on them, as if even with that remote contact they might come closer to that to which they aspire." And other comments here and there: "I never saw H— when he didn't inspire a feeling of revulsion in me," and, "H— seems to go out of his way to make things unpleasant for all involved," and "H— cares only for confirming his perverse and cynical views of everyone and everything;" and, "He's a literary Theodore Roosevelt, a charging rhinoceros, creating mayhem wherever he goes."

I couldn't find anything that referred to what had happened to the girl. Joe was injured, and Hemingway went on being Hemingway. But much of his hatred for the man, I noted, preceded all this, and had to do with the writing, aside from the personal reason: "There is as much to dislike in H—'s writing as there is to dislike in the man himself, writing as vacuous and humorless, as cold and cruel as the man who penned them."

19

Baron, *whose* brain did you say you used?

I dove deeper into the bookstore, propelled by lust, love, and longing, twisted into some hideous caricature of myself—The Grinning Imp, as my wife called me—I delved into more of Joe Melkert's notes. I went out and made deals, bought the strangest, oddest things in and out of print: *The Art of Growing A Beard*, *How to Survive on Nothing*, *Welsh Dictionary*, *How to Curse in Swahili*—these were the titles I brought in, and more, including ancient books on such popular topics as hydrodynamics.

I continued to buy books no one would buy—I dropped by Moses' shop, purchased a pile of Freud, copies of *The Denial of Death*, and *Beyond Evil*, by Ernest Becker, some Bertrand Russell, Geza Roheim and Theodore Reik, Camus and Sartre. The prices, of course, were ridiculously low, plus with the discount he gave me, they cost me next to nothing. I hit thrift stores, and on the weekends, yard sales. I usually paid no more than twenty-five cents or less per book. I loaded up my car and carted them back to my shop.

There, I took pains to show off these literary treasures to all the business men and women who came in on their lunch breaks to rummage through the magazines before going about their business, their parting shot being: "I used to read, but I don't have the time any more." That's right, back to your cubicles, play with your computers and your electronic games while this dust heap of a planet sinks ever farther into the mire of no return.

As in the case of Norman O. Brown, I often ended up buying the same titles that Moses had bought from me. How many times a particular book was resold between us, I couldn't say with any accuracy, but I believed steadfastly in what I saw as an under-researched law of physics, which stated that the more noise and/or movement generated around a given object the greater the attraction that object holds for others. I suspected that the mere kinetic energy released with the constant passing back and forth of these books, would in fact, cause others to eventually catch on, and pick up where we had left off.

While there may have been less and less of what customers asked for, there was more and more of what were for me worlds I longed to explore. I found names new to me—Flann O'Brien, Clarice Lispector, Fernando Pessoa, Eduardo Galeano—writers whose books I knew I had to educate myself with so I could in turn know what writers and books I should recommend to people.

Was it important, after all, to make money, to succeed as a bookseller just to satisfy creditors, to become an upstanding member of the community, such as it was, and pay money into the coffers of the government, or was it my mission to uncover great poets and essayists, playwrights and historians, and to share these discoveries with others, to keep these writers from fading into oblivion?

The choice was clear.

I struggled to make sense of Joe Melkert's writings: "H— was an absolute shit to V—. I didn't blame her for how things ended. It was unpleasant, but she had every right to do what she did."

V—, I pondered. Who was this woman? What was her name? Vera, Vanessa, Veronica? I pictured Veronica Lake. Then I too wanted to smash H—'s ugly mug.

While I struggled to keep my head above the rising water and maintain some semblance of sanity, I ruminated heavily upon what made time tick, on why everything I touched seemed doomed to an abysmal end, but also upon the likes of Fante, my god, whose *Ask the Dust* I reread for the umpteenth time. His Arturo Bandini, had inspired Bukowski, who had stumbled upon Fante's classic novel in the library in Downtown L.A. in 1940.

By a fluke I had stumbled upon Bukowski's work, and was later surprised to discover that he resided in San Pedro, where fate saw fit for me to have the bookstore fall into my lap. *The Road to Los Angeles*, by Fante, was set in Wilmington and San Pedro. The circumlocutions of chance and synchronicity, serendipity and circumstance, had brought us all together. And when my brother who had just started to read fiction read *The Road to Los Angeles*, as I insisted he do, "My God," he said. "This guy is you!"

My assistant, Mike, returned from whatever black hole he had disappeared into. He began telling me about his life in detox centers, and halfway houses, his failed attempts at love, and his striving to find a mission in life.

"I want to make up for lost time," he said. "All those years, the decades I've wasted. They're a blank. I remember nothing." He sounded wistful. "I want to read, to catch up on what I've missed." I let him help himself to a number of books, the only payment being his agreement to listen to my speeches on literary matters.

Mike took note of the numerous stacks of Bukowski and Fante books—every title in print. He asked me about them and I told him what I thought, what I liked and disliked.

On occasion my nostrils captured a vagrant waft of a delicate perfume. Light and tantalizing, it excited me into a full-on frenzy of desire. *Katherine.* She wore this delicious scent, right, but if so, where was she? I sniffed around, tried to pinpoint its source, turned the bookstore upside down. But just as suddenly as it had appeared, the scent eluded me, was gone, dissipated like so many idle daydreams and false hopes. Ghost scents.

20

Striking While the Iron is Hot

I bought books even more frantically, more crazily, like some paranoid survivalist stockpiling food, medical supplies, and weapons, storing them away against impending disaster. After all, books were a precious commodity. The one thing that reading the ancient Greeks teaches is that nothing in human behavior ever changes. They'd burnt the fucking Library of Alexandria, hadn't they? I expected they would soon do the very same thing here. I could see the headlines now: America lashes out against Intellectuals! Modern Inquisition! Purges! Buy a Gun, Burn a Book!

The pogroms in Russia would pale in comparison to the lynchings of writers, college professors and sundry poets. People would make huge bonfires of books, Twain and Salinger first on the heap, the way all those Southern Baptists burned Beatles' records in the sixties.

I sneaked away now and again, drove all over L.A., stopped off at any and all bookstores, in any out of the way place. I bought up every copy of every book by my favorite writers. This way if people wanted these books there would be only one place to go for them. They wouldn't be found anywhere else, and therefore being scarce, in no time would become valuable; the prices people would be willing to pay for them would soar. And we would have every last copy.

Books, I was convinced, would soon become obsolete. Possibly all writing would be banned, writers shot on sight or stuck in some lightless airless hole. A little risk, a bit of danger and we might start to see an uptick in the quality of American fiction. A bit of torture and whatnot, and we'd finally be sure to see writing that mattered. Here we lived in the freest country on earth, yet the vast majority of writers played it as safe as a paint-by-numbers scene, as opposed to writing with any conscious sense of the responsibility that the possession of those very freedoms entailed; they'd grown complaisant. They were content to write about college professors having affairs with their students, or—here's an original—a story of an alcoholic, abusive writer unable to maintain a decent relationship. Gee, now why hasn't anyone tackled that subject before? There were writers in many countries around the world where freedom of speech wasn't guaranteed, and they risked being imprisoned and tortured or shot if they wrote about a host of forbidden subjects. And those who did possess those freedoms, the lack of restrictions, frittered and squandered the precious gifts they had on the trivial. American writers don't get fatwahs against them.

In other places in the world writers were revered, their books treasured, saved, handed down or passed round to friends, shared; they were smuggled by people eager to read them; some were copied and hidden, like underground newspapers. Here, books were the lowest of commodities, produced by the millions, dumped, stripped, returned, remaindered; more titles by more authors than one could count—mere product, insignificant, inconsequential, wholly forgettable. Here writers died deaths in obscurity, the news too cluttered with reports of the passing of this actor or that pop musician, to give any notice to the death of a literary giant.

In fact, what I began to see as the salvation of the bookstore was not to slash prices, not to offer big sales—as we had done again and again with little result—but to raise the prices of the books, charge 5 to 10 times what they were worth. Then folks would think, Hey, expensive, hmm, must be valuable. And in trying to get an edge up over their neighbors, to beat the prices before they went even higher, and while

supplies were still available, they'd buy books, and think they were getting a bargain.

I thought of Hank. What might Chinaski have written with a gun
up against his head? Or stuck in a prison cell for ten years? Success was
a killer. Hank should have been locked up on Terminal Island. Fante, too,
instead of playing golf, gambling, or sitting in a Hollywood Studio—
books would have poured out of him with the loss of his freedom and
monetary success.

I sat drafting scathing insults to the world outside. I collected bits
and pieces about writers who had been maimed or who had died hero-
ically: Cornel Woolrich, who'd written "Rear Window" and many, many
delightful mysteries and suspense stories, like Fante, had gone blind, and
had also lost his legs, to diabetes as well; Tom Reamy had died at his
typewriter having only just completed two books; Jorge Luis Borges
had gone blind, as had Joyce and Homer and Milton; Luís de Camões,
the greatest of Portuguese poets, had lost an eye in battle; Cervantes, too,
had been maimed at the battle of Lepanto. These were my friends, my
compatriots.

I compiled lists of writers who died before their time: Poe, Stephen
Crane, Sylvia Plath, John Kennedy Toole, Virginia Woolf, Hart Crane,
Shirley Jackson, Nathanial West, the Brontes—all the siblings. It was clear
that writing was a dangerous profession.

What drove these people to write? What possessed them? Was it
the promise of wealth, fame and prestige, or perhaps the urge to cheat
death, their names immortalized by the printed word, leaving something
behind to say, I was here, I lived, I loved, I wrote, I died? It was difficult
to imagine a good number of these writers thinking their books would
keep their names alive, not when so many had fared poorly, some whose
books were never republished during the author's lifetime, and those
whose work were consigned to obscurity.

Perhaps they wrote simply because they enjoyed writing. But there
must be as many reasons to write as there are reasons why people go
into any profession. Perhaps a parent or other family member wrote

and inspired a protégé; maybe a favorite book made the reader identify with the author and wish to emulate him or her; maybe someone saw their adolescence or youth fading from memory, saw the world changing drastically right under their feet, and wanted to preserve that aspect of their life in a moment of nostalgia.

Real writers, of course, were incapable of *not* writing, even when circumstances made it extremely difficult or dangerous; they didn't dabble at it, or do it just to land themselves a cushy academic position; no, they *had* to write, if they wished to sleep at night, or remain sane; characters came unbidden, tales wove themselves amid their daydreams, their work, their conversations, their sleep. Ideas flitted and fluttered like hummingbirds trapped inside their minds, bouncing against the limits to escape. Like the child for whom nothing is impossible, these writers saw other worlds, other pasts, other presents, and undreamt futures; they toyed with their visions with total disregard for propriety, for rules and appearances. They remade the world on paper, where anything goes; or they followed the subtle unspoken dictates of their characters who took on a life and logic of their own, with the story insisting it go where it must, bending the author to its will.

Some people read *Ulysses* and thought it the end-all, be-all, while others disliked it, found it self-indulgent, murky and dense, and preferred instead to absorb the magic of *The Night of the Hunter.*

I slipped a naked sheet of white paper into the manual typewriter and began a finger-dance upon the keys, although I only used two fingers at the most. "America has endured the world's longest adolescence," I typed. "To paraphrase the Lincoln of literature, who wrote that, 'all one needs is ignorance and confidence and one is guaranteed success,' and of course our writers have made a great practice of this, substituting a childish fascination with war, killing, fishing, hunting, womanizing, drinking—all symptoms of our lingering childhood, which we cling to as our most precious and treasured things. And if we are to acknowledge any writer it must be one who embodies these noble attributes."

I telephoned Mrs. Fante, who with the patience of a saint did not hang up on me, but humored me and allowed me to lose my head. "Don't worry about John Fante slipping into obscurity," I assured her. "I can't keep your husband's books on the shelves. I'm selling record numbers of *Ask the Dust*, and the others."

"That's very nice," she said.

"I'd love to do your husband's biography. It's criminal that there is no biography on the life of John Fante."

She told me that she too hoped someone would write her husband's biography, but a complete one, not a book that portrayed one aspect, just what a marvelous writer he was, but the whole man warts and all.

"There's no one better," I told her. "I only wish he had written more."

"I think he wrote all he had in him," Mrs. Fante said.

I couldn't accept that. Surely, had he received more acclaim, and stayed away from the distractions that plagued him, he might have written more.

"I feel like he could be my father," I confessed to her. "Like perhaps I am an illegitimate offspring of his."

She coughed and replied coldly that she didn't much appreciate that particular sentiment. I apologized over and over, until she had to forgive me.

"I got carried away," I said. "I didn't know what I was saying."

I didn't have the heart to tell her I had written to Budd Schulberg asking him if he would be so kind as to sign my copy of *What Makes Sammy Run*? I'd inquired about his experiences in Hollywood, hanging out with the likes of Fante, and other writers, and mentioned what I had said to Mrs. Fante. When I got the book back, Schulberg had inscribed the book: "To Johnny Fante's illegitimate son, Nicholas Kastinovich!"

I telephoned Mrs. Fante time and time again to keep her apprised of the progress I was making, spreading the faith to the infidels and heathens who hadn't yet heard the word.

I no longer recognized the sorry figure that gazed back at me from the other side of the mirror. My hair had sprouted strands of gray, lines appeared on my face, my skin showed an unhealthful pallor. Still, I had a hell of a long way to go if I was going to compete with Bukowski in the arena of ugliness. Pretty, I wasn't. So far, however, life hadn't ravaged me, but only given a glancing blow.

A San Pedro book buyer approached my counter. "I'm not who I appear to be," I said. "More than this I cannot say."

"I'd like this book, please." He handed me a ragged paperback priced at fifty cents. Something kept these people from buying anything of recent production. No, it had to be old and weathered, on the verge of having pages fall out, stitched and scotch-taped back together by my own shaky hands.

"I may look like myself, but I am of another time and place," I croaked.

He looked at me, puzzled.

"Don't ask."

He glanced around as if to see whether this was all part of some joke.

"It is true. There are strange and unnatural acts occurring in this shop. If someone dreams up a monumental book but doesn't set it down on paper, does anyone...there, I've gone and said too much."

He took his change and began to leave.

"Thanks."

"Don't mention it."

More and more I ignored the day-to-day goings-on. I was a machinegunner hidden away in his turret with an endless supply of ammunition, like Poe, firing indiscriminately, at friend and foe alike, alienating everyone.

Locked away in the cold confines of my dark tower, I retreated from the world, spoke with fewer and fewer people, one man pitted against his enemies, who were manifold. If I could only somehow gain financially by making enemies, I'd have an instant fortune.

I heard the Father's favorite words just then, lifted from the great bard, as they frequently were: "I could be bounded in a nutshell and call myself a king of infinite space!"

21

Biting the Hand that

I'm not certain exactly what perverse streak made me lash out at Hank, of all people, my lone benefactor (aside, of course, from Moses); a man who had only shown kindness and favor while the rest of town waited anxiously for me to clear out. That most of it was due to my failure to have even the barest shred of an affair with Katherine I had no doubt. An affair would have meant unbridled pleasures, hot steamy nights, endless sex, not this perpetual state of despair, this painful torture, this unwilling monk's interminable and unbearable celibacy.

We were locked in a strange intricate cycle, riding the seesaw of desire. When she had given me indications that she wanted to become intimate, I hadn't been ready, and later when I was ready, she wasn't.

The frustrations of running the store and trying to make a success of it, and myself, of dealing with my wife's on again, off again love-hate relationship, of Katherine who fluttered like a hummingbird just beyond my reach, to say nothing of reading Joe Melkert's ramblings, culminated, and the result was that some other being reared its ugly head.

Or maybe I was simply tired of feeling like I'd been caught wetting the bed whenever Hank deigned to notice me.

Bukowski now strolled past the bookshop, and kept right on going. He gave a quick wave as if to say he couldn't afford to stop by and listen to someone who spoke as if he were confessing a lifetime of sins and had only five minutes left of life in which to make his peace. Or maybe he just didn't want to sink with us, worried that the taint of failure might prove contagious.

I waved him on. Don't worry, Hank, I know you can't be bothered.

I mused over the work of Bukowski, and Hemingway, Dostoyevsky and Mark Twain. In the midst of all this it suddenly dawned on me that Hank really wasn't half so great as he might have been, as he should have been. Some of his writings, like so much of Hollywood—the endless violence and drinking, the smoking, sex, retching—seemed gratuitous, became as numbing as the death tallies on the evening news. It got in the way of, or was there in place of the story itself.

I read Bukowski's poems, stories, and novels. Okay, Hank, so where's the humor here? Where's the emotion that resounds deep within you, a wellspring of truth, of memory echoing but with a newness that feels like something seen, heard, touched for the very first time? Sure, there was violence, savagery, even, and a fair amount of filth. But where was the enchantment of words that grabbed hold of you even before you know what has happened?

I read aloud line after line. Too flat, Hank. Too journalistic. Give them at least one redeeming quality. It's troubling, here the character seems too pedestrian, as if it's manual for how to be the lowest of the low. If you're going to use JoeSchmoe, at least make the story compelling, make the characters interesting; at least put them into extraordinary circumstances. Not: "'Don't cum in me,' she said. 'Don't worry, I won't,' he said. He came and got up." That's not really all that compelling, Hank, not poetry, not funny, not if you're older than thirteen. Neither were all the stories of sex and drinking, vomit and sex, men and women, shit and sex, and drinking, and pissing, and cuming.

Very gritty, Hank, but lacking meter, rhythm, magic, and music. Like Hemingway, far too many characters who you can do nothing but despise. If you want real life, there's the nightly news. There's the street just outside your door.

I accused Chinaski of not going far enough, of not living up to his ideal. Sure, go on, write stories about men and women on the street, or in the gutter, but never, never ever forget humor. The sort of humor that Fante's best work fairly brims with.

At some point in time, I noted, Americans began equating humor with the commonplace, much to the detriment of our culture.

If people wanted American realism, that was fine, but how many stories, poems and novels do we really need to enlighten us about the American drunks, about American misogynists, American cheating wives, American ruined marriages, American men and women who lived lives of desperation and despair? I feared that people liked Bukowski because his stories either mirrored the lives of the reader, or else projected a fantasy they aspired to live.

Enough was enough already.

"Bukowski is," I boldly wrote, "one of the three forces who for several decades have caused the decline of American literature." There it was, the fact staring me in the face. I couldn't shake it. All my frustration, my resentment, my disgust, all the efforts of holding my mind together against the onslaught from external forces, comingled and culminated and blew like Mount St. Helens at that moment.

I wrote it up as best I could. The entire ugly thesis.

Once I began, I found it impossible to resist raking Bukowski and Hemingway over the coals, not so much for what they'd written, but for the legion of imitators who'd followed, those who held them up as the Icons of American Literature, and emulated their writing as well as their lifestyles.

I took an unnatural savage glee in personally swinging in every direction, and read aloud as I wrote. Mike listened in wonder to my words, nodded his head and smiled the smile of the medicated man. He commented on occasion how absolutely right, how brilliant I was, which was a hell of a lot more courtesy than anyone else who entered the store gave me. As a result it was hard to find fault with the man.

Hemingway and Bukowski. They had done it. Oh, not alone. No, not by a long shot. I mentioned three forces, right? And just who was the third part of this unholy trinity? Academia, of course. Academia championed and qualified the writers they saw as fit and produced new writers who had suckled from their own narrow and purified fonts. Give us two or four years and you too can join the ranks. They positioned themselves to proclaim and herald who the great writers were. And hey, if poetry and art from the intellectual word game circle jerks are too much for you, you have the reaction to that from the numerous spinoff Bukowskis and Hemingways writing for the common man, the regular Joe.

"Bukowski," I scribbled furiously, "You and Hemingway have spawned the simplification of writing pared to the bone, to the level of grunts and groans and other ejaculations, dragged it down to a uniform mediocrity, stripped of imagination, stories about nothing, aimed to meet the hordes at eye level, content matching the cranial capacity of the least discerning of readers, and not one blessed iota more.

"Every scraggly headed semiliterate punk who's ever had a pimple, who's ever gotten laid, or who's thrown up after a long night of drinking, takes it upon themselves to think they too can write a story or a poem. Furthermore, they presume that this very first poem of theirs is as good as any other poem ever written and to prove it they promptly mail it off to *The New Yorker*. When it's returned without comment they chalk it up as yet another example of bias against women, if they are female, and if they're male, then it's an obvious case of the powers that be being aligned against them.

"Every man or woman who's reached middle age and added up their lives to find it amounts to just shy of zero feels they have a book or two in them. Every young woman who believes she has known feelings both intense and unique, who has tingled with love and loss, is compelled to pour them out in free form verse to share with the rest of humanity. Anyone and everyone who has ever rafted down a river, or caught a fish or panned for gold or caught a right hook to their jaw is bound to become the next Hemingway.

"It doesn't matter who. There are no limits or restrictions; both the well-read and unread, the literate and the unlettered, the unwashed as well as the clean. They simply all seem to be born blessed with the innate ability to sit down and produce a classic formed of words.

"I want to grab hold of these people by the scruff of the neck. 'Look here, schmuck, Don Quixote is not an exercise in selfexpression; Shakespeare's plays are not character studies; Emily Dickinson's work is not the result of someone merely pouring out their excess of feelings onto the printed page. It is Art; a creative, imaginative activity. Warning! It is absolutely not reporting, or autobiography, certainly not reality, any more than a cake is a list of ingredients. It is making something out of nothing, taking a few elements and practicing a bit of alchemy, the magical process of creating a story, get it? STORY!' which is the product of storytelling."

Igor, Mike, whatever you want to call him, giggled and laughed. He thought I was doing a comic routine.

"Hey, listen up, you, this is deadly serious," I warned him.

"I read more of the Bukowski stories," he said, now cackling like some mad monk and dancing a few lively steps. "Those were good, especially the way you do the voices."

"I'm not doing this to be funny or to entertain," I said. "I am risking my life to illustrate a serious point."

"What was wrong with the story?" Mike asked.

"What's wrong with the story? I'll tell you what. A story means making things up; I believe that's why they refer to it as creative writing, emphasis on creative, fiction, meaning a literary work of imagination. There's a whole world of difference, say, between creating a setting and simply writing down what I did last week."

But then so many of the people who came into the shop had apparently missed that class, for when I pointed people to the fiction section, or mentioned that a book they were searching for was a novel, they often asked, "Is it real or made up?"

"Why don't these people," I continued, "who, struck by lightning suddenly decide they want to be a writer, why don't they go off to become the next Picasso, or Rembrandt, or Van Gogh, or Mozart, instead of dragging down all literary endeavor to their level, which is stripped clean of anything literary?"

"I thought it was pretty funny," Mike said, scratching the side of his head, the side with the hole, the sight of which made my knees buckle. I never glanced to closely at that wound, but always averted my eyes.

"Funny? *Funny*, he says. What the hell's so funny about people screwing one another and getting screwed in return? What's so funny about sloppy drunks? Or bar fights, or throwing up, or lousy marriages? Nothing witty, or droll, or clever.

He shrugged. No answer.

I thought of all the countless Bukowski and Hemingway imitators, wondered how many of these neophytes had gone into writing, how many had gone into editorial jobs and the like, or teaching, thus spawning more and more of the same? More writers, more editors, copyists, readers, critics, publishers, agents. Clones and clones of clones of their heroes, watered down to the nth degree. And those who didn't make it were the ones to buy the books, to read the stuff, to keep those others in business, to keep them writing more, ultimately causing more people to copy, imitate, etc., and so on ad infinitum. To prove my point the current darling of academia was none other than Raymond Carver, a man who out-Hemingwayed even Hemingway! What next? Where will it end? Would someone weaned solely on stewed prunes, Hemingway and Raymond Carver come along to be the next wunderkind of the literary world?

"Will a Bukowski wannabe ejaculate on sheets of beer-stained paper and hand it in to class?" I asked. "How pared down, how stripped to the bone can you possibly get: 'See Mike. See Mike run?'"

Mike continued nodding and laughing. "Oh, you're really letting them have it, all right!"

Page after page I delineated my attack, putting Hank through the wringer. Still, Hank's legion of fans came in search of him. They rummaged through his books, mishandling them in the process, asked if he often came into the store, and oh, by the way, where, perchance might I find his house?

I saw them day in and day out, conversed with them, and spouted off to outdo their hyperbole. "Oh, yes, Hemingway, Buk, they're gods, man." The fans nodded, lapping it up. "Genius," I said. "Writers of the earth, the streets, the alleys, the filth, the reality of life. Why, you can smell the booze, the piss, the vomit and the sex just reading those stories."

"Yeah, yeah," they said nodding in agreement.

"Why, the pages positively reek of the man," I said.

"That's why he's so great," they said. "It's so real you can taste it."

Real. How real was real enough? These weren't people interested in a good yarn, a beautifully constructed tale or poem. No, they wanted to peer into the most intimate, dirty, ugly aspects of a man they wholly believed had lived out everything he had ever written. They were getting their jollies and thrills vicariously; titillation for the literary voyeur. It was only a trifle better than peeking in at someone's bedroom window. Some of them gleaned ideas from their master and practiced following in his footsteps, lived their wretched squalid lives in wretched imitation of the great man, as his unchosen disciples. Only these wannabes obviously rarely bathed. Bukowski, at least, bathed regularly. They went home to get shit-faced drunk, hit their girlfriends and puke. They gravitated toward a writer whose life was *simpatico* with theirs, or at least their aspirations, the way so many men over the past few decades have looked to Hugh Hefner as a mentor, as having lived the ideal life. Perhaps they longed to outdo Hank.

I actually saw this in its inception, when some of his readers proudly proclaimed that they had done worse than the old boy. *Sure, Bukowski is badass, but I've been in and out of jails my whole life, I treat women even worse than he does, I've been in more fights, and gotten laid more.*

Just like copycat killers and method actors, these people imitated and hoped to outdo their idol.

"He's the best," they said. "Nobody's nastier than Bukowski."

"Yes, and such scope and depth," I carried on. "Such style, such inventive settings and subplots. Stories and novels of such incredible scope and depth, such heartwrenching dialogue: yes, yes, my rabbit, my little rabbit, Hemingway, Bukowski, like father like son, such welldrawn characters, such imaginative plots...."

My hapless audience stood staring dumbly.

I went on and on, but it was too late. My listeners had beat a hasty and silent retreat, leaving the resident lunatic to babble to himself, sitting on a stool in a twentyeight hundred square foot asylum that might otherwise be a paradise could I only lock the doors and keep the shadows outside while I conversed with the ghosts of dead writers from centuries past.

I continued to babble how lamentable it was that anyone who read Bukowski, who had done the things his characters in his stories did—or who wished they had done those very things—people who related to his *ouvre*, all jumped at the chance to write a "Bukowski poem" —these uncouth bards of the barrooms, the strip joints and whorehouses.

Why weren't they content to write a journal or keep a diary? Want to record your every thought, feeling, daily activity? Fine, but publish them in book form, distribute them to bookstores and subject the rest of the world to reading it? Everybody, as far as I knew was born of man and woman; most fall in love and hate, get burned, grow old and die—so what? Does that mean that each and every last one of them must write a book about it?

Your modern confessional, accusatorial, sliceoffuckinglife novels and stories were no better than the cheesy television talk schlock shows like Geraldo and Sally Jessie Rafael and their thousand-and-one bastard offspring.

"Why do all the Bukowski clones sound so monotonously alike, one indistinguishable from the next? Why the unbroken uniformity amongst all the offspring of Hemingway? How minimal can minimalist be? Strip a story of plot, of imagination, of creativity, and all you have left are words. But mere words do not a story make."

Yes, sirree, I wrote it out longhand for all the world to see, then punched it out in a marathon session at the typewriter, ensconced in the bookstore after hours, where I escaped from the smoldering ruins of my home life and the beautiful blond who haunted the nocturnal caverns of my mind, and who I knew would cause me more turmoil than I would know how to handle.

Bukowski and Hemingway weren't the only writers I went after, either. I pulled books from the shelves, authors who had failed to write books of lasting value over the past few decades. I pored over best story collections from the 30's, 40's, 50's, and 60's, marveling at how many of their authors were unknown, forgotten. I unearthed old magazines and discovered the same thing. Magazines like *Collier's* and *Esquire* and *Saturday Evening Post* which once published four or five short stories per issue, not to mention poems and serializations, and which now published one, if that many. *Playboy*, which, during the fifties and sixties, published three or four stories per issue, along with a whole flurry of other men's magazines. There were some, too, now long defunct, like the truly amazing *American Mercury, that which had first published John Fante,* to forgotten treasures like *The World Book*, and *Horizons*—magazines that published stories, poems, essays, reviews, art work—all of it.

I reprimanded novelists by the score for writing books that were clearly short stories puffed up and stretched out to make a novel; books by authors who churned them out faster than they could be read, who cannibalized their old books, reshuffled them into new ones; books about the same tired predictable themes, done—not only a hundred thousand times before—but done far better; books that were poorly written, books that had nothing to recommend them to any intelligent, discerning reader.

I quickly mailed off my essay on Bukowski and Hemingway to *The New Yorker, Harper's and The Atlantic.* The New Yorker had once published Shirley Jackson, but now published John Updike and that dismal slice-of-lifer, Ann Beattie, in whose stories you struggled to get the slightest whiff that indicated something had occurred. Would they publish today a story like "The Lottery" as they had in the 40's? Or the fabulous John Collier? No, the corruption had reached the highest pinnacles of the literary establishment, to be sure, and *The New Yorker* had in recent years heralded in a new era of fiction, a new style, a movement, as it were, American Bland—stories of the inconsequential life.

People lauded Updike for constructing beautiful sentences, but nobody was willing to point out that the emperor wore no clothes: for while beautifully constructed sentences were nice and all, a string of them did not necessarily a brilliant story or a book make. No, they merely called attention to the writer, see ma, no plot, but one hell of a metaphor, eh?

I was going to change the world of American letters with this essay, even if I had to do so with everyone in the industry kicking and screaming. People would read it, see for themselves how corrupt and inconsequential the publishing world had become, and a new day would soon dawn, a renaissance of American fiction—a real renaissance, not this crappy sappy farce for which David Brin was apparently the self-appointed spokesman—a rediscovery of stories about *something*, a reawakening of genius, past, present and future.

I dodged phone calls from a bewildered Harlan Ellison to whom I had allegedly sent some halfcrazed, barely coherent missives demanding justice or retribution or some such foolishness relating to some real or imagined slight I had borne, back when Moses and I held an imagined bloody Tribunal against the powers that be.

I received concerned phone calls from the likes of John Martin, Bukowski's publisher, who too had recently received some questionable if not lunatic missive from yours truly.

"Are you okay?" he asked. "You really had us worried."

"No, I am fine, really, John. It has passed; a momentary affliction, probably something I ate."

"Are you sure?"

"Don't worry. It's nothing serious."

"I didn't know what to think. You sounded pretty desperate."

"Me, desperate?" Nah, I could take it. I still had my sense of humor, didn't I? I could still laugh with the best of them. In fact, I laughed too much. In the mornings, at mid-day, throughout the night, I howled and wailed with laughter, uncontrollable, unstoppable, laughed until tears streamed down my face.

"You're sure you're all right?"

"Really, John, I'm fine."

"I had a bad feeling," he said, "thought maybe you'd gone."

"Gone? Where?"

"I don't know, jumped a train or hid as a stowaway aboard a ship bound for Panama."

"I'm still here, John. I'm not going anywhere, as far as I know." Though I did like his suggestion and saved it for possible future use. Go to the store one night for a pack of diapers or a new baby bottle and never come back. Hop a freight train to New Orleans or some such place. Ride the rails like Woody Guthrie, or a tramp steamer, end up like Pippip in *The Death Ship*, by B. Traven, a man without a country, with no destination.

There were others, too, who called up, hoping to catch me before I jumped from the Terminal Island Bridge.

I brushed aside the concerned and the curious and retyped my scathing proclamation accusing Bukowski, Hemingway, and Academia of the crime of causing the decline, nay, the death of American literature, all twenty-seven pages, and this one I addressed to Mr. Charles Bukowski. I mailed the copy to Hank and held my breath, waiting for the coming storm.

I was biting the proverbial hand that fed and signing my own death warrant at the same moment. Not pretty, perhaps, but this was how far things had gone, and how badly I wanted my body to be riddled with scars; I longed for the inevitable end to come now and not dally or dance poised above my head like the Sword of Damocles, while I choked on anticipation. If half of what they said about him was true, Hank would most likely rearrange my face, in which case I stood a chance to end up even uglier than the old man himself, if that was humanly possible. 'Course, he might take my machete, instead, and lop off my head, take it for a trophy, stick my severed head on the gate outside to serve as a warning.

After I mailed it off, I immediately regretted having done the evil deed. He would be crushed, wounded by so callous and careless, by so thoughtless an act. Beneath that tough gnarled exterior, wasn't he as sensitive and insecure as anyone else? Wouldn't he, at the very least, feel betrayed by an ingrate to whom he had graciously done a favor? I thought of retrieving the letter, but of course in the miasma that was the San Pedro Post Office that would be impossible. The Post Office—more so than most—was a morass of ineffectuality. A permanent cloud of suspicious origin, a haze of narcolepsy, rendered its workers into a state wherein numbers and letters appeared jumbled and confused. I was told they held the record for lost parcels and letters miss-delivered, and had no cause to doubt it.

Dealing with the employees of the post office convinced me that the inmates from the halfway house on occasion got mixed up with the postal workers, switching places with one another.

In fact, I'd gone down earlier that day to the Post Office and bought stamps from the guy behind the counter, who sat in his little cage. He was somewhat bleary-eyed, but friendly. He made a little joke, something about a Jew, a Catholic, and a Protestant all walking into a bar. There was alcohol on his breath. He'd been hitting the bottle. Probably had a fifth of Scotch right there in his cage with him. With every word a waft of whisky came my way.

Realizing I had to take matters into my own hands, I drove past Bukowski's home. I tried to summon the nerve to intercept the letter in his mailbox, before he got his hands on it. But nerves were a scarce commodity. I could write a scathing attack on the man and yet couldn't muster the courage to retrieve it from his mailbox.

For two or three days I returned and parked in front of his house, stared at the mailbox, at the hedge and the house itself, stared at the windows. Was he in there? Was he reading it, and rereading it, formulating a plan of extermination, of revenge? Could I tell him I was sorry, that I'd written it on a dare, which I could never refuse, or as a sick joke?

Someone—a lunatic fan, perhaps—appeared to be stealing the mail out of Hank's mailbox. Days went by and the old man didn't receive anything. Where were the letters from fellow poets and editors? Where were the perfumed missives by female English literature majors a third his age, who found him a beautiful and sensitive soul: "I've read your poems, Mr. Bukowski, and I'm left breathless by how perceptive you are, how thoroughly you understand women. I know that you know me completely, though we've never met. I'll fly out in two weeks and rent a hotel. I'd love nothing more than to meet you, to offer my body to you. I've enclosed a recent photo, so you can see I'm attractive and sincere." Was there a letter from Red Stodolsky reminding Hank what a great writer he was? Or maybe a chatty note from John Martin: "Hank, remember when I upped your monthly fee from $150 a month to $200. Now look at you. Things sure have changed, haven't they? Who would have known? You're as great as Shakespeare!"

Perhaps there were one or two letters written by one of the multitudes of Bukowski imitators. "Dear Hank, That putz you mentioned, the creep in the bookstore, if you want I should go make short work of this mug, just let me know. Sounds like a real case, this one. After all, now that you are a big somebody you shouldn't soil your hands. You want I should strangle him?"

The neighbors began noticing me, parked like a stalker in front of Hank's house. Probably another fanatic, they thought. A lunatic on stakeout waiting to glimpse the famous author. I had to face the facts; it was likely that Hank had received my letter, and chewed it up. I left, crawled back to the bookshop to await my fate. There was no undoing what had already been done.

I got me a bottle, picked at random, for to tell you the truth I didn't know my whiskey from my rye. But I wasn't yet so damned young or green. I was as tough as anyone, even if I did look like a mere babe. I never backed down from a challenge, never refused a dare. I'd taken on Hank Chinaski; San Pedro's celebrated poet, and soon I'd reap what I had sown.

I bought a pack of cigarettes, though I didn't smoke, and got carded, and it took all I had to keep it in, to walk out without a word, simmering the whole while. After all, I was about to be tracked down like a dog by none other than Charles Bukowski; I'd hit the big-time. This was akin to having the mob come after you; better, even. The mob killed people as a matter of course. Bukowski wouldn't just kill anybody, no sir. It took someone especially deserving, someone particularly vile to warrant Buk coming after them.

I settled down hoping against hope that the Post Office true to form had misdirected the letter. Perhaps it would end up at Moses' shop. I was certain that Moses at least would have a good laugh over the matter, because he detested Hemingway and Bukowski both, and because the Post Office had taken such liberties with his mail. Usually it arrived two to four weeks late, delivered by the owner or manager of a business on Gaffey St, or some place on 9th Street, who had received mail addressed to Moses' bookstore.

Meanwhile, I expected the worst from Mr. Bukowski. I kept waiting for him to walk in, or to bump into him on the streets, to grab me by the scruff of my neck and growl, "Here's that sorry little son-of-a-bitch, Kastinovich. I'm going to tear you apart limb from limb."

I fondled my machete while I envisioned Hank and me squaring down like something out of *High Noon* or *The Good, the Bad and the Ugly*.

I practiced my final words, what I would say to Bukowski when he finally showed up. I only hoped Hank didn't take me by surprise, that he gave me a moment to utter my last words, a fitting pithy salvo, or at least a suitable epitaph. I wracked my brains for something memorable to say to the man before he planted me in the ground, but I was at a complete loss of words. Would I let him kill me in silence, without so much as a final wisecrack, perhaps just grinning my impish grin? When would he show up? What would Buk say? "This is it, baby. Say your prayers."

I fussed and fretted over how he might rearrange my face, whether he would strangle me, or knife me, bludgeon me with a baseball bat, or roast me over a slow fire. I had my wife open the mail in case I was sent a letter bomb, and refused to answer the phone. Every time he showed up at the Ka-bob place I sweated bullets and began my prayers: "This is it, God. If you are there, looks like I'll be seeing you momentarily. My life may be through, but while I've got your attention it could have been a better life, you know? I mean you could have done a whole hell of a lot better than this."

I began doing situps. I even bought a chinup bar and began using that, strengthening my body, getting myself into shape for the confrontation with "the Buk." Sure, he had size and an innate viciousness, not to mention centuries of experience on his side, but I had youth and quickness, as well as a keen instinct for survival.

After closing and before opening the shop I sparred with an invisible Hank. Though he towered over me and swung a fist that was like a sledgehammer, I was quick as the devil. I took jabs at his paunchy belly.

My daughter stood in her crib, her tiny hands gripping the rails as she watched, laughing.

"Look at daddy," she said.

"Not daddy," I said. "A killer. The annihilator."

She repeated the word syllable by syllable, "Annihilator."

"That's it, kiddo." I swung at my invisible opponent, a feint jab with my left, a right hook.

"You're funny, daddy," the kid said.

I hit the floor and did twenty push-ups. Was that enough? I did five more. Back on my feet, I danced on the cement floor, working it, shadowboxing with Bukowski.

On my side, I was light on my feet. My punches, however, lacked Hank's ferocity. I was a featherweight going up against a heavyweight.

Assailed by repeated gory nightmares I saw he was coming to decapitate me. Night after bloody night he held the prize of my head aloft for all to see.

He might kill me, but at least he wouldn't look at me like I was still in diapers any longer. The headlines alone would be a fair tribute: Bookstore Owner Killed By Notorious San Pedro Writer!

People would finally start spending money in the bookstore. They'd buy books in the place where Bukowski had personally dismantled me. All those people who flew in from overseas would make this a regular stop. The Little Big Bookshop, a holy site. A shrine to my detached head. They'd take photographs of themselves in my store. It would become the most famous incident in the already fantastic repertoire of Hank's many devious deeds.

I was in need of some strong medicine, a tonic. What to do, how to alleviate the crushing weight of nerves I was experiencing? I slipped another clean sheet of paper into the typewriter and began an essay on the spot.

"Some sentences flow so exquisitely, so smoothly, so effortlessly," I wrote, "as if the words come together of their own volition, as if they teach the hand that writes them, leaving the reader with the feeling that the sentence has always existed." — This was it! I'd write about those miracles of prose, the geniuses of letters, and the impossibility of their task. Okay, so it sounded familiar. Maybe I had dreamed it before writing it. Maybe I had it twirling in some remote back corner of my mind before it surfaced in my conscious thoughts? Or maybe I had read it somewhere, I don't know. "If you read any current magazine from cover to cover," I typed furiously on my 1950's manual typewriter, "It'd be difficult if not impossible to distinguish one writer from another. What was the last story you read in a literary magazine that could be called memorable? Their motto seemed to be, 'Heaven forbid a story or poem should stand out.' Instead, they lined them all up and lopped off everything above the shoulders. Institutionalized conformity.

"The net effect of all this conformity and derivative work is that the level of writing, be it mainstream, popular, or genre, has become increasingly bland, more and more like journalism, or worse, bad television."

I'd go down fighting, all right. I'd come out shooting at anything and everything. I'd show them that this was America, land of diversity, so what the hell in tarnation were they doing by all conforming to the same tired themes, where were the iconoclasts?

While I was at it I decided to go after bookstores as well. They had to accept some of the responsibility for things being as they were. It was because the vast majority of them didn't stock books like *The Personal*

Recollections of Joan of Arc, that no one appeared to know Mark Twain had written it. Of his own books, it was his personal favorite, but I never met anyone who'd actually sat down and read it.

I sat up late and honed my words, the sword by which I would teach the world that had ignored the likes of John Fante decade after decade; those who consigned Gerald Kersh's extensive list of titles to the dust heap of oblivion. I would rise to the challenge, take up guerrilla tactics, and start a campaign of journalistic terrorism against the entire literary establishment.

I degenerated into a cornered, desperate beast; nothing more than a twisted caricature of my former self. I knew it was only a matter of time before something finally snapped. Every shadow, every sound represented the end, took on shape and substance, metamorphosed into Buk coming after me. I was wound tighter than the bowels of a man about to walk the last mile on his way to the gas chamber.

What did it matter anyway? By now Hemingway was probably dragging himself out of the grave to come and help Bukowski throw me to the sharks. My days were numbered, and like many who were taken to the executioner's block before me, I would go wearing an enigmatic smile, let them lop my head off, let them eat cake, or read Jackie Collins!

22

When the Going Gets Really Weird...

Late at night, curled in a corner, I listened to the eerie sounds of the bookstore. It was uncomfortable as hell, but I endured it with the Father's words ringing in my ears, "Pain is sweet. Suffering is good for the soul."

Occasionally, I roamed the corridors, following the ghosts that came and went, and listened to the murmurings, shuffling noises now and then, as of something being moved, the moans and groans, and the unmistakable sound of thousands upon thousands of books whispering to one another. I held a feeble flashlight that flickered on and off at whim, and pointed it at the back of the store from whence emanated all manner of strange commotion. I explored the aisles in an agitated state of dazed exhaustion and frustration, knowing I was being observed, that a hundred thousand eyes hidden peered out at me from the shadows. The hairs on my arms rose.

My eyes welled with tears, either because of what I saw and heard, or perhaps it was the result of the bottle of brandy I nursed to keep me warm during the long nights in the bookstore.

I clung to my new friends: Joan of Arc, Don Quixote and Sancho Panza. I watched their excursions and adventures, and longed to hang out with Scout and Atticus, with Huck Finn and Tom Sawyer.

Things rapidly deteriorated and blurred before my eyes. The familiar world erupted into a frenzied nightmarish landscape that could only have been concocted by Hieronymous Bosch on a binge: vivid visions of earthquakes and tidal waves, the downtown reduced to rubble; creatures, only halfhuman, or human yet with monstrous distortions, their features disproportionate and hideous, swarmed all about. They shouted and pointed and moved things around. The earth erupted, and the sounds were deafening.

I fidgeted, realizing Bukowski would choose the right moment to strike, to maul me. Maimed and crippled, at least missing a limb or two, I'd finally able to look at others proudly, scarred—provided I survived the encounter.

Somehow or other I ended up on the street, and there was Hank, at my side. Bukowski and me. The poet and the bookseller. He grinned, laughed the sound of a landslide of rocks, and slapped my back. We were the best of pals. The two of us ended up at some sleazy noisy bar on Mesa Street, where we drank lousy beer that wasn't even properly chilled. He drank me under the table.

"People who fawn over me and my work annoy me," he said in that Bukowski drawl. "The ones who hate me, I don't care about." Had my insulting him endeared him to me, the way people had told me the best way to deal with Harlan Ellison was to insult him right off the bat?

"It must be something being fawned over," I said. "I wouldn't know."

Hank shrugged but I don't know that he heard what I said.

"I prefer the company of cats," he said. "Cats don't give a fuck who you are or what you do."

Some burly loudmouthed lout then interrupted, said something to Hank, and after I blinked I saw the guy lying on the floor. I hadn't even seen Hank swing at him. I looked at my fists and wondered if I had done it. The guy crawled away. No, it must have been Hank who'd clobbered him. I couldn't have clobbered a hamster.

Hank ordered two more beers. Instead of feeling bigger and stronger beside him, I felt diminished. I snarled and looked round for someone to fight, but people looked right through me, and ignored my words of provocation. Nothing I said or did registered, let alone made an impression.

Gigantic holes appeared in the ground. Concrete and steel shot up everywhere, while machinery created an earsplitting cacophony of gnashing and scraping. The nightmare spilled over into my day-to-day affairs. Everything was caught up and swept along and jumbled: fish flew, birds tumbled and rolled, water flowed upstream, boats sailed through the air, and clouds crawled around on all fours. The rotting heart of Terminal Island gnawed at San Pedro with an eager appetite, threatening to engulf everything. A sickening convergence of time, a dissonance of events rang in my ears. My sweatfilled sleepless nights in the bookstore were disturbed by numerous inexplicable sounds, the building shifted, groaned. Some things creaked and moaned, others went bump in the night.

I later recalled my attempts to dig, yes, though I must admit the recollection of it is somewhat confused and muddled with *The Great Escape*. I was tunneling, however, in a mad, desperate, if not Herculean effort to reach Katherine's lair, to awaken her with a kiss. But don't believe for a second that that's where it would stop, no siree, Bob. No more of this endless, unendurable platonic agony. Not for me, thank you just the same. I'd had enough of that, God knows, with my wife.

23

The Man in the Mirror

Anxious, suffering insomnia, as well as a possible ulcer, I made a protective ring around me of my idols: Poe, Twain, Dostoyevsky, Cervantes and Fante. They would keep the nasties at bay. What a lovely group, they were. Mark meet Edgar and Fyodor, Miguel and John. They got along swimmingly. I urged them to discuss whatever suited their fancy and brought in Shirley Jackson to help ward off any ugly spirits, especially if they happened to be the ghosts of any thirdrate hacks lurking in the bookstore.

In the wee hours it was a regular watering hole for these writers. A small group in the far corner mostly sat and played cards as they drank. They had nothing to do with anyone else, and were generally disliked and looked upon with contempt by the rest of the writers. I couldn't identify all of them; however, I noted that most looked to be the Paris crowd of expatriates.

Fante, William Saroyan and Carey McWilliams, and others I didn't recognize sparred playfully with one another in a bantering, brotherly sort of way. The art of good-natured putdowns and insinuation. I listened and laughed, nonplussed by the crowd who made my bookstore their hangout.

I moseyed my way around, observing the goings-on, but realized, after some time, that I had become the object of ridicule. Twain, Poe, Dostoyevsky,

Cervantes and Fante were laughing it up, pointing at me. Between bursts of laughter they argued as to my unbelievability as a character.

"And I thought Prince Myshkin was ridiculous," Fyodor said. "Now *this* is an Idiot!"

"Truly fantastic," Poe said. "His implausibility stretches all credulity, a pastiche of fantastical incongruities."

"Preposterous jackass," Twain grumbled good-humoredly, "A right first-class jackass at that. Reminds me of a particular S.O.B. I made the acquaintance of during my gold-panning days in California!"

Dorothy Parker was there, too, slightly tipsy, leering and winking at Twain, who blushed profusely and stammered helplessly as he sat back down, uttering a grunt of consternation.

They asked Ambrose Bierce to stand up and do an imitation of me, which was so hilarious it even had me doubled over in hysterics along with the rest of them.

"I've got a new definition for you," Ambrose said. "Kastinovich, a—" but the rest of what he said was drowned out in a flood of raucous laughter.

One table in particular erupted in a bustle of activity and more noise than the others combined. I heard catcalls and whoops, shrieks of laughter and shouts of encouragement. I ambled over to take a look and much to my surprise found Nellie Bly arm wrestling with H.L. Mencken, while Oscar Wilde, Gerald Kersh, an elegant elderly woman I later learned was Marguerite of Navarre, and none other than my friend Moses himself competed in a verbal contest of some sort. Elsewhere, T. S. Eliot attempted to woo Emily Dickinson with disastrous results.

Nellie appeared to be beating Mencken, who turned bright blue in the face, and began stomping one of his feet on a small stack of books on the ground—Gertrude Stein's, and, yes, I'm sure it was *For Whom The Bell Tolls*, which oddly appeared to spurt blood with every stomp—amid the shouting and stomping, the crowd hurtled epithets and one-liners with a dizzying ferocity.

The next thing I knew I was being eased down onto a couch . A moment later Bukowski was there, but a younger, bearded version. He smoked a cigar and was dressed rather spiffy.

"Eeasy, baaby," he said, as I struggled to speak and upright myself.

"But wha—I mean, who, uh?"

"Reelaax." I stared at the man wondering if he could speak without drawing out every single syllable, as if the words stuck to his gums and teeth. Books were suddenly piling up everywhere, all around us.

"My god," I said, "They're multiplying!" Stacks of paperbacks and hardcovers sprang up like plants growing in time-elapsed photography in some nature film.

"Why isn't Céline here?" Bukowski demanded to know.

I gulped. "I don't know?" I answered. "We would sell his books, but, to tell you the truth I could never read him, not cover to cover. Anymore than I could read Joyce. "

"What do you mean!" he roared.

"So many books, so little time. How does one choose what to read now, what to read later? I have books I've been carrying around for years intending to read, dying to read, but there are new books published every day, and books I find out about from the writers I read, their favorite books. There are hundreds of classics lying around unread."

"You talk too much," Hank said.

"I know, I know, I'm sorry. It's a nervous habit, one attenuated over the centuries by my clan, I'm afraid. I've tried to rein it in, really I have." I realized he wasn't saying anything. I glanced over. Bukowski had fallen asleep, was snoring with his mouth open.

Then the scene changed. I was alone, but I heard sounds, terrible sounds, the sound of death, of my bones being ground to dust. I groped in the darkness, lost. Still, I moved along, used my hands to feel my way. I found something smooth, cold, hard. Slowly I began to see. A faint glimmer at first, growing brighter and brighter. Shapes, shadows. There was someone in front of me. No, an image. It became clearer, sharper. An old man. A tired old man. It was me. I was facing a mirror.

Okay, enough of the damned clues already. The attack on Hank had not been written by me, it had been written by Joe, the old man of the bookstore. I realized at that moment that along with everything else, I had in some way become Joe Melkert's double. He was me. I was he. We were one and the same. Goo goo g'joob!

The ghastly sight of Bukowski coming to get me snapped me out of my delirium. He stood outside the shop and shook the bars, clawed toward the doors, attempting to break into the bookstore. He held what looked like a scythe in his hand.

"I want your head, Kastinovich, you groveling son-of-a-bitch" he said, swinging the blade at me, spitting out my name as if he would stomp me into the ground, and I remember thinking, Oh, so now he remembers me. "If you weren't a little cockroach I'd squish you under my foot." Then he roared with laughter. A future warning to all who might dare antagonize Mr. Charles Bukowski.

The Father began singing Ben E. King: "I, I who have nothing!" a song *he* had always tried his damndest to sing, not me. Only, I felt my jaws move, the voice appeared to be coming from me.

24

Running Amuck in the Sierra Madre

I needed an exorcist, and one arrived in the form of my friend, Carl England, who I'd known since the third grade.

"You need a break," he said. "The bookstore is making a mess of you. You should go before it gets any worse." He suggested we go off to Mexico to ride the Copper Canyon railroad and mingle with the Indians in a canyon larger than the Grand Canyon, and through which there wasn't so much as a single road. He said he'd read something in a magazine about it.

I must have hesitated for Carl began to whisper, "Gold, gold, gold. Just think, there must be tons of it waiting to be found. Maybe an old abandoned gold mine where we could dig for a rich new vein."

I mulled this over. The thought of having a gold mine in Mexico that funded the bookstore didn't seem too unreasonable to me.

"Let's go explore," Carl said. "When's the last time we went anywhere?"

Truth be told, he was right, even though I feared the bookstore wouldn't easily release me from its grip. My dreams of venturing forth into the deepest darkest regions of Mexico in search of adventure, going off like Ambrose Bierce, however, got the upper hand. I wouldn't hide in the festering bowels of the bookstore any longer. Maybe I too would vanish off the face of the earth. It seemed just the thing.

Before I could even bring up the Mexico plan to my wife she came home and announced that she'd been laid off from her job, and was going to spend her time at the bookstore once again. I wondered at the convenience of fate, and then mentioned Mexico, thinking she would never let me go. "I need you here," I could hear her say. "Let's work together and get things done."

That wasn't her reaction, however. "That's a great idea," she said. "You should go."

"Are you sure?" I asked. "It won't be too big a burden on you, having the baby and the shop?" I'd be a liar if I said part of me didn't hope to hear her plead for me to stay.

"No, we'll be fine," she said. "It'll be fun." So, there it was: I was as dispensable as the disposable diapers the baby wore and took off in the window to toss through the railings at those who lingered and goo-gooed at her. Perhaps my wife had secret connections with the Mexican authorities or Mexican bandits, who would put an end to yours truly in some vile and painful way.

The rows of floor-to-ceiling shelves of books shifted and merged, replaced by vistas of stark mountain ranges, and deep lonely valleys, of heat baked train tracks and errant sagebrush.

I imagined Bukowski accompanying me to Mexico. Two desperados doing missionary work, spreading the word south of the border: The word of Fante.

Maybe a typed manuscript would mysteriously find its way to the bookstore. Left behind at closing time, or deposited on the doorstep of the shop during the night. Whose manuscript? A rough draft, but it somewhat resembles Bukowski's writing. Could he have left it behind in a drunken stupor? Or is it Bukowski's breakthrough book, a departure from his usual fare, one that will assure him of a lasting place among the geniuses of our time, a truly great novel? Bukowski's Unknown Adventures in Mexico.

I revisited *For Whom the Bell Tolls* and the pages concerning Spain that Joe Melkert had left behind. I got a chill up my spine when I saw the name of the protagonist's predecessor in Hemingway's book: Kashkin. I remembered something about one of my relatives having left Russia and going to Spain just before the Spanish Civil War. I had an uncle who went by the name Caspian, in a vain attempt to escape being a Kastinovich. There appeared to be some confusion as to our real name, which had changed several times since my great-grandfather arrived at Ellis Island. Great-grandpa had left Russia under dire circumstances, either stemming from the antagonism toward Jews, an insult that he had hurled at the czar, anti-governmental activities in the Russian army, or simply under threat for being a Kastinovich. Perhaps a combination of all these. This great-grandfather never spoke a word about Russia once he landed on American soil. He became a plumber, and in no time was known far and wide as the plumber who plumbing always leaked. He was busy both day and night if for no other reason than he personally guaranteed his work, which meant he was constantly returning to the scene of the crime, allegedly to fix what was supposed to be already fixed, and chase after the lady of the house. To say he had a reputation is to say the sea is wet.

Hemingway had probably seen fit to change Caspian or Kastinovich, or else he heard from one of my relatives that Kashkin was the name that had been changed to either Caspian or Kastinovich, no one could quite remember which. Regardless, the same gnawing bid for justice, for fighting against the oppressors, rose in my gut. To journey to Mexico, to see for myself the drug lords in action, then take notes on the corrupt government and the social injustices, much the way my hero Nellie Bly had done and written about nearly one hundred years earlier in *Six Months in Mexico*, until the government forced her to leave the country, was all the incentive I needed. The enemy was out there; it was just a matter of pinpointing his position and determining a course of battle.

"Sure," I said, "and if we get killed at least then I'll be able to look Bukowski in the eye."

I'd been holed up for long enough. I needed to go out into the real world.

The décor shifted, like fine sands blown by gusting winds. It blurred and faded completely. The scenery changed. Mexico? Yes, that was it. My wife informed me that I had fretted for weeks, and in order to avoid a high school reunion I had booked a trip to Mexico. I didn't remember. After all, how could I show up among successful people, people who had lived, who had done something with their lives, I, who was still called baby by Bukowski, and kid by Harlan Ellison? I'd have to mingle among men who had gone bald, women who had had a number of babies and divorces, people who'd been in jail, who had drug and alcohol addictions, who attended AA meetings, perhaps some who'd come out of the closet, or who'd had sex change operations, people, I was sure I would no longer recognize, while I hadn't changed one iota. I was still exactly the same as when I was in junior high and high school. I'd never spent a single day in jail, had never gone to a prostitute for sex, had no venereal diseases, wasn't gay, and had never even knifed someone. No wonder Hank called me baby.

Carl and I went off, headed for the Mexican border. I left my wife, my daughter and bookstore (my entire life, in other words) for ten days. I promised to do the same for her someday.

"I have to do this," I said, "Not only for my own sake, but for all of our sakes."

"I'll see you when you come back," she said. "If you come back."

Such humor, such confidence. What did she think? That I was running off to escape my home life and obligations, the sweet serenity of wedded bliss?

We took the bus to San Diego, but the bus that was supposed to take us from there to some other border town, where we would catch the train didn't show up. There wouldn't be another bus until 8:30 the next morning. We waited, walked around downtown San Diego some, found an all-night diner, and waited some more in the depot, amused by the goings-on around us; what with some people trying to sleep, others trying to get drunk or score drugs, people having marital difficulties, kids going haywire, security guards and police, unruly customers, we had no problem staying awake.

We tried reading, to kill time. Carl brought a stack of get-rich-quick books and get-smart-quick books. He always rummaged through my store in search of the definitive text on the subject: *The Lazy Man's Guide to Making it Big*, and such, while I read a Raymond Chandler mystery. Aside from the requisite copy of *Ask the Dust*, I'd brought several books, not that I really thought I'd have the time to read them all, but it was best to be prepared for any eventuality; who knew but that we might get stranded somewhere, or arrested on some trumped-up charge and made to spend months, if not years, in a Mexican jail? I'd also brought a thick notebook upon which I had planned to sketch my latest essay entitled: "Confessions of a Bibliophile."

However, distracted by the disruptive mode of our fellow travelers, we felt it'd be best to keep an sharp eye on our belongings, so we didn't get much reading done that first night.

We caught the bus the next morning, then finally the train. It was crowded and comfortable, but we had the whole country ahead of us— where would we go? We glanced at a map after climbing aboard, and looked at points like the Yucatan and Oaxaca, places where we were sure to find ruins and jungle and God only knows what, but those places were far, the train less than luxurious, and Los Mochis was close, so our decision wasn't a difficult one.

After debarking we realized the train station was in the middle of nowhere. We were lucky to find a ride to town with some friendly fellow travelers, and then got ourselves a hotel room. Suffice it to say it was very cheap and not much to look at.

We slept the sleep of the road-weary. The next day we roamed about town, ate and drank. Two hombres, two desperadoes in a foreign land; Stanley and Livingstone, if not Don Quixote and Sancho Panza.

There was an upstairs cantina just down the street from the hotel that Carl discovered. We went in for a drink. A group of cowboys in full-fledged attire, fresh off the range, whooped it up and downed beer and multiple shots of tequila like it was nothing. They slammed their bottles and mugs down on the tabletop with a blood-curdling coyote yelp. We ordered some beer. A guy came over and sat down at our table. He started talking to us first in Spanish, then in English and back to Spanish, but I couldn't understand a word he said in either language.

He was pretty well toasted already, but ordered more beer, first for himself, and then for us. "Drink with me," he said, pushing the beers toward us. "Come on. You're my friends!" Or had he said, "You look famished!" I couldn't be certain, or "Drink before you are finished?" It did sound more like a demand than a request. I looked toward Carl to see if he had picked up on this possible hint of impending doom. Carl, however, was busy conversing with this gentleman though Carl didn't know a word of Spanish, and kept up with the drinks toss for toss, while I still nursed my first beer.

Our new friend laughed and cried himself silly. "Why is he so emotional?" I wondered. Is it tradition to be heartbroken over your intended victim's demise, before you knife them?

As we drank, I began to understand a word now and then of what he said, though it was still impossible to hear with all the noise around us; the cowboys screamed and yelled as a mariachi band took up their instruments. His going from Spanish to English and back again made my head spin, and he slurred his words in both languages, which didn't help matters.

"I'm a Mexican," our friend said. "But I grew up in the United States. I came here to try to find myself," I think he said. Either that or he said, "I am jealous of your wealth."

He said he felt sad because he didn't fit in as an American, was often called a wetback, treated like dirt, looked down upon by gringos, and yet, he found, to his dismay, that he didn't fit in in Mexico either. For to the Mexicans he was Americanized. "I'm disliked by both people," he said. But even then I wasn't sure I was hearing the words correctly. What he said sounded an awful lot like, he didn't like Americans, especially weak little white boys who came down to Mexico looking for a good time, showing off to the Mexicans, who were poor, but who were a noble and strong people.

Carl was particularly moved by his friend's story. The two of them practically fell into each other's arms as they soaked up beer and shared tears, never mind the looks I was giving him, the non-verbal clues that we might well be in for it as soon as our backs were turned.

For all I knew this guy sold freshly harvested human livers and kidneys to the local hospitals.

I might have been touched by his story, too, had I not been so busy trying to decipher what he was saying, trying to decide if he was welcoming us as *compañeros* or introducing himself as our executioner. Though he kept smiling at us with a mouthful of broken teeth, he still looked to me like one mean son-of-a-bitch. And while I empathized with his plight, what with the shrieks of the cowboys and the loudness of the band, I was getting restless. The state of my nerves had me feeling quite on edge. Even the waitress coming back to our table with platters of beers made me jump up once or twice, all too ready to demonstrate the classic fight/flight response to danger.

Sure, this guy seemed friendly and all, but, hell, might not Ambrose Bierce have been taken in by some friendly *caballeros* before they shot him? Might they not have drunk together before deciding to plug him full of holes?

"Hey, Poncho, let's see how a gringo dies."

Had it been any other day and place I too might have cried over our beers with him. However, the atmosphere and the noise, coupled with fresh memories of my friend Ron's advice on the dos and don'ts of being a gringo in Mexico, saying that sitting in a bar with your back to everyone was fine, but that turning around and facing the crowd was as good as challenging any and all to a fight, made me feel I had walked into a lion's den. And then, just when the waitress startled me, I had turned and faced down the entire room! Me, Nick Kastinovich, challenging these hard and desperate men; it was ludicrous. One look at them and it was clear these hombres lived by the knife, if not the gun and the bullwhip. They likely wrestled steers with their bare hands. Their skin was rough as rawhide, and their eyes revealed vistas of the vast desert and ever-present death. They drank tequila by the bottle, and amused one another by knifing themselves, just to watch their wounds bleed out. No, my life wasn't worth so much as a plugged peso.

The mariachi band closed in on our table. Carl told me that our Mexican friend was inviting us over to his place for more drinks, and I was saying, "Look, we don't know this guy from Adam, nor even Paco. He could want to have us stuffed and mounted on his wall or something even worse."

The thought of dying in such a place as this, not just the cantina, but Los Mochis—The Flies? Was that where I wanted to be known to have met my death? Where we knew no one, and where, more likely than not, no one would ever learn what happened to us, where no one would come to visit our graves—probably unmarked—because no one would know where we were buried, filled me with dismay.

I tried by mute signs to indicate to Carl that I didn't think traipsing off with this dubious chap was in our best interest, but he was too busy chumming it up with his new best friend, even though I wondered how. They spoke the language of beer.

They laughed and drank another round, when I felt someone touch my shoulder. I looked up. A Mexican Goliath towered over me, his black mustache drooped with malevolence, his enormous belly the only thing that separated us.

He spoke, or rather snarled something incoherent.

"*No hablo español*," I said, in what I thought was a pretty decent accent.

Goliath repeated whatever he had said and glared down over his protruding belly at me. I repeated that I didn't speak Spanish. The two of us stared at one another. I looked over at the waitress and our Mexican friend. They shook their heads. "What did jolly man here say?" I asked. They didn't say anything but shook their heads again. "Ignore him," someone said, though I didn't know who.

I looked up at Goliath, squinting one eye. He glowered down at me like I wasn't fit to spit on. I tried to see if he had a gun or machete. Perhaps I was finally going to get that scar I had dreamt so long about.

"Is laughing boy asking me to dance or to step outside and fight?" I asked.

I had a sneaking feeling I was no longer going to have any problem facing Bukowski, if I survived the encounter with this behemoth.

The cowboys at the other table became even louder, screeching, making animals calls and whistling between dranks, with steely-eyed glances that were dark and impenetrable as the graves I imagined they were thinking of digging for Carl and me. Perhaps they cheered the giant on, encouraging him to dismantle me right then and there. Goliath clearly out-weighed me by at least a factor of five or six. His arms and legs were as thick as my torso, for God's sake. He reeked, too. Maybe this was it, my number was up. Hell, our newfound Mexican friend sitting at our table was at least twice my size. Why didn't Goliath tango with him instead of me? Even if I had unconsciously challenged him and everyone else to a fight. If some pint-sized brat in kindergarten challenged me would I flatten the little sucker for it? Perhaps it was because we were the only two gringos in the place. Come to think of it, it really didn't look like the type of cantina that catered to tourists. We were probably the first gringos to ever venture inside, and now they weren't about to let us go. I silently cursed Carl; leave it to him to steer us into a den from which we wouldn't likely be walking out. First Los Mochis, now this!

Then again, perhaps the giant just didn't like my face, that ridiculous sneer of which I was no longer capable of ridding myself.

"What the fuck is this fat lummox saying?" I said, feeling a bit more belligerent and indignant at this vile ogre slobbering down at me. His breath was worse than the rancid stench one encountered in the trash bins behind fast food restaurants.

I turned my back on him and wished I knew how to call him a fifteen-day-old pig shit in Spanish, or at least a degenerate oaf with an unsavory interest in somewhat innocent boys, but alas I knew none of the choice phrases that might have served me under such adverse circumstances. What few words in Spanish I'd known from growing up in Los Angeles lay dead and buried in my throat.

At last he lumbered off, snorting and huffing, disappointed that he had no dance partner for the night, or feeling cocky that I had proved a yellow gringo who had backed down from a fight.

Carl said he was ready to go off with our new friend. I knew they planned to drink away the rest of the night together. However, given the experience I had just survived, I preferred to go back to the hotel instead. Carl left, and I returned to our room.

He came back to the hotel drunker than when he had left. I found that I couldn't sleep what with the sticky heat, the unbreathable air of the hotel room, and wondering what sort of demise Carl had met, before he returned, miraculously alive, and unscarred.

We went out to see if we could find a café that was still open. We finally found a place, where we drank enough coffee to sober Carl up. After that, we walked back to the hotel. A block away someone approached us on the sidewalk, first on one side, then on the other, weaving back and forth. Was this another dancer, or was he trying to block our path?

I saw something in his hand.

"Run." Carl shouted. "He's got a gun." I'd seen guns before. This was no gun; it was a fucking cannon.

We took off into the street, trying to dodge bullets, to avoid having our brains splattered. We ran for our lives. I knew then what the cliché meant, of having your life flash before your eyes. It was apt. Carl and I ducked behind some cars parked along the side of the street. As we ran, the gunslinger, obviously drunk, perhaps one of the drunken cowboys from the bar upstairs, raised his cannon and pointed it at us. He couldn't hold it steady. He tried aiming it, though I'm sure that in his condition he saw not just two of us but perhaps four or more and couldn't make up his mind quickly enough which to shoot.

We took off and didn't stop running until we were several blocks away. We stopped off at the café where we had coffee and ordered two beers to celebrate our narrow escape. Now even I was in the mood for a drink or two.

"I thought we were dead for sure," Carl said. He held out his hand. It shook. I held out mine. Same thing. All I thought was, Buk look at me now, though of course it would have been better to face our assassin down, instead of running away. Still, we'd been threatened with death, and I wasn't about to quibble.

A brochure we found during breakfast promised glorious sights, a hotel, Indian tribes and inaccessible canyons. We were instantly swept along by descriptions of more adventures awaiting us. The brochure promised ruins, too. I didn't know if we would make it back, so I left a copy of *Ask the Dust* in the hotel for future tourists to luck upon.

We'd survived the night and the next day found ourselves riding the rails along the Copper Canyon, The train took us into the interior of Mexico. It was a great ride through the mountains, on trestles that overlooked gaping abysses. The train rode through the canyons on the very edge of doom. Even here, in the desert wastelands of Mexico Bukowski haunted me, hunted me, every step I took.

When we arrived, we found a place quite different from what we'd been promised. The ruins were nothing more than buildings built in the fifties to house the men who had worked on the railroad, which had deteriorated. Certainly nothing remotely Mayan or Aztecan about them. The hotel was no hotel but some dilapidated shack, the dining room and restaurant, nothing but a kitchen and a single table. We were the only customers. An American woman ran the place. She had designed the brochures and had made up the itinerary of the trip, she proudly informed us. We asked her about each aspect of the tour and about each one she informed us it hadn't yet been completed; this and that were still in the planning stage.

"In other words," we said, "none of this is true?" We brandished the brochure.

"No," she said, sheepishly. "We didn't think people would come so soon. But if you come back in a year or two it should be really great."

A year or two.

Carl and I discussed the possibility of going through the Copper Canyon on foot. Gazing out over the whole thing from where we got

off the train, seeing all that uncharted terrain, one could very well imagine a thousand secret gold mines hidden away in those hills. Visions of
The Treasure of the Sierra Madre filled our heads. Had B. Traven roamed
through these very canyons?

We lay back under the sun, drowsy with the heat, the beers, our
fantasies, and the flies buzzing round our heads. We dreamed of treasure,
though neither of us had ever mined for gold. How difficult could it be?
We'd simply dig and dig, keeping our eyes peeled for shiny yellow metal.
Perhaps some of the local Indians could be persuaded to point us in the
right direction. We could stumble upon the biggest vein in all of Mexico.
The celebrations we would have. We had a field day imagining how our
lives would change, coming home rich men, or maybe buying a fancy
ranch and staying put in Mexico.

Carl and I explored the place. The sides of the canyon were extremely steep; one didn't see much in the way of paths or trails, but
somehow these Indians came and went, up and down without trouble. I
observed the indigenous people who lived there without roads, cars, or
modern conveniences. Perhaps I could crawl down the canyon and find
a small cave to inhabit. Would these people accept me? Moses' brother,
an anthropologist, had spent a year among the Tarahumara Indians. He'd
commented that it had taken months for the Indians to get over their
suspicions that he had come to steal their women.

I approached one of the Indians who sold beautiful hand-woven
short blankets from a wooden stand. The Indians wore these things like a
shawl. I expressed my interest by pointing, and he replied, "Serapa" in a
voice that sounded like water running over small round stones.

I scratched my stubble, thinking it would make a nice souvenir to
take back home, maybe as a peace offering to my distressed wife. I'd hand
it to her beaming, "Don't let it be said a Kastinovich never delivers."
Perhaps it would buy me several weeks of detente.

I showed the Indian a copy of *Ask the Dust*, made him to understand
that it was worth all the *serapas* in the world. "This is the Good book," I
said in crippled Spanish. "*Sagrado y fantastico.*"

Again, in broken Spanish I conveyed to him what a treasure I was offering him. "Better than gold," I said. "*Muy mejor.*"

He nodded, but without expression. I gestured that I would do him the greatest service by accepting his blanket as a token for receiving this book, which would change his life.

We spent forty-five minutes haggling back and forth, Carl tugging at my sleeve, saying "Come on, Nick, let's get the hell out of here, already."

But I couldn't give up. The thought of this man sitting up late around the fire reading Fante to his fellow Indians, the Tarahumara people telling and retelling the adventures of Arturo Bandini, was something I had to do my best to enact.

The Indian and I finally came to an understanding about the book and the blanket. I paid him his measly twenty bucks and kept my copy of *Ask the Dust*. He had no desire for the book. John Fante meant nothing to him. All he wanted was money.

"Corruption's rot has reached everywhere," I said, disgusted to my core. I had a passing thought of leaving the book behind, but was afraid it would end up being used for toilet paper, or to fuel a fire.

We left feeling rather crestfallen, convinced that people coming here from the United States like this woman who ran the resort were the scourge of the land, the ruination of Mexico. We returned to Los Mochis sorely disillusioned.

"What should we do?" Carl said. "Go to Mexico City, or catch a boat to Cabo San Lucas?"

"Forget Cabo," I said. "Too damn many unpleasant associations. I don't need to be reminded of all that." It was, of course, where my wife and I had honeymooned. I couldn't help but think of my bookstore, my wife and child back home. Here I was having grand adventures, living it up, having the time of a lifetime. Meanwhile, what was happening back at the store? I had visions of people from the halfway home holding my wife and child hostage in the bowels of the bookstore.

We were pretty fed up with our Mexican adventure so far, and knew we couldn't stay in Los Mochis. We had to go somewhere else. But where?

We looked into finding information on train arrivals and departures, but no one seemed willing or capable of answering our questions. One would tell us one thing. "No, that's not right," someone else would say, and before you knew it they were arguing back and forth, and then a third person would join the fray with yet another opinion, on and on. We narrowed it down with their assistance: the train would pass some time between ten o'clock in the evening and three o'clock in the morning.

Enough was enough. We were sure that if we booked a boat it would sink, that if we headed for Mexico City disaster would soon follow. If an earthquake didn't level the city upon our arrival, then a volcano would surely erupt from a nearby patch of cornfield. We checked out of the hotel, and hurriedly made ready to catch the next train no matter where it was bound, north, south, east or west.

Carl and I took a taxi to the train station. It was closed, but we weren't worried since we stood waiting for a train with a crowd of people who did the same. After an hour or so we sat down and leaned against our bags. We'd brought a bottle of tequila to keep us warm and ward off sleep.

We passed the bottle back and forth and watched creatures crawling across the still-hot, dry sand, scuttling like crabs, but too large, with cruel stingers or pincers that were made for business. Freight trains occasionally passed in the dark, but didn't stop, or we might have jumped aboard. Still, as they slowed, hordes of dark, shadowy shapes ran toward them, and climbed aboard. We watched, wondering where they were bound, these shadowy vagabonds, creatures of the night, and how they managed to jump aboard the trains that though they slowed were still too fast for our gringo feet to catch, especially carrying our belongings and running along the iffy path of railroad tracks. Carl swore he wasn't about to hop a train that didn't have the decency to stop.

A couple of hours later we were feeling no pain, or cold.

"Maybe they do have the right idea," I said, peering at the dark shapes that scrambled toward yet another passing train. We were tired of waiting, tired of wondering if and when the train station would open so we could purchase our tickets.

I got up and walked around the tracks. Where do these steel rails lead, I wondered? To fame, fortune, anonymity or death? Carl came crawling after me, reaching for the bottle of tequila. I fought him off.

He yelled something at me but I couldn't understand a word he said. Disgusted, I walked away from him. "I have no respect for someone who can't hold his alcohol," I chirped, then took another swig.

The train tracks and the night loomed before me, like the mouth of Jonah's whale about to swallow me whole. But I didn't give a damn.

"Go on, swallow me," I said to the darkness, waving my bottle as I had earlier waved my talisman of *Ask the Dust*.

Something happened at that moment I never told anyone about. If I did I'd be told it was the tequila, or the night, my exhaustion and homesickness, perhaps even Katherine and the ongoing situation with my wife, or all these things. But I know better.

For some reason, I set the bottle down on the train track. The bottle began to glow, and I swear it filled nearly to overflowing. I heard a shriek. I can't be sure, but I think it might have come from my mouth. Either that or it came from the bottle itself.

I issued some kind of prayer, or at least an equivalent of sorts. "Oh, great Goddess Tequila"—(pronounced Ta-Kill-Ya), "Thou mysterious beauty, practitioner of mystical arts, sublime, be my bride!" I bowed down before the bottle.

When I looked up again, a deeper, darker shadow rose in the darkness, a thin billow of shimmering smoke. What was this, Black magic? I was still on my knees as it swayed and swooned seductively above my head. Black, blue, brown and green smoke that assumed the unmistakable curvaceous shape of a woman.

I reached out to touch it, and felt warmth on my hands. I held it closer, tighter, as a thousand thoughts raced and churned in my mind: this is death, a muse, a goddess I had invoked, or some poor stray Mexican woman who'd taken a shine to me. She enveloped me, and as I opened my mouth to speak, she became mist that filled me the way the tequila had coursed through my body earlier. It was like drinking fire and ice at the same time.

I shut my eyes, and when I opened them again, something else entirely stood on the tracks. It was a monster, a giant that rose to the height of a four-story building and wore a toga, had one eye, and raised a huge club. It shouted something vile at me in Spanish.

I grabbed the tequila bottle and raised it invoking its protection with one hand, and my Bantam paperback of *Ask the Dust* in the other. I was about to be creamed, slaughtered, annihilated. One more Kastinovich about to get his just desserts. So, what did I do? Did I spout off a line of poetry, or sing, "Lonely, I'm Mister Lonely, I have nobody to for my own," like the Father would have done? Did I quote a line from *Ask the Dust*? Did I cower and try to hide, turn and run? No, I laughed. I laughed and laughed and couldn't stop laughing. I laughed until I cried because I laughed so hard. I laughed and began choking. The thought of dying from laughing made me laugh even more.

By this time Carl had found me and took the bottle from my hands.

"You're a sick freak," was all he said.

I managed to follow him back to the train station. It was finally open. I looked at the clock. Somehow I was completely sober. It was 1:30 a.m. We crowded to the ticket booth and I bought two tickets. I asked for a sleeping compartment. The man laughed as he handed me my tickets.

"What's he laughing about?" I said.

"Maybe it was your Spanish," Carl said.

"Nah, it was more malicious than that."

We went back to the spot where we had sat earlier, and waited for the train, which would come soon, or so they said. We were shaken awake around 2:30 a.m. by the passenger train's arrival. We ran with our bundles and packs, my *serape* and other souvenirs we had purchased to take home, and jumped aboard. The horror that greeted us I could long afterwards taste in the back of my mouth. Filled, absolutely; no room for so much as a shiver to pass through that car. Even between the cars, standing room only. Packed as I'd never have imagined a train could ever be so stuffed.

Carl and I acted upon the same thought and jumped off together. We ran to another car, but found the same crush of passengers. No wonder the bastard who'd sold me the tickets had laughed. The train was filled to capacity and beyond. Somehow we squeezed and sandwiched our way in between cars just as the train began moving. We stood and crouched the entire night. I took out the *serape* from my pack, as we were all shivering. A woman without a coat, wearing nothing but a thin faded dress that went down just below her knees, was pressed up against me. I offered her some of the *serape*. She smiled and accepted.

The ride was long, cold and uncomfortable. Everyone's bodies were packed tightly together, for all the paltry body-heat it provided us. There was no room to move, not even to scratch an itch. I doubt any of us actually slept.

With the morning came a pause. We got off, stretched our legs as the train coupled and uncoupled, added more cars—we assumed—in order to alleviate the overcrowded conditions. We watched the maneuvers with happy hearts, longing to grab a seat in one of the new cars.

The trains separated. A voice on the intercom spoke out something in Spanish, but we didn't understand a word of it. We stood scratching our heads as one half of the train went on and on and didn't look as if it were about to stop or return. We grabbed someone in uniform, made ourselves understood with a word in Spanish, another in English and hand signals thrown in for good measure.

"Texas," the man said, pointing at the other half of the train, the half which had just departed, the half that contained our luggage. It was headed for Texas.

We stood staring in disbelief. We asked people what we could do. "Do? Nothing," they said. "It's gone, brother. Someone will make good use of your things."

We watched the train carrying our belongings as it headed toward Texas.

25

A Return to Sanity?

Somehow, we made it home again; beaten, bloodied and battered, to be sure, and with nothing but the clothes on our backs—but alive. Barely. My head was abuzz, my thoughts jumbled with somersaulting visions of Hank and Fante, my recent escapades in Mexico—all of it spun and swirled round and round my brain. Toss in Joe Melkert, Hemingway, Katherine, my wife, my daughter, and the bookstore, and you might get an idea of my state of mind.

I wore a wrist bracelet from a hospital. A vague memory of food poisoning or some such thing, crawled like a worm along the edges of my brain. I was lying in a hospital bed, sick as a dog, watching the space shuttle explode over and over before my assaulted eyes. Was this instant replay, memory shuffling the deck?

My wife took a sudden, if temporary, liking to me; perhaps distance had worked some fondness into a chink in her heart, or maybe it was just that she enjoyed seeing me so completely helpless and debilitated. I had gotten violently ill on my return from the remote southern regions, one of the inner circles of Hell.

After several days of recuperation, I was released on my own recognizance, weak, and still feeling like death warmed over. All my insides had been sucked out, and replaced with hot simmering tar.

The bookstore, I was surprised to find, hadn't been washed away in the interim. It wasn't reduced to rubble, or even under the sway of San Pedro's less stable inhabitants, though it was no longer in the same place. Somehow sometime it had hopped, skipped and jumped to a spot farther down the street.

It also remained just a bookstore, and did not front a bordello. For the life of me I couldn't find a tunnel leading to Katherine's house—or anywhere else for that matter—though I retained a memory of crawling on all fours to what I at least thought was her house, baying like some wounded animal, and making love to her in some mad frenzy. Now I wasn't so sure. Maybe I had made love to a complete stranger who had only slightly resembled Katherine. Hell, it might have been a Bougainvillea or a Rhododendron growing just below her window that I'd made love to, for all I knew.

I was especially surprised, too, that my head wasn't stuck on a spike in front of the bookstore but was still attached to the rest of me, although it throbbed and hurt like hell, as if it had been pummeled pretty badly.

"What happened to the bookstore?" I asked. "It isn't where it was."

My wife explained that we had spent several weeks moving the store before I had left for Mexico, after some initial though characteristic resistance on my part.

"I'm not going anywhere," she claimed I had said in a fit of pique. "I don't care what they say!" Apparently, I had attempted to barricade myself into the bowels of the store, screaming obscenities, threats and pleas, some nonsense about tunnels, a love nest, and a waiting lover, but after some gentle inducement, I had finally given in.

The persuasion they had utilized was that either the entire building would be retrofitted to meet new earthquake standards, or they would close the bookstore for good. We were assured it would only be a week or two, not much of an imposition at all. Well, their one or two weeks dragged out into many weeks. They took apart the whole bookstore, dug trenches, tore down walls, ceilings, and erected steel beams. A nightmare. We moved into an available space two doors down. I hadn't dreamt it, after all, which left me wondering what else hadn't been a dream?

I had put out a plea to everyone I knew. New friends, old friends, family, people I hadn't seen in years, showed up to help us move every shelf, stand and rack, every book in the building. We worked day and night, moving the entire bookstore, which created a chaotic mess, what with people phoning or stopping by, with trying to fit everything into the new shop, trying to maintain sections, to keep everything in order in the midst of complete disorder. We put up big signs, saying: Bookstore Has Moved Two Doors Down! A large arrow pointed the way. But notices and banners didn't prevent customers from losing their way, from not seeing the obvious, from turning and walking away, thinking we had closed down for good.

People drove up and down the street, gazed at the former bookstore and wondered where it had gone, while I waved my arms, over here. Here we are. We're still here.

Katherine showed up, and for one moment my former troubles dissipated into much nothing one by one.

"I wish things could be different between us," she said. Different? Was this a euphemism for, See ya later, bub? "If it was another time, some other place. If the situation was different."

Another time, some other place, the great if onlys, whatevers, and what ifs. One look in her eyes told me the whole story. She didn't wish to be simply friends any more than I did, but—and it was a big but— Obstacles. Oh, how I cursed the tyranny of fate's timing, how if we'd only met earlier, or…what if, what if?

"We'll stay friends, okay?"

Friends. The word tasted hard and bitter in my mouth. I didn't want her as a friend; I wanted to ravish her. I wanted to be with her permanently.

"But, *Love's Body*," I stammered incoherently.

She smiled. Silly boy. Poor dear. I was unmoored. Lost.

After a too brief conversation, a quick touch of her hand on mine, I reached out to caress her shoulder. We kissed and parted.

I was no longer Joe Melkert, for a true Melkert would have fought like hell to have Katherine by his side. Somehow the former owner had shaken me off, rightly rejected inhabiting the body of a Kastinovich, leaving me high and dry. A man at odds and ends, at sixes and sevens, who couldn't make up his mind and follow through. Perhaps it was the sojourn down to Mexico, nearly getting shot, challenged to a duel, the misadventures through the Copper Canyon and the trains, getting sick—the doctor said he was surprised I hadn't died. I wasn't so sure I hadn't. Moving the bookstore, and the end of any hope for Katherine had contributed to ridding me of the specter of Joe Melkert, had worked an exorcism, purged me of the old man's angry, restless spirit.

I'd never felt so weak and puny. Not even in Mexico. Or standing beside Hank. I peered in the mirror, studied my face. I was myself once again; a Kastinovich through and through. My denouncements of Hemingway and Bukowski weighed on my conscience, a terrible guilt. My God, I wanted to crawl under a rock and hide. Had I really written up such scathing attacks? Had I really sent off letters? Mad letters! Written by a deranged lunatic. Everything I'd been through had taken their toll, wrought changes and left me a shaken, unstable wreck and ruin, someone only Dostoyevsky could have rightly depicted.

I had all the Bukowski titles. I hadn't burned them or torn them into shreds. I had Hemingway, as well, and Faulkner, and Fitzgerald, all set beside Dorothy Parker, Lillian Hellman, James Joyce, even Gertrude Stein.

I pleaded temporary insanity. "The real me is back," I said, ready to set things right once again, to correct all the terrible wrongs that other, raving doppelganger had done.

Lovely towers of Fante's books observed me as I dove back into work. Had they merely been the writings of another American author, like so many others? I grabbed one and began reading, no, see, there I was laughing and crying, because in the 1930s no one wrote the way John Fante wrote. He set the standard. The only problem was that nobody was listening, outside of such luminaries as Lawrence Clark Powell and Carey McWilliams and a handful of others.

I attacked the business with renewed vigor, received a New Year's greeting from Black Sparrow, a poem, signed by Mr. Bukowski—he apparently didn't hold any grudges against me—and gave the everdelayed Harlan Ellison book yet another month.

I still fretted and worried over what would happen when Hank saw me, but when he did show up all Hank did was smile, wave, and call me baby like he always did.

That was it. My recent fear gave way to incredulity. Could this be so? Had my missive been lost in the mail, after all? Incredulousness soon gave sway to guilt and shame, which ultimately gave way to twinges of annoyance. After all, why shouldn't Hank come and slug it out with me? Wasn't what I'd done deserving of his wrath and vengeance? Was I too young and innocent a lamb for him to bother doing me any harm?

However, all this irritation and insult quickly had to give way to my no longer giving a flying shit because our money was drying up faster than a teardrop falling onto the steaming strip of asphalt running between L.A. and Mojave in the dead middle of August, and creditors called at all hours, demanding I pay up.

I was forced to move my little family into a tiny one-bedroom apartment downtown in order to save money, giving up our apartment at Land's End. After two months in that tiny crackerbox of a place we were forced to leave and rent out one of the mysterious offices above the bookstore, using the bathroom down the hall. We were kept awake at night by the obnoxiously loud, as well as out of tune, Mariachi band that played in the Mexican bar just around the corner, on Mesa Street. Every night drunks straggled by, retched, argued, conversed, demeaned themselves, yelled to God knows who or what, fought, and shook the steel gate that accordioned out across the bookstore windows to prevent all those overeager book fiends from breaking through the windows to get at the books they simply couldn't get enough of.

We sneaked in and out so no one would know we were living there. And what a strange, dark, claustrophobic little universe it was. This stuffy, dingy office housed the three of us. Only a few of the other offices were being used: an accountant, a lawyer, and someone else we never saw or heard. God only knew what this mysterious ghost did within the confines of that particular room down the hall.

"Can't get much worse than this," I reassured my wife.

"No?" she said. "I suppose next we'll be sleeping in the car."

"I am loathe to say this," I said, "but the more we suffer now, I'm convinced, the more reward we shall reap in the future."

"I'd rather have an ordinary comfortable existence like everybody else, a normal life."

"You'll see. I admit, things may be bad now, but I tell you in a month or two, things will turn around and we'll be living the good life. We'll look back at all this and laugh."

She looked at me with skepticism written all over her face.

There we sat night after night, staring at the four walls, at each other, out the one window, at piles and stacked boxes containing our belongings, in a room that was maybe fifteen by fifteen feet.

The universe shrank daily around me, the bookstore itself was the center, the black hole, the very bottomless hell that would consume me in the end. I noted how my living quarters had steadily gravitated to within spitting distance of the shop. Each day we were dragged closer and closer to its insatiable maw, swept toward utter oblivion. This ranked as one of those inexplicable phenomena like the Oregon Vortex or the Mystery Spot in Santa Cruz, California; the bookstore was voracious, a structure of otherworldly forces. It devoured everything that came within its sphere of gravity, and didn't bother to spit out the pieces.

I clung by my fingernails to all I had—my marriage, whatever scrap of sanity remained, the bookstore—not out of sensibility, nor practicality, but sheer obstinacy. I kept the damned creditors at bay with my winning charm, my promises, not to mention a fair amount of pleading and begging. Time, time. I only need a bit more time. Wait and see, I'd pull a miracle out of my hat.

My wife left me with the store and the baby and went off to work another job, so that at least we would once again have something of an income.

A phone call informed me that the members of my immediate family were about to fly off to the South Pacific to make a reconnaissance trip with hopes of founding a family style commune, a paradise of their own devising complete with tennis courts, snorkeling and houses for all members, and docile servants who'd wait on them hand and foot.

"It'll be like Ben Cartwright and his boys in the Ponderosa," the Father intoned. "We could each have our own house."

"And just what will you do after a couple days of this life of Riley?"

"Oh, I don't know, play, relax, fool around with the servants."

I wished them well, bon voyage, and count me out. That was just what the world needed: a village of Kastinoviches, breeding, running amuck.

I went out for long walks through the streets of San Pedro, passed by crowds of people. My people, I thought. How lucky you are to live here, where Fante himself had once worked and strolled in his youth, and where Bukowski lives. Warren Zevon, too, had grown up here. I contemplated the harbor and the breakwater, tried to coax the hordes of feral cats out from the rocks, and eyed the pretty strip of shoreline, the dark shape of Catalina slouched along the horizon.

It was a sleepy, quiet town. A small town, where everyone knew everyone, or at least knew the outsiders from the hometown crowd, and didn't take too kindly to strangers moving in. I pondered the many questions I'd been asked. I knew of course that this was why the very people who owned the stores in which we shopped would not purchase from us. I was constantly reminded of the fact that I, unlike everyone who mattered, wasn't born here, didn't grow up here, and I only hoped and prayed that I would not be so unfortunate as to ever be buried here.

I stopped by to commiserate with Moses, yet another estranged outsider boycotted by the denizens of San Pedro. I bought some books, because somebody had to keep the bookstores in town going. There were always remarkable books to be found on his shelves, and he practically gave them away, they were priced so low. I found solace in the company of this poet who cared about meter and rhyme, the beauty of language, who looked for a spark of intelligence and originality in what he read. He showed me his latest column for the local free paper, *The New Devil's Dictionary*, after Ambrose Bierce, taking to task those who fell under his withering glare, who deserved to be put in their place: politicians, reactionary whackos, public icons, the cheap, the mean and the rotten.

I couldn't help but wonder if Moses was how I'd end up in another forty years or so, a man who celebrated the birthdays of dead geniuses, a man who busied himself with the seriousness of art.

I hadn't forgotten what had happened on the railroad tracks in Mexico, nor what I had seen. While I wasn't Joe Melkert anymore, I wasn't my old self either. Something had happened to me, left me altered in some mysterious way, as if a stray spirit, a whiff of Mexico perhaps, had entered me and remained. My body was electric and I whispered chants from God knows where.

Before I knew it I had written up several satirical articles on the after-hours writers club in the bookstore and an account of the trip to Mexico. They made me chuckle, so I Xeroxed a number of them and sent them off to various people, hoping to rattle their cages. Don't ask me who, I'm not one to kiss and tell.

I tried desperate new measures to save the bookstore, bought more new books; horror was big, why not horror, mystery, science fiction, fantasy. There was a deluge of books, all purchased on credit, which they inexplicably kept extending, as if the banks wanted nothing other than to plunge me deeper and deeper into debt.

We tried contacting Ray Bradbury, and a score of other writers. We left messages begging for favors, wrote letters imploring them to help save a chunk of society and civilization, by helping to save the Little Big Bookshop. But we heard only dead silence in response. Perhaps word had gotten round town. My name conjured evil associations. These folks had been warned about my troubled state of mind.

I rummaged through the newspaper looking for upcoming book signings and the like. It seemed the opportune place to corner a writer and wring a promise out of him or her to pay the bookstore a visit.

I found one where Robert Bloch was to make an appearance. I loaded up as many Robert Bloch books as I could possibly find into the back of the car and went off dragging wife and child in search of the famed writer of *Psycho*.

We showed up and found the place swarming with die-hard science fiction fans, a species of humanity I'm at a complete loss to explain or describe. Suffice it to say after a quick perusal I didn't stick around. I looked at the swarming mass of Star Trek outfits, alien garb etc., and hightailed it out of there.

I marched to my car and was about to depart when I noticed a beat up, old, yellow Impala, an old man driving this monstrous ship. He appeared to be searching for a parking space.

I got out and realized it was none other than Robert Bloch. I motioned toward him, indicated my car, the space I was about to vacate. He aimed his tank toward me. I pulled out, he pulled in, and I parked my car behind his Impala.

"Mr. Bloch," I cried. "I don't know if it's safe for you to go in there. There are hoardes of people in there and I use the term quite loosely."

He laughed. He had a nice laugh. He was elderly, or at least he appeared so to my eyes, and frail, but kindly, too, generous of heart. "Look, Mr. Bloch," I continued. "I came hoping to have you sign some books. But I gotta leave, see my kid and my wife are there in the car, this isn't the proper kind of place for them. Would you mind signing some of them for me, I have them here in my car."

"Sure," he said, with no hesitation. "I understand. Be happy to."

I popped the trunk, and lo and behold, it was as if the handful of books that had been there but a few hours had gone and multiplied like rabbits. "Lord, how'd these all get here?" I said, scratching my head. There were two large boxes filled to overflowing with Robert Bloch books.

He didn't so much as bat an eye. He was probably used to dealing with hardcore fanatics. He proceeded to sign each and every one of them, bless his heart. Paperbacks, hardcover, new and old.

We shook hands and parted company. "There goes a living saint," I said. "A mensch of the first water." I got back into the car and hightailed it back to the shop to adorn the shelves with these signed Robert Bloch books.

"Well, after this, I hope those books sell," my wife said.

"A breeze," I said. "With his signature the books will go, just you see. We won't be able to keep people away from them."

Bradbury and the rest were no shows. They wouldn't answer my letters or return my phone calls, but avoided me as if someone had my every move monitored and was informing them of my actions.

What can I do? I wondered. What drastic action might bring these people my way? I tried to encourage my wife to write the kind of notes that had brought us Bukowski, but she felt it was like using a bucket to prevent the Titanic from sinking. I made ever-more frantic calls to Harlan and to John Fante's widow, Joyce.

"Dear Mrs. Fante, I'm selling tons of your husband's books. Can't keep them in stock."

"I'm happy to hear that, young man." I even told her that I had spread the word of Fante to Mexico, which seemed to please her.

I made anonymous calls to certain late-night radio programs delivering messages of doom and gloom.

"Don't look now," I said. "But your days are numbered. You'll see. Annihilation will be swift and sure. Renaissance my eye!"

Bernie's Bordello was momentarily resurrected in the guise of a new improved idea the Father conjured up in his spare time, after he, my brothers, and one wife had returned from the South Pacific with their tails between their legs. They were having second thoughts. It wasn't quite what they'd expected, and so on.

The Father threatened to run the bookstore, again as a front; he'd put a massage parlor in the back, and import girls from Southeast Asia, who could give terrific massages, yes, but who could also provide help working in the bookstore when we needed it, and if sex happened to come into the picture now and then in the back after hours, especially as he would be the proprietor, well, then, so much the better. Maybe it wouldn't be so bad, after all, although I wondered where my father would be found were the cops to raid the joint.

I urged him to face reality; the bookstore was sinking fast. And I was being dragged down with it.

He stopped by to survey the wreckage. "Varlets," he said as he crossed the threshold, causing no one to take notice. "Avaunt, and quit my sight! Let the earth hide thee! Thy bones are marrowless, thy blood is cold." He held his clenched fists side by side, near his chin.

"Hello, dad."

"Go prick the face and over-red thy fear, Thou lily-livered boy."

The Father was in his element, gesturing wildly at the shelves and ceiling. He stepped behind the counter, opened the till, and examined with dismay the paltry amount we had taken in that day. He couldn't comprehend our lack of sales.

"You must be scaring away customers," was the best he could think of to explain our sorrowful tallies.

"What'll I do? I have a family," I said. "I need to earn something. What else can be done?""

He made his way over to an enormous shelf of Shakespeare's books, volume after volume, multiple copies of each. They were inexpensive. We usually sold them to students at the high school or Harbor College. If it wasn't *Hamlet* or *Macbeth*, my dad might pull out a copy of *King Lear*, another of his favorites: "As flies are to wanton boys are we to the gods. They kill us for their sport." He stepped to the center of the clearing, arms raised as if in supplication. "Thou shouldst not have been old till thou hadst been wise."

He momentarily rallied. "You could give something away with the books, something that would bring people in, pot for instance, a few joints with each book," he said, much the way a child might state it could fly if he flapped his arms hard and fast enough.

"I won't do my family much good from inside a jail," I said, as a couple left the store emptyhanded.

"When we are born we cry that we come to this great stage of fools," the Father spake, as he roamed the aisles, shaking his head as he thought long and hard. He thumbed through the shelves of books and finally walked to the counter with a few erotica titles in hand.

"Sell," he finally said. "Sell everything for next to nothing. All the books they can carry for a dollar."

"That's it?" I said. "No more brainstorms, no ideas?"

He shrugged. "Out, out brief candle! Life's but a walking shadow, a poor player, and then is heard no more. It is a tale told by an idiot, full of sound and fury, signifying nothing."

On that note he walked out of the store, leaving me alone to decide our fate.

I struggled uselessly against the tide and the prevailing winds. Maybe that was my character flaw. Perhaps I should have just given in and sold porno, brought on the sex magazines, sold paperbacks written by that excessively prolific Mr. Anonymous. Give the people what they want, my new credo. Why not drugs, too? The way things were going, if I did resort to crime, at least I'd get clothed, housed and fed in prison. Caryl Chessmen had written four books in jail. Perhaps, I could earn a law degree, become a modern-day Oliver Wendell Holmes and take on corporate America, the NRA, and organized religion, single-handedly.

To while away the frivolous hours, I fielded questions by people who wandered into the store, curious about the history of San Pedro. "A crazed Portuguese criminal," I said with a straight face, "discovered this strip of land, although of course Native Americans lived here, quite nicely too, though not the Indians most people think of. No, these were black and ruled by a warrior woman, named Califia, whose kingdom was rich with gold and pearls, and who had 500 griffins to fight against her enemies."

Distracted, I fretted over what would happen to the little club of writers who met in the bookstore late at night, all the greats of literature. Where would they go once everything was sold off or given away, all the books blown hither and thither to the ends of the planet? Would they be dispersed, too, or simply move off to hold their nightly sessions in some other hospitable locale?

26

Aftermath

A terrific sound echoed and vibrated. The whir of a rope being swung, a wet fingertip rubbing the rim of a crystal glass, a strange buzzing that comes of extreme heat, insects, and dry inhospitable regions; the sound of hope having the life squeezed out of it—an anguished wail, a howl, rising in intensity and volume. A sound that would have come from the painting "The Scream," if it were alive.

I followed that frenzied cacophony down to the waterside, through the streets of downtown, which had been left to the downtrodden derelicts, while those of means and money flocked in droves to the malls. I followed in mad pursuit that terrible cry that filled the atmosphere, which radiated and resonated from the heart of San Pedro itself. Or perhaps the sound filled my own lungs, the signal of a defeated man; beaten, but not down. Not yet vanquished.

Katherine left, sauntered off to Santa Monica to work for some graphics firm. Her parting shot took all the wind out of my sails. "If you had left your wife we would have had something," she said. Eleven words perfectly spoken by an angel slipping out of my life forever. Eleven words, so tantalizing, so poignant, so gutwrenching. I prostrated myself and wished I had the strength to tear off that damned nuisance that dangled between my legs and hurl it across the untenable distance, the gulf that stood between me and the object of my desire.

"Let those eleven words be my epitaph," I shouted in the muffled asylum called the Little Big Bookshop.

My wife and I finally admitted we were beat. Although we had given the bookstore our best, the debts were rising and our sales just weren't keeping up. We announced a going-out-of-business sale. Everything half-priced. People up and down the street came out to have a look, "Yes, see, they're finally throwing in the towel, leaving, no more bookstore!" Self-satisfaction beamed in their eyes. They could barely restrain the elation they felt knowing the bookstore was closing its doors for good. They never thought for a moment that while the bookstore going under may not hurt their business, it certainly didn't do it any good either. Moreover, it was a black eye for San Pedro. It was a sad testimonial to our time, and to the city, that it couldn't support a used bookstore.

After a few weeks we slashed the books to 1/3, then 1/4 the prices. People seemed to be holding out for when we'd just give them away.

Friends and family stopped in to say good-bye to the bookstore. They grabbed what few books they were interested in and fled before the store caved in on their heads. Carl made a nice stack: every book ever published—or so it seemed—on the art of getting rich and scoring with women. As soon as the banners were unfurled the ghouls came round, buying up books finally for a dollar, hell we're giving 'em away. Buy one book, take a handful for free.

They wanted everything.

"Is the cash register for sale?"

"You selling the shelves?" A shop owner from down the street. Had I but known this was how to get them to buy from me.

"How about the magazine racks?"

"The sign?"

No, the sign I wouldn't part with. I paid good money for that hand-crafted sign. I may not have the Little Big Bookshop any longer but the sign would stay; it was all we had left. Perhaps I would hang it like an albatross around my neck, and sell books from a pushcart by the side of the road.

The bookstore fell by the wayside, and my wife and I even discussed splitting up, giving up the ghost, parting company.

"Do you want to divorce?" I asked.

"I don't know, do you?" I wasn't about to forsake my child, not even for Katherine. Without the baby in the bookstore window in the equation the solution would have been simple. And obvious. In the end, I figured I could take it if she could. We decided to try to salvage what there was of our marriage, to remain in our familiar if uncomfortable ways. She reclaimed her maiden name, not that I blamed her for wanting to be rid of the onerous stigma of Kastinovich. I stopped using my wife's maiden name, as well. Not only because it wasn't fair to her, but because I knew it hadn't done me any good. I couldn't escape the onus of my own name.

We were to leave San Pedro behind, but not before I saw Hank Chinaski, who didn't get angry when I blamed him (in part) for the decline of American letters, but who blamed me, he said, for ruining his peace of mind and privacy by sending crazies coming after him.

It was one of these typical loonies, Mike, none other than my former assistant and guinea pig in my experiment for the Little Big Bookshop School for Iconoclastic Wanna-be Writers. He returned as suddenly as he had disappeared from whatever dank nether region he normally inhabited. The last few weeks or so of the bookstore's existence he made himself a regular, often dropping in to chat, knowing damned well I was a captive audience, if not a prisoner. My doors were open to the public, and I couldn't very well throw out everyone who was strange or friendly, or bothersome, for then I would be left with an empty store. This ex-alcoholic with a wild gleam in his eye, and a proclivity for telling me the intimate details of his life story, came into the bookstore with a Bukowski book in hand. "It's my Bible," he said. He had discovered Bukowski—this after I had loaded him up with the greatest classics of modern literature, drama and poetry, after handing him Fante on a silver platter. After wasting most of his life drinking, and living in institutions of one kind or another, he had finally found his calling. And he owed it all to Hank, for he too was going to be a poet. In fact, he brought some with him. Would I care to have a look? Mike had bought himself a notebook, of all things, and within the notebook had scribbled his attempts at poetry with the scrawl of a child.

"Here, read this one," he said flipping the pages.

I read. "Uh huh," I said, nodding my head. "Hmm."

"And what about this one?" he said, pointing. "I just wrote it last night."

"Oh, yeah," I said. It went on and on. He had filled practically the entire notebook with poems about Bukowski, about an ex-wife who no longer spoke to him, about halfway homes, the alcoholic haze in which he had spent the past few decades and which he now attempted to remember, about his damaged brain.

I happened to look out the door. I was trying to pretend I was working. Anything, just so long as I didn't have to read another of his poems, which, of course, weren't poems at all, but merely notes he'd jotted down, notes to himself. Clumsy, awkward, embarrassing, like stick drawings of people. Nothing remotely poetic about them, to be sure. Hank sat with the Romanian and I prayed this guy, this latest, most recent of converts to poetry, didn't see Hank, didn't run over to sit with him. But that's exactly what happened. Before I could stop him, Mike ran across the street, waving his Bukowski book and his notebook of poetry to go chum it up with Hank Chinaski. I prayed for a car to hit him before he reached the other side.

I retreated to the very farthest corner of the bookstore, loudly protested, swearing my innocence, but Hank figured I had sent the loony after him. I could certainly be cruel, but never that thoughtless, never that mean. If nothing else, Hank should have known that.

Someone showed up at the bookstore with a proposition to buy all the remaining paperbacks we had, every single last one of them, no matter what they were, for pennies a book. We didn't ask questions. They supplied people to come in and box them up, and ship the books off to the Philippines.

Moses eventually packed up all his books, too, and moved clear out of town, in search of a locale more conducive to commerce and culture, after another year or two of struggle and strife. If I wanted a true iconoclast there he was, just down the road. When I stopped by Moses' shop to say good-bye, once again I couldn't resist a book or two for the road. I grabbed a book by Edwin Corle, *Mojave Tales*, because it sounded interesting and I thought perhaps I would end my days out in the desert, a wandering nomad, and because it was priced more than just about any other book in his shop. It happened to be a signed first edition, and the point was to hand over some cash and take a book off his hands. Instead of the usual one or two dollars, this tome was a whopping eight. I knew damned well that it was worth much more.

"I think this was mistakenly underpriced," I said, showing Moses the book in question.

"I won't take more than what it's priced," he said.

Obstinate, stubborn, ornery old cuss. "Come on, Moses," I argued, "At least take fifteen for it. You can't give books away like this."

"Take the damn book and get out," he shouted. "Nobody's going to tell me how o run my business." Ever true to himself. It was good to know some things never changed.

I was a character who had wandered off the pages of a book, who now no longer knew the plot, the story line of his life. Left suddenly in a vacuum, I drifted in a world haunted by the familiar characters invented by all the authors whose books I read and admired. All I had left was my name. A terrible burden, to be sure, under the weight of which I buckled and stumbled, for with that name I carried the sins of all my ancestor's who preceded me, all the wretched amends and retribution that was coming due. I knew there was no escaping their legacy.

Bukowski's parting shot was a good one. "I read what you sent me. It was good. Made me laugh. You should write. Look at me. I've never written for money, but because of some imbecilic urge. I was one of the lucky ones. You should do the same. Just work at it."

"Me?" I said. "All I read are dead writers."

He chuckled. Or, at least I thought that's what he did. I'd heard t

who preceded me, all the wretched amends and retribution that was coming due. I knew there was no escaping their legacy.

Bukowski's parting shot was a good one. "I read what you sent me. It was good. Made me laugh. You should write. Look at me. I've never written for money, but because of some imbecilic urge. I was one of the lucky ones. You should do the same. Just work at it."

"Me?" I said. "All I read are dead writers."

He chuckled. Or, at least I thought that's what he did. I'd heard he'd been sick and wondered how he was faring. "You're doing okay?" I asked.

"Yeah, baby." He brushed away the subject with a wave of his hand. "Remember, work is where the vigor come from, the creative fucking process. Puts dance in the bones. About all I can read without agony is the daily newspaper. I don't fear good writing, I only wish there was more of it. There's room, even for someone like you. It's a large stage, if a shaky one. Give a man a bit of solitude and a good night's sleep and then he can just about beat anything except that last card."

That was the last I saw of Buk. I felt bad. San Pedro was no longer the same. It had lost an essential essence, a spirit. Things moved along, and people acted as though nothing had changed but it was now drab, colorless.

To pay homage to the man I went to the Vietnamese restaurant just past 22nd Street, and ate a meal for Buk. It had been one his favorite places to eat. The woman who owned the place and I talked a bit about Hank and Linda. She missed him, too.

•   •   •

Nick Kastinovich stopped abruptly.

"Is that all?" I said.

"That's it. The whole enchilada," he said, looking like he was about to crawl off, or as if he were on the verge of disappearing.

So, there you have it. The story just as I heard it from one Nick Kastinovich, who might or might not be related to me. He gave me the story, he said, to do with as I saw fit.

"Publish it or burn it," he said. "I really don't care which."

"What do you do now?" I asked.

"Not much," he said. "An odd job here, an odd job there."

"And books?"

"Ahh! I content myself to reading. I'm rereading Dostoyevsky, all of his writings."

"Wasn't he anti-Semitic?" I asked.

"Who isn't?" he growled. "He hated everybody, not just Jews. His world is the only place I feel at home."

I never saw Nick Kastinovich after that, nor do I care to. Relative or not, he wasn't someone with whom I was at all eager to associate. I knew even before he had finished that I would use the name, Kastinovich—there seemed to be no avoiding it. One is what one is. His life had more or less mirrored my own; there was a resonance of familiarity, a frisson resulting from the horror of recognition, as if I knew deep down what I hadn't known on the surface. There is more than one kind of knowledge.

I did a bit of research on my own, enough to discover that we were both from branches broken off the same withered tree.

He'd assured me that there were more of us out there, somewhere, like shadows lurking in unfrequented places. His last words to me were this: "My advice to anyone, if they should be so unlucky as to meet one of us on the road is to turn and run in the other direction, don't speak, just follow your toes and count your blessings that you too are not a Kastinovich."

THE END

Afterward

Some weeks later I returned to the bar. Not sure what drew me back. Ron Voss, the bartender handed me a packet of paper, as soon as he saw me. "Hey, that guy left this for you."

It was something Nick Kastinovich had written up, a parting shot, so to speak. Read it at your own risk:

Before the bookstore closed down, Bukowski would stop by now and again, mostly to chat and have a drink with the Romanian across the street. He didn't linger long in the bookstore, which threatened to fold like a house of cards in a sixty-mile-an-hour wind, but would ask, "How's it goin', baby," in that distinctive gravelly drawl the way he always did, and waved whenever he saw me on the street, or in the doorway of the bookstore. I sat and imagined him in films with the likes of Edward G. Robinson and Bogey. With that voice and that face it was a shame to let that go to waste.

Hank referred to my writing. He'd seen my piece on Mexico, which some thoughtful stranger had mysteriously slipped into his mailbox; go figure. He said it had amused him. I looked forward to discussing the one thing we did have in common, John Fante, for it was clear to anyone who read his prose that Bukowski had been spurred on to write prose from the memorable experience of having found and read such books as *Ask the Dust,* and others by Fante, that writer's god, that unsung champion who was so incredibly good as to make it appear so sinfully effortless, like watching Rubinstein play the piano, or Perlman the violin, who made fools like me still green in their youth think that they too could do it. Bukowski wasn't the only one to go about calling himself Arturo Bandini. Many of us did. Even if we didn't say it aloud to a living soul; it was written in neon all over our walk, our talk, that cocky crazed bravado we fairly radiated that said we were the best, that we could do anything.

That Fante had been permitted to die was something I couldn't accept. I agonized over it because he had died before I even knew he existed, before I could have phoned him or written to him. It shook Hank up pretty badly, too. You simply could not find writing so clean, so pure, so heavenly hilarious and warm and bursting with emotion as his; even when his character/alter ego Arturo Bandini was a bastard you just couldn't help but love him. And without him the world seemed a colder, lonelier, uglier place to inhabit.

Society should have waited on the man hand and foot, brought him an infinite supply of sheets of virginwhite paper, ream upon ream, lapped up his every word, so he could have finished that Filipino novel, so he could have finally written that brilliant book about a Catholic couple caught in the typical, painful struggle of a life of poverty while being forbidden by their church to ameliorate their hardships by the use of birth control.

"Dear Fante," I'd have written. "Won't you resurrect Arturo Bandini one last time? Just one more book. I know you have it in you. For us, for posterity, for all humanity? Let us laugh and cry with Arturo once again."

People should have bestowed upon him praise and adulation, taken away his golf clubs, kept him away from gambling, taken away his screen writing and all the other diversions and distractions, and set him in front of the typewriter locked in a room until he produced yet another masterpiece. For what could a man do when he was faced with the prospect, reinforced by decade after decade of obscurity, that the world cared so little for his books? I believed that he only needed to know he had an eager audience. Then he would have gladly carried on, come diabetes, come blindness, come amputations, come whatever; for there he was even after all that still dictating books at the very end to his dear wife, Joyce. It never left him the way it left others; even his letters ring with his genius for laughter, his uncanny ability to capture a scene or a character, letters that could wring tears out of anyone with half a heart.

About my own character, I thought the least I could do was to help out future writers, live my life in such a way as to offer all manner of choice anecdotes and experiences from which they could compile book after book. I paused to wonder how my character might develop, how close it might be to the real me, what liberties writers would take. In the future I had many occasions to consider before I acted upon things, to think, now what would my character do in a situation like this? I tried to foresee the novels and stories they would write: *The Man Nobody Thought Was Real*, *The Pathetic End of a Ridiculous Man*, *The Life of a Grinning Imp*.

I foresaw too the difficulties these writers would have with publishers: "No one will believe it," "Nobody would do such a thing," "Look, the story's fine but the character really seems far-fetched." Perhaps the greatest of these tales would be the ones written concerning my fate at the hands of Bukowski; would the old man take me under his wing, be my mentor; perhaps we'd get drunk one night in the bookstore, surprise someone attempting to break into the store and accidentally kill the person, then try and pin it on one another. Or would we decide that since Bukowski's fame was on the upswing and I was the respectable owner of a business that the best thing would be to hide the body, and somewhere deep inside the Little Big Bookshop would be the rotting corpse of the man murdered by Bukowski and Nick Kastinovich. Or maybe the two of us would ride off, hit the road. A modern-day Butch Cassidy and the Sundance Kid.

Though Hank was responsible for wreaking such offenses by letting loose his progeny, those legions of emulators, you had to admire him. He had survived, like some terrible stone icon that remained after storms, wars, earthquakes and centuries of wear, the Sphinx itself. He'd not only weathered all that life had thrown his way, he didn't give a damn either; not about what others thought, not what others did. He didn't need people to like him. He didn't need their approval, or acceptance. He'd written what he wanted to write. He never once relied on a single soul out there to inform him who or what he was, unlike Hemingway, who was ruined by his success. Chinaski, after all, had made it, which in the eyes of some made it all worthwhile—the money, that is. At least it gave him the last laugh.

But to illustrate just how bad things had gotten, if Huck Finn was the pinnacle of American fiction—which it is, no ifs ands or buts—look what followed in its footsteps. Compare the best books of the thirties, the forties, the fifties, and so on with that one book. What you have? A mere handful qualified to sit on the same shelf.

Bukowski was always the first to deprecate his own writing. He knew that ninety-nine point nine per cent of his readers couldn't tell good Bukowski from bad, that those who rushed up to sing his praises wouldn't know good anything from bad, and certainly wouldn't recognize genius, not in a million years, not even to save their souls from an eternal damnation of being forced to read the likes of Sidney Sheldon, Danielle Steel and Judith Krantz. He knew too that poetry had slid to new lows, a rising babble of selfabsorbed rantings with a perspective of the universe limited to the view from the depths of the writer's own navel. Everything was selfexpression, I, me, mine. There were no distinctions to be made anymore. Who could say whether a poem was good or bad? It's me. It says what I want it to say. Or just jumble a bunch of nonsense words together with some artful line breaks. If you don't get it, then piss off.

Of course, in truth, you couldn't altogether blame Hank, or even Hemingway. On the other hand, academia and publishers you couldn't possibly blame enough. I shuddered to think what the literary giants thought of the literature of this soontofold century of ours. Twain, Hawthorne, Wharton, Poe, were probably spinning in their graves. A hundred or two hundred years from now what will they still be reading from the last hundred years, and how will they look back upon our writers? The age when a writer's life and personality became far more important as to overshadow what they wrote? The age of minimalism, writing stripped to the bone, bereft of plot and beauty of emotion, of writers with little or nothing to say, writing devoid of imagination, of humor? Satire? No longer even in the vocabulary, my boy.

Oh, sure there were exceptions. Problem is they were too far and few between. Now and then a novel that made a splash, but point me to the last truly great collection of short stories, will you? What collection of stories out there will still be cherished, will appear as bright and fresh, will help to illuminate the dawn of this next millennium?

Chinaski knew all this. He joked about his writing, knew he could sell his soiled hankies and toilet paper as easily as his poetry. What did it matter? The world, after all, had consigned Fante's books to near total obscurity for fifty years. And I heard the choice words Bukowski saved for those fans who actually thought he was a better writer than Fante. They were beneath contempt.

Meanwhile, Bukowski's film, *Barfly* had been released and now he was hot stuff. The literary establishment had discovered him. No longer was he the favorite poet of the underground, of literate actors and musicians, and a handful of fellow writers. Bukowski was a huge commodity, a big name, hanging out with the likes of Micky Rourke and Faye Dunaway, film producers, directors.

I spoke with him, asked him how things were. "Pretty good, baby. Pretty nice." He seemed amused by the whole Hollywood episode of his life.

"You look like you're having a good time," I said.

"Oh, yeah. They're treating me well. Mickey Rourke, he's great." The affection was written all over his face. "The woman, well, what can you say?" He winked.

He would capture the whole experience in his novel *Hollywood*.

I still watched the fans go after him, fools who never seemed to realize poetry was the last thing Hank wanted to discuss—his or anyone else's—that all he really wanted was to be left alone. Wanna-be poets in drug rehab, vagrants who roamed the range in downtown San Pedro came into the store, read his books, and waited for him to show up so they could get their books signed.

I was glad to have known him and to have learned a valuable lesson from him, if nothing else; the lesson of the iconoclast: that you did what you did to the very best of your ability, with open honesty, and fuck what everyone else thought. What they thought didn't matter one whit, as long as you were true to yourself. Yet at the same time there was a world of difference between writing for the public and writing words that belonged in a diary or a journal. That was what so many people failed to see.

Like dying, it wasn't whether you were going to do it or even when, but how you went about dying that really mattered. If you wrote for acclaim, fame, a pat on the back, you were lost. An iconoclast blazed his or her own trail, regardless of what the rest of the world was doing or thinking, whether they received scorn, contempt or a firing squad. Integrity; that was the upshot. Whether you were good, bad, or indifferent, a genius or a hack was besides the point. You simply did your best.

If the masses were asses, as some declared, unable to tell quality from crap, well, they certainly weren't alone, for the vast majority of the educated, the intelligent, the artistically savvy couldn't tell you who will last and who will fade into a well-deserved obscurity, who will be adored and revered in fifty or a hundred years' time and who will be reviled. It was anyone's guess, which was why they now had to resort to million-dollar advertising blitzes and talk shows to convince people they should read this or that hot new writer.

Geniuses were seldom recognized in their own time and place. Popular and successful today, forgotten the day after tomorrow; the unknown greats of today may be discovered in a century, or never. Hell, even now Fante sold far more in France than he did in the U.S. It would take those in the United States to see him on the big screen, a film version of *Ask the Dust* or *Brotherhood of the Grape*—provided they didn't screw it up—before he'd get any kind of serious recognition here. For that was the earmark of fame, reality, even—what's on the big screen. And most people need to be told what to read, just as they are told by critics which films to view—hence the popularity of Crown Bookstores. Why have hundreds of thousands of titles that only serve to confuse the book buyer? We'll narrow it down to the most popular, the bestsellers. You needn't go searching anymore. We've got the book you need! After all, this is America, *El Norte*, where popularity equals success, equals wealth, which of course equates with "It must be good!" Success measured by the profit margin.

Or, better yet just listen to Oprah Winfrey.

Hank lived well those last few years, and I certainly wouldn't begrudge him that. His popularity flourished, notwithstanding the essay I'd written, which was roundly rejected by everyone I had sent it to.

One day, years later, I found Hank at a Coco's restaurant—always seeking out those places where he could sit unrecognized, and be left alone. He was seated at the counter. I promptly sat down beside him. His eyes shifted toward me. He turned ever so slowly, and sized me up—I actually saw my insignificance register instantly in his eyes: zero, zip, nada! Before he turned his head away I said, "Hi, Hank, how're things?" I reminded him of the bookstore, my name. Finally, a grin. I saw myself raised a whole one-and-a-half notches, as there was a flicker of recognition. Then, giving me a nod, he said, "Hey, baby, how're ya doin'?" in his deep, slow and gravelly voice; a voice that could float boulders. "What 'cha ya doin' with yourself?"

What could I say to this man who had seen it all, done it all. This beer swilling behemoth who could fit me into one of his pockets and forget I was there? "I've got six months to live, Hank. Rare disease, incurable." He might swallow that, perhaps. Or maybe I was on the lam, laying low for a while since paying some guy to feed a case of rotten fish through the mail slot of a bankruptcy lawyer who had made a pass at my wife. I doubted that would impress him, though. He'd wonder why I hadn't done it myself.

"Not much, Hank, been thinking of taking up writing a script for Hollywood, something about my family, all its sordid secrets, a filthy exposé."

"Stay away from Hollywood," Hank said. "It'll ruin you. It's ruined the best of 'em. Fante, Frank Fenton, Fitzgerald, Faulkner."

"I'm safe," I said. "My name doesn't begin with an 'F.'"

He leveled a puzzled look at me.

"Speaking of "F" I'd like to join the French Foreign Legion. I wouldn't mind going off halfway around the world to die in some desert wasteland. But I'm asthmatic and so I'm certain they wouldn't have me."

He cocked an eyebrow at me. "You always were a bit strange."

Now, at last, he remembered me!

We parted with smiles and best wishes. He patted my back. "Good luck, baby."

Even after Hank died I continued to see him; the ghost of Chinaski hovering above the skies of L.A., his tough arms embracing the entire city, the one reflecting the other, as if neither could possibly exist alone. I saw it happening right before my eyes. We closed the shop and hid from the creditors and lawyers. Of course the Father, who actually owned the nightmare was nowhere to be found. The Kabob place went under right after the Little Big Bookshop, went the same way as the Red cars which Fante had ridden from downtown L.A. to Long Beach and Bunker Hill, where he had lived, the way so many of the things, people and places which inhabited his world were gone. Bukowski's world, too, was slowly disappearing, as if the city was little more than a mirage that evaporated with time, remaining only in his books, his stories and poems.

I carried my copy of *Ask the Dust* with me everywhere I went, raised it against the onslaught of commercialism, of stupidity and lack of culture, of ignorance and cheapness and mediocrity, that specter which loomed everywhere, on all sides.

More novels and novellas from Fomite...

Joshua Amses
During This, Our Nadir
Ghats
Raven or Crow
The Moment Before an Injury
Raymond Barfield
Dreams of a Spirit Seer
Charles Bell
The Married Land
The Half Gods
Jaysinh Birjepatel
Nothing Beside Remains
The Good Muslim of Jackson Heights
David Borofka
The End of Good Intnetions
David Brizer
Cacademonomania
The Secret Doctrine of V. H. Rand
Victor Rand
L. M Brown
Hinterland
Paula Closson Buck
Summer on the Cold War Planet
Ann Abelson/L.enny Cavallaro
Paganini Agitato
Dan Chodorkoff
Loisaida
Sugaring Down
David Adams Cleveland
Time's Betrayal
Paul Cody
Sphyxia
Jaimee Wriston Colbert
Vanishing Acts
Roger Coleman
Skywreck Afternoons
Stephen Downes
The Hands of Pianists

Fomite

Marc Estrin
  Et Resurrexit
  Hyde
  Kafka's Roach
  Proceedings of the Hebrew Free Burial Society
  Speckled Vanities
  The Annotated Nose
  The Penseés of Alan Krieger
Zdravka Evtimova
  Asylum for Men and Dogs
  In the Town of Joy and Peace
  Sinfonia Bulgarica
  To Weave a Grasshopper's Cage
  You Can Smile on Wednesdays
John Michael Flynn
  Answer Only
Daniel Forbes
  Derail This Train Wreck
Peter Fortunato
  Carnevale
Greg Guma
  Dons of Time
Ramsey Hanhan
  Fugitive Dreams
Richard Hawley
  The Three Lives of Jonathan Force
Lamar Herrin
  Father Figure
Michael Horner
  Damage Control
Ron Jacobs
  All the Sinners Saints
  Short Order Frame Up
  The Co-conspirator's Tale
Scott Archer Jones
  A Rising Tide of People Swept Away
  And Throw Away the Skins
  The Moth
Julie Justicz
  Conch Pearl
  Degrees of Difficulty

Fomite

Maggie Kast
A Free Unsullied Land
Coleen Kearon
#triggerwarning
Feminist on Fire
Jan English Leary
Thicker Than Blood
Town and Gown
Diane Lefer
Confessions of a Carnivore
Out of Place
Rob Lenihan
Born Speaking Lies
Cynthia Newberry Martin
The Art of Her Life
Colin McGinnis
Roadman
Douglas W. Milliken
Our Shadows' Voice
Ilan Mochari
Zinsky the Obscure
Peter Nash
Ghost Story
In the Place Where We Thought We Stood
Parsimony
The Least of It
The Perfection of Things
Michael Okulitch
Toward Him Still
George Ovitt
Stillpoint
Tribunal
Gregory Papadoyiannis
The Baby Jazz
Pelham
The Walking Poor
Christopher S. Peterson
Butter, or the Dairy of a Madman: Book One and Book Two
Andy Potok
My Father's Keeper

Fomite

Frederick Ramey
  Comes A Time
Howard Rappaport
  Arnold and Igor
Joseph Rathgeber
  Mixedbloods
Kathryn Roberts
  Companion Plants
Robert Rosenberg
  Isles of the Blind
Fred Russell
  Rafi's World
Ron Savage
  Voyeur in Tangier
David Schein
  The Adoption
Rana Shubair
  And No Net Ensnares Me
Charles Simpson
  Uncertain Harvest
Lynn Sloan
  Midstream
  Principles of Navigation
L.E. Smith
  The Consequence of Gesture
  Travers' Inferno
  Untimely RIPped
Robert Sommer
  A Great Fullness
Caitlin Hamilton Summie
  Geographies of the Heart
Tom Walker
  A Day in the Life
Susan V. Weiss
  My God, What Have We Done?
Peter M. Wheelwright
  As It Is on Earth
  The Door-Man
Suzie Wizowaty
  The Return of Jason Green

Writing a review on social media sites for readers will help the progress of independent publishing. To submit a review, go to the book page on any of the sites and follow the links for reviews. Books from independent presses rely on reader-to-reader communications